Ms Behaviour

With the tip of the pencil I lifted my skirts
ever so slightly away so that my underwear
was showing and then I sat quietly again for a
few moments. I leant forwards and jotted
down some notes like the rest of the students.
In short order, I subsequently positioned my
naughty pencil back down in the vicinity of my
panties, and, with the tip of it, I pushed aside
my underwear and touched my clit with the
eraser of the pencil. Oh, what a good student
she was. Terrible me.

This made me pulse unbearably as I slid
the pencil back and forth. I was hungry and
unsatisfied. I wanted MacLean to see; I was
wishing the professor would touch it someday.
Will he sit down at his desk so he can see me
masturbate for him, please?

Ms Behaviour
Mini Lee

BLACK LACE

Black Lace books contain sexual fantasies.
In real life, always practise safe sex.

First published in 2005 by
Black Lace
Thames Wharf Studios
Rainville Road
London W6 9HA

Design by Smith & Gilmour, London
Printed and bound by Mackays of Chatham PLC

ISBN 0 352 33962 4

1

In class I squirmed in my seat. It was so boring. All I wanted was to go to the girls' and have a cigarette. Re-apply whatever. I needn't worry about looking good necessarily, to go put on my lipstick and all, because I knew I already looked good. It was just an excuse to have some time of my own, and, plus, I must confess that I loved to piss off my professor. He was such a nasty, crusty character and his terrible eyes followed me like a mangy vulture's every time I'd get up to leave his class. Ours was a huge lecture hall, and students would often be coming in late or leaving early, but I had consistently bad manners in this regard and I would feel his disapproving gaze burning into me every time I got up to leave. He wanted to see me naked, possibly spank me, even. I knew it and I loved it. And during these frequent cigarette breaks I would indulge my inappropriate erotic thoughts about him.

It was a small university; a place where the more obscure academic professionals might wash up at some point with worn shoes on the worn shores of their careers. It seemed to collect burned-out professors who had become indifferent to whatever discipline they taught. They were matched by students who had the lower GPAs, such as myself – a woman who was moti-vated by things other than her studies. In fact, I was beginning to think I may have something horribly in common with my professor insofar as his distracted attitude concerning the work.

It was entirely possible that Professor MacLean

taught in the faculty of law at this university for immoral reasons. In my fevered imagination, access to young female students and the authority he could have over them was likely the guiding reason for his dubious academic career.

I'd enrolled two years ago as a freshman and, though uninterested in the whole system and process, this year my marks did count more, whether I liked it or not. But school didn't stimulate me. I hadn't yet grown passionate about the study of law and I was doing my courses half-assed. Had I wanted, top grades could have been mine, though, I'm sure of it, but I was just plain lazy when it came to academia. If I'd studied harder I could have gotten into an entirely different school, but here I was, attending the university where Professor MacLean presided as law professor. His course was 'Crime and Law Enforcement'.

Actually, with a title like that, the potential was there for a really interesting course so, in this spirit, I took a sly interest in watching MacLean and his approach to the class. I gathered that he knew his stuff, but he was holding an even and steady attitude of competent indifference when it came to the instruction of the subject. And so it was dull. *He* was dull, with his faded suits and out-of-date ties. There was, however, a certain erotic restlessness about him that caught my questionable attention. And I certainly knew I had his.

Anyway, I sometimes met my friend, Bee, another third-year law student, on these frequent breaks from his class.

'Call me on my mobile when you're ready to meet,' she had said to me. This was our regular plan.

Fifteen minutes into the lecture I rose to leave. That was doubly belligerent of me since the class had just begun. But, as I alluded, I enjoyed getting the good professor's ire up. According to plan, once in the hallway, I rang Bee's mobile. I heard her feign the importance of the call and murmur an apology to those other students around her whom she might be disturbing as she was trying to make her own smooth exit.

We loved these games. Beyond that, we both contrived all sorts of stories and plots about our alluring selves and our greying, preying professors and their silly, ignorant wives. And us, the female students who were oh so amused by the old professor's longing gaze upon our young bodies. Like the way MacLean would look at me. I asserted to Bee that my own husband, if I ever married, would never be like that.

The women's bathroom was dimly lit, which gave it an air of secrecy, as if our illegal behaviour was hidden underground. We lit up our smokes. The grey haze caused by our cigarettes seemed suitable to the surroundings, and the smoke swirled lazily upwards towards the weak lights above to form a mellow fog just below the ceiling and above our heads. It was like a delicious underground rebellion – us, armed with our cigarettes.

'Did you get the big stern frown?' Bee asked me.

'Sure did, pardner,' I said through clenched teeth around my cigarette like a western cowpoke.

'Bet you're driving him nuts, Santa,' she said and I secretly hoped so, in more ways than one. Some of the female students, I suspected, seemed to be genuinely flattered by the obvious exhibited lust of the tutors. And I have to confess that I was one of those girls. While I sat in the classroom, the other students would be jotting down notes, and MacLean all the while would be noticing my legs, long and dangling beneath my slight skirts. I liked being the object of his gaze; it titillated and thrilled me.

'Did I ever tell you how MacLean spied on John and me, late one night when we getting it on in the univer-

3

sity library?' I asked Bee. I knew I had told her before, but I liked recounting it. We enjoyed sharing stories of our sexual escapades. Bee was a bit of a naughty one, and I was a terribly naughty one, so I went on to tell her: 'Well, I knew MacLean had been watching us for a long time before he made his presence known, the dirty pervert. I could see him watching us. I swear that I could even hear him breathing his heavy-with-sex breath while John was exposing my breasts in the library.'

'You're such an incredible slut,' Bee said with feigned disproval.

'I do confess to that,' I replied. 'And to do something like that in such a stiff, sanctified space as a library! What kind of girl . . .' And we both laughed.

Naughty me. 'I do enjoy a voyeur,' I admitted to Bee, and I thought of my bare tits that night in the dark library, so raw, pert and exposed in the dead library air. How sweet – my bare tenderness, my nipples, my raisin-sized dark nipples. My buds were on breezy show for my professor and I arched my back, reaching out with my bare breasts that ached to be touched by the intrepid voyeur in this quiet place filled with books. John was lightly caressing my exposed breasts and touching me so seductively all along the length of my body. God, we were being bad in the library. I let him do as he wished and I was gasping a little too loudly because I was so erotically charged. And I would have let my professor feel me with his bare hands if he was of a mind to; he who was standing by and watching. 'Join in,' I wanted to call out.

I told Bee, 'Since then he watches me very closely. I have observed this, my friend. MacLean hopes to catch a glimpse of my breasts again and, since that time, he's taken to leaning over me in class and peering down into my low-cut shirts every chance he gets. I once purposely wore a very revealing top and I knew he could almost see my nipples. I even dared to lean over for his pleasure once or twice. His beady little eyes were well satisfied. You know what he said to me then, Bee?'

She laughed. 'Don't hold me in suspense.'

I mimicked my professor's serious tone. 'I'm concerned about your work.'

'Is that all?' she asked.

'Bee, there was something to that remark that suggested he intended to make good on it. That he meant to do something about it.' I relished in telling her the details.

'You wouldn't like that, would you? He's such a dirty old letch. He gives me the creeps. Not you?'

She let the question hang when I didn't answer right away. In my mind I knew full well that he gave me the creeps too, yet it was for that reason I had this inexplicable attraction to him.

I went on to diffuse her curiosity and tried to explain my way out of it. 'My God, no, Bee,' I insisted. 'In fact, after that episode, I grew anxious about what I was provoking. I wanted to regain control over this whole weird situation. That was when the high button-up shirts were in fashion for me. No one else was wearing them, let me tell you!

'I do believe I suffer greatly from the whore/saint complex, probably why my parents named me Santa, hoping the saint-part would win out, ' I joked.

Bee laughed appreciatively.

But, in fact, when it came to Professor MacLean, I was creating a situation that stirred a fabulous fear and excitement in me. Any increase in tension with him served to fuel me further in my fantasies. It was most unfortunate that such thoughts preyed on my mind. At any rate, I was helpless to it. I was inexplicably drawn to the idea that someday he would have to punish me for my misbehaviour and my panties were wet just thinking about it.

Bee and I had half-finished our cigarettes in the now smoky campus bathroom, and it was my turn to swish out the sink from the ashes. As always the water pressure came out with a gushing blast and sprayed all across the front of my shirt. But it was worse than usual this time, and it wouldn't go unnoticed when I got back to class. I could feel my nipples hardening already from chill of the water and MacLean would register this, no doubt.

It was our Friday class and so Bee and I talked about some plans for the weekend. She wanted to introduce me to a friend of her boyfriend's.

'I don't know much about him other than he is in the faculty of commerce. He's from a filthy rich family and there's some scandal around his father: some liaisons with organised crime, or something. But his son's terribly handsome, that's all I know for sure.' Bee's eyes twinkled playfully.

'I like your offer. Introduce me to Joey's friend, then,' I said to her.

This blind date sounded intriguing. The only problem was I had difficulty with monogamy, should we get serious. Moreover, I had a hard time getting rid of old boyfriends, because they'd continue to try and seduce me even after we'd broken up. The fact was, I was very willing to let a man have his way with me. I liked to lie there and simply submit to my ex-lovers. I couldn't help myself. I knew I should tone down my sex drive, but still, I would lie there for them and would let them undress me and play with my naked body. All the while I got a thrill from knowing that they too knew they shouldn't be touching me there, doing that.

Bee and I cautiously exited the women's bathroom.

No one saw us or the billow of smoke that followed us out of the door. We parted just outside and each headed back to our respective classes.

I returned to MacLean's lecture hall. Friday was the best day of the week, I thought, and class would soon come to an end. I had a date set up for that night and I was really determined to stop obsessing about my professor and think about a potential romance with someone my own age; someone more suitable for a girl like me. It helped that MacLean seemed to be ignoring me too. I watched him in his deliberate, mechanical way of lecturing, but I soon found myself falling into one of my many fantasies about him.

One of my favourite fantasies was set in the very class I was in.

In my little daydream, I am asked to stay after the other students have left. It is about my work, MacLean says, for asking to be excused to the bathroom too often. Have I learned nothing about classroom etiquette? Here I was in third year university! I sit in my seat, the professor in his. I wait. He taps his desk a few times with his long finger. He addresses me in a low, stern voice. 'Your work is very poor, and your classroom etiquette worse. I know you are smoking in the women's bathroom during class-time. That's lacking respect and breaking university rules.'

My heartbeat picks up, me always being such a bad girl and now caught by the professor.

'Do you like breaking the rules?' he asks as he rises from his chair. He moves around to the front of his desk with the utmost precision of movement and he stands there for a few moments, quietly looking at me. 'Look at me,' he orders coolly. At this point in my fantasy, I am starting in reality to feel moistness on my underwear, seated at my very desk. Wait, I am wearing none! I can't bear to look at him! I cross my legs uncomfortably.

'Do you need a spanking? Is that what you need?'

And suddenly there he is, right beside my chair. Though he isn't that close to my ear, it seems as though he is lightly blowing his hot breath right onto my ticklish neck. He speaks words of condemnation about my academic work, the same work he is holding in his hands, my terrible file – the negative data of my performance so far that semester. He brushes the file lightly across my breasts as he slides it onto my desk. 'I could fail you. Suspend you for smoking in the building.' I nervously touch the edge of my skirt. To my horror, his cool, snaky eyes follow my trembling hands.

In my daydream, everything he says now is discharged with the most quiet and sombre of voices. 'Where's your underwear? I can see right through your skirt to your nakedness. Stop squirming. You need a spanking for being such a bad girl – parading around in my classroom without any panties on.'

My pussy tingles miserably at the prospect of him disciplining me on my bare bottom. I can't help it. I quiver and shiver with terror at the thought that he might bring me to orgasm while I lie over his knee. I am in a great state of willingness that he should know about my now wet clitoris too. Though he should never know about such a thing – how in my fantasy, how my clit was waiting for him, crouched and ready for him in among the many folds of my drenched pussy.

While I sit at my desk, he leans over and flips up my skirt and spies my bare pussy. 'You bad girl. If you wish to act like a child, then I shall treat you like one. Stand up,' he orders, now sounding really cross. He straightens up from his leant-over pose to allow me to stand. Bare bottom, hot slaps of his palm is all I care for at the moment, it is too true, but I cannot stand for fear my legs will shake so and not hold me up. Next, with his finger, he taps one of my breasts so as to make it wobble embarrassingly. 'Stand up!' he says, and I stand up. Now he would be able to pull up my skirt more easily. I knew, oh I knew too well . . .

I am transported by his mastery of me and his terrible devotion to this devilish script of ours. I have provoked him in many ways, and now he has complete control and it is time to discipline me. 'I'm going to make your bare bottom sting,' he explains darkly as he stands behind me and tugs on the hem of my skirt. I am ready to lift my skirt for him myself, so obedient am I to his will, but he does it first. Up across my bare bottom my skirt slides up, so slowly that I gasp with shame. He makes my skirt tickle me so as he slides it up my bare ass and also along the front of my pussy. I even feel the light fabric glide up and slowly slip across my wet clit. Suddenly, seven sharp slaps of his hand beat against my now fully exposed buttocks. This has the unfortunate effect of making my pussy gush forth quite unreasonably. And, much to my chagrin and pleasure, his long fingers come from behind me and in-between the back of my legs, and he touches my asshole. He goes in deeper to find my wet and embarrassed private parts. My professor whispers close and too warm in my ear that I needed another spanking. Yet another! My bare bottom is already hot in his hands, he is feeling my hot buttocks and with his long fingers he gives my shy pussy long strokes that make me so warm. Sliding up between my thighs, slowly his fingers glide all along the slippery folds.

'You're all wet, you bad girl,' he says.

Soon he is going to make my ass burn again, he tells me. 'And make it hotter yet,' he threatens. In one smooth move, he is sitting in my chair, and from there he pulls me over his knee. He has me ready to spank again, and this time I can't help but squirm in a most helpless, sexual and highly stimulated way. I am literally grinding myself down onto his knee. He moves his leg in rhythm with my pelvic gyrations as he spanks me hard with his hand and he intensifies his terrible voice and says, 'Stop squirming, you dirty girl.' Impossible, though, since I am already orgasming. And so he disciplines me with his finger that thrusts itself in and out almost angrily from in-between my legs, while I grind, oh my God please ...

'I'm sorry,' I plead to the fantasy professor, but the MacLean of my imaginings keeps probing my clit with his middle finger so insistently. His finger slides back and forth and I climax away, for ever more, him telling me always that I am such a dirty girl.

Such was how my fantasies went. They clearly implicated me as the deviant that I was. And not only that, but how I believed the same to be true of my terrible professor.

Back to reality: the Friday class with MacLean was finally coming to an end and I was anxious to get out of that lecture hall, realising I hadn't listened to a single word of it. As I was leaving, my professor stepped in my path and seemed to deliberately bump into me. At this, he barely apologised, bearing down on my small frame with his eyes. He said with cool intensity, 'Miss Santa Pertog, explain why you continually disturb my class. Your frequent exits from my lectures and my lecture hall are in poor form. You know that, don't you? You don't wish to make me angry, do you?'

'I see,' was all I found to say. As I continued past him in the doorway and I thought, he hates me, I loved the feeling of rousing his angry authority. I had to do something with all my pent-up energy.

The university had a pool which I used frequently and so I decided to go there before heading home. Swimming laps always calmed me with the added bonus of giving me a lift in my physical energy. I loved swimming so much that I had the fabulous habit of keeping a swimsuit on me at all times for my spontaneous swims. It was a one-piece – and never a two-piece – for doing lap after lap. Breast stroke, front crawl, breast stroke, side stroke and so forth until I'd exhausted all the strokes that I knew how to do. One day I would have to get some coaching on how to do the powerful butterfly stroke. I just couldn't seem to get the dolphin kick down, which was ironic as it required such deliberate pelvic movements.

There were a few other women in the changing room – the bunch who regularly swam at the same time as me. We chatted amicably as we put on our bathing suits and challenged each other to races in the pool. Though we all had different body types, we were all fit and toned. One of the best swimmers, Marcia, could always beat me in the back-crawl. But I remained unbeatable in the free-style stroke. So great was my relationship to the water, so intense, that I almost felt I could breathe in it.

After a hot shower, I slipped into the pool. The cold was momentary and I started to warm up within the first few strokes. The water felt like velvet along my smooth body and I couldn't get enough of it. It was better than sex, I thought. Well, different, but so splendid all the same.

In the lane beside me, Marcia was doing her warm-up lap too and we smiled at each other. My, she was a beautiful swimmer. At the other end of the pool, we looked at each other and laughed, setting off in a race to the other side. Freestyle. It was my fastest time yet!

As I plunged through the water continuing my laps, I thought, yes, I wanted to make MacLean angry. What an immensely perverted thing I was. Would he go so far as to fail me, I wondered? I was neglecting my work and I was always going to the women's for a smoke. He might put a black mark on my transcripts. My work was half-assed at best; I had to admit to that. Or maybe he would have to spank me and teach me a lesson in his own way. Lap after lap, I swam. How to escape this terrible mind of mine while my entire body yearned for a sound lesson from the good professor? Dirty fun it was in fantasy, and dirty fun it would turn out to be in reality.

2

That night we were all going to Sergeant's Bar for cocktails. We lived in a small town, so there weren't many nightspots to choose from; but Sergeant's catered mostly to the university crowd and it was an obvious place for a blind date as there were loads of young people around, and a lively atmosphere to avoid the situation getting too awkward. I decided I would wear my new blue crimp dress on my blind date. It was not too low-cut, and skimmed just above the knee. I didn't even know my date's name yet, which was a strange oversight on my part. Had she told me, and I'd been thinking so much about my professor that I wasn't concentrating? I vaguely remembered that it was an unusual name, and that's why I couldn't recall it, but I did know that his family owned a well-established restaurant.

Bee was over at my place while we were getting ready for the evening. 'Let's do it, to it,' I said, suggesting a joint, and I pulled one out from my secret place at the back of my kitchen cupboard. 'It's particularly called for under the circumstances,' I continued. 'Wouldn't you agree? Blind date and all? This is no time to get real!'

'Ha! Go for it,' she encouraged as she flicked her lighter for me.

'Thank you so very much.' I inhaled deeply. 'Hope this isn't going to be a night from hell.'

'Don't get into a weird space, Santa. This stuff sometimes makes you a wee bit anxious, or just plain crazy,' she joked. Anxious wasn't quite the word for it. Restless, horny, that really was what the sweet weed did to me.

'I'm holding you responsible for anything inappropriate,' I warned her, thinking that if I wanted deviant activity, surely I could make it happen tonight; and it could be raunchy enough with this reportedly handsome mystery man – like, if it turned out that me and the blind date screwed in the parking lot or something.

Bee and I were toasty now with the joint. Who knew what the night had to bring; what the night had to offer.

In the club we joined up with Joey and Fez. Fez was my blind date. Fez . . . I found his name rather romantic. He was handsome and he could have me, as far as I was concerned. I instantly thought of him as an objective for me, for he had a magnetic glow about him; it was apparent from the first moment when I'd caught sight of his handsome face, in spite of the sporadic light show going on in the bar around us.

I watched him from behind as he ushered us to the back of the murky bar. By the way he led us around I could sense his sexual confidence.

We all followed him to a table in the back. It was there that I caught a sudden glimpse of my professor. The lights in the bar cast sharp blade-like rays across MacLean's devilish face, so I couldn't quite tell if he really was there – which was very disorienting and disturbing. But finally I knew it; it wasn't just the weed playing tricks. He was there, and in the company of a couple of the more shamelessly lecherous among the other professors from the university. From the other side of the room, I observed him; he had an air of chaperoning the whole affair, such as was his way. Seeing him there made my spine crawl with terrible excitement at what I secretly hoped he might try to do to me in this dark and discreet environment! Well, I didn't have to wait long to find out!

At first, he certainly didn't seem to take any notice of me. I wondered that he quite possibly had made a point of ignoring me while he seemed to be watching the rest of the crowd so intensely. What was so alluring about him when I was out with such a perfectly handsome date of my own age?

Fez was smart, sexy, polite, and had a sense of humour about life. There was seemingly nothing wrong with him. I felt self-conscious, being truly unprepared for someone so attractive. I was so devilish in my ways, but I wanted him to think me pure, a good girl, someone he might like to eventually marry. I'd gone out with a good many men, but that night, it suddenly meant a great deal to me that Fez would like me, and love me even. Moreover, a romantic relationship could bring me to clean up my dirty thoughts and chase away my perverse fantasies about my professor. And Fez did seem to be falling for me. Later that night we did kiss. It could have been more than that, but something strange had happened at the club; something that completely affected the evening.

It was a queer event – one that might never be explained – and later I badly wanted to erase the mysterious happening. Originally I thought it had involved Fez. In the end, however, it turned out to have nothing at all to do with him.

I'd been clever that night, brilliant even, with Fez and I making jokes. We got on well, clowning around, stimulating each other with our wit and stealing brief moments of intimacy. He would lightly place his hand on my thigh when he was talking to me; everything he did was subtle and smooth. He really had my head swirling. I felt like a blushing maid, and after a few drinks it seemed that we could be totally meant for each other. I was hoping with all my being that he felt the same way.

He led me up onto the dance floor. The music was great; some of my favourite songs. I loved those tunes and I was a good dancer – one who got noticed by men and women alike. Several fast dances had gone by and I felt in a sexy sweat. Fez loved my dancing and was watching me, admiring my figure. He didn't seem to mind that I was twirling and twisting with everyone else dancing around us. Of course, my greatest attention was on him and he moved just great, too.

Then came the slow dance, the one where Fez held me close, his arms about me, his groin subtly suggesting sex. It wasn't like I wasn't up for a discreet little romp on the dance floor, but when he started putting his hands up my skirt, and even under my panties, fingering my most private place, searching my folds, well, I wasn't really ready for that, especially in public. Although it felt so good, that slippery finger, I didn't want him to think I was that kind of girl, because I so liked him and wanted to see him again. So, out of strict reflex, I roughly pushed Fez away.

He looked completely surprised and stunned, and held up his hands in seeming innocence and anger and walked away from me, leaving me alone on the dance floor. Just as shocked myself, I spun around, seeking perhaps some other culprit, and only found my professor dancing with some woman a few feet away. Could it have been him? No matter how aghast my face must have looked, MacLean wouldn't meet my gaze.

As I made my way back to our table I wasn't sure if I shouldn't just go out the back exit door. I realised I'd acted sleazy on the dance floor, as was my usual way; and it could have been anyone, someone with a sense of humour who had copped a feel. And it would have been out of character for Fez, given that he'd been so subtle earlier. God, what did he think of me at this point? I wondered. At our table, I could see he was visibly perturbed by me. Bee was also giving me questioning looks.

I could only stand there stupidly and say, 'I'm really sorry, Fez, I thought you, or someone ...' I couldn't carry on. I was completely baffled and wondered if I hadn't imagined the whole thing. Was I losing my mind? I slurped my drink and I could feel a tear stream down my face, leaving a black mascara trail. Before this, the night had been unbelievably fabulous. What was this weird twist? It challenged my perception of things. What indeed had happened? It was ages since we'd smoked the joint.

Fez would ask me out again, perhaps. And maybe the next time, there wouldn't be these complications – the same haunting complications that I was later to grow convinced must have had to do with my suspicious professor.

'I think you need to go freshen up,' Fez said dryly. Well, I hated him at that moment. Go freshen up. Of all the nerve!

'I'll go with you,' Bee offered.

Bee and I went along the corridor to the women's washroom, and I caught sight of MacLean standing there alone against the wall. I just about died then and there. We had to pass right by him. To my utmost shock, there he was licking his fingers, tasting them just as we went by. He nodded almost imperceptibly at me and I shuddered. My pussy fluttered. It couldn't be possible, I thought. He couldn't be sampling my own personal, private sex scent right off his devilish fingers, could he? The same scent that he seemed to have so deviously stolen from me on the dance floor? Among the moving crowd, had his hand stole up dress and under my panties? His probing finger had even slid into my cunt! It was so covert and so blatant all at the same time. And how incredibly menacing! Was it truly him?

It could have been anyone.

I had to admit that I had been provoking MacLean since the beginning of the first term at university this year. This is what you get, then, isn't it, girl? I chastised myself. But if he had perpetrated such a thing, he'd done so of his own perverse volition. Like he'd stepped over the line and had become an active agent in my fantasy world. He touched me where I wanted him to touch me. He was now tasting his fingers and looking at me. It was awful, and yet I was finding the whole thing unbearably exciting. I had butterflies in my stomach, not to mention that my underwear was quite wet indeed. I hurried to the door of the women's bathroom.

When I burst in, I didn't know what to say to Bee any more. At first I was going to tell her my suspicions, but then I thought I must be going mad, and not even one's best friend should be let in to that kind of paranoia. People talk, even best girlfriends, and I didn't want a reputation. In any case, the bathroom was too crowded and noisy for us to speak candidly at that moment.

I checked my mascara in the mirror. It was a bit smudged and as I leant in closer, I looked over and saw Bee was re-applying her lipstick. And so while we waited to talk I dwelt on the manner in which we crossed each other's paths, me and MacLean. Tensions were mounting. Our exchanges had a hypnotic effect on me. This was not a good sign, I admitted to myself. In the end, in my very heart of hearts, I deeply hoped for things to work out with Fez and that I could get a regular thing going with him, and dedicate myself only to him.

But I knew I couldn't resist this game with MacLean. And now it was moving up a notch. My rule-breaking behaviour was bringing him to play the game on his terms. I revelled in the idea of coming up against his power. It felt inevitable. But little did I know what I was in for with the good professor. In my present state of mind, then, it was flesh to touch and flesh to fear. Let it come up against me, I thought, that flesh to lick, that muscle to beat, that sweat to taste. God help me, I intended to rile my stern professor! What with my shameful behaviour as his student and all the other things I could plan to do, just wait and see, I thought. And tonight – when he fingered me on the dance floor – marked his first disciplinary measure.

With the restroom finally cleared out, Bee turned to me and said, 'What happened out there?'

I took a deep breath and shook my head. 'I think I've had too much to drink,' I said. 'I really like Fez, though, and now he must hate me.'

'Did you really shove him?' Bee asked, her voice echoing in my ears as the adrenaline continued to pulse through me from my encounter with MacLean.

'Well, I guess I did. I thought he was touching my ass, my legs, my … you know. If he was, I want him to know it was a real turn on, only it shocked me on the dance floor. It was just a reflex action. Bee, is he leaving right now? We should go back.'

'OK, sure, hon. But I hope you're not scared of him.' She looked genuinely concerned, then smiled and gently asked, 'Did he really cop a feel? I hope not, I mean, it is a first date. A first dance, for God's sake!' Bee further commented with a laugh, 'I mean, I don't really know this guy.'

'It is a first date and I have to tell him he's too hot for his own good, that's all.' I shot these words over my shoulder as I led the way out of the bathroom, leaving my nervous giggle to be swallowed up by the stale air behind us.

Outside, MacLean was nowhere to be seen.

Back at the table, I sat close to Fez. He hadn't left after all, and I was relieved. Without a word, I drew myself closer to him. There was something about him that made me feel good, even though I still felt very silly. I tried to convince myself that what I'd just done had a lot of style.

Luckily Fez didn't make any sign to move away. We were going to forget the incident, I thought thankfully. Or maybe talk about it when we were alone. For now, Joey was telling a funny story about his landlord.

Fez was enjoying the story and chortling at Joey's pin-sharp character analysis. I looked up at Fez's profile; he was divine. I was keen to tell him I was just teasing him on the dance floor when I pushed him away; that I was just trying to tantalise him. That someone bumped against me, or so I thought, and had gotten fresh. An approach that wasn't my style.

I didn't mean to hurt Fez. That is, unless he liked that sort of thing. Later I did tell him all of this.

'What is your style, then?' he asked.

'I'm used to men, in a sense. I know what they're like, what they think about with girls. And I like you,' I replied coquettishly.

'I'll bet you're used to men,' he replied. 'How much do you like me?'

He accepted my overtures of affection, embracing me too. He apologised for 'grinding' me on the dance floor. I told him that I had liked it. He kissed me deep, but as much as I urged him on later, on the front stoop of my apartment building, he wouldn't come up to my flat. And he only left once he'd seen that I'd entered my apartment building safely. I fell more in love with him for seeming to be so gallant and protective of me. And my feelings for him intensified even more as I worried that he might not love me back in the same way and that was why he wouldn't come upstairs.

When I did get inside my apartment, and with the night behind me, I ran myself a bath. My strong feelings for Fez seemed to have unnerved me; the whole crazy night had, in fact. A bath would do me good; unwind the tension.

But it wasn't long before I started to imagine another lewd encounter with MacLean.

God help me, I couldn't rid my mind of him. I took out my razor and slowly began soaping my armpits. With a light touch, I shaved under one arm. The soap smelt like sea mist: clean, yet fecund.

I shaved and thought about the incident on the dance floor. The fingers that stole up my skirt in public had felt terribly erotic and had made me so wet. I wanted my professor to touch me again in the nether regions, and at greater length – if it had indeed been him.

I rinsed and began shaving under the other arm. The blade was keen, and it had to be guided carefully across my skin. In a moment, my tender underarm was shaved smooth and it felt wonderfully sensitive as I stroked it with my fingertips. It felt like my pussy would if it was also shaved clean. So many raw undulations; my clit especially would love to be freed from all the hair around it. I sank back into the tub and my breasts felt light and warm in the water. My nipples were dark and erect and I raised them up and down against the liquid surface. My, how sexually charged up I felt.

I had to shave my legs and that was a chore, for I was waiting to shave something else. I had intended it all along.

My legs were shaved clean, but for one little nick. It stung slightly under the water, but I was more interested in the feeling of bringing my clitoris up and down out of the water. Slowly, so slowly; I did this repeatedly until I could no longer bear it. I rose out of the bath.

Astride my toilet, I sat backwards from the usual position, causing me to separate my legs to accommodate the toilet bowl. It was the best position to allow for a proper shave. I had done this sort of thing before and it would always occur when I was on the sexual edge, so to speak, like in a MacLean situation. It was one of those times when I was trying to get myself into trouble with a man I shouldn't be toying with. I was shaving my cunt for my professor, wasn't I?

Yes, my razor was sharp and it did the trick. First and foremost, the area around my clit had to be shorn. It felt so good to denude it of fluff. My clit was responding, so full, so achingly, to the shedding of the hair. Soon my pussy was mostly bare. My protruding lips were barely covering a clit that was so excited to be more exposed. I was getting wet doing this procedure and I had to return to the bath frequently to rinse away my slippery juices. My razor could slide on the horny wetness.

It was all I could do to not orgasm throughout the grooming of my cunt. But I'd wanted to save the final exquisite pleasure for my bed. My, how soft my pussy felt now that it was all shaved. It wanted to be stroked and stroke it I did, after rinsing it off in the tub. There was no hair left, just a softness that was indescribable. Rising finally from the tub, I stood in front of the mirror and saw the expressive shape of my shaved-bare pussy. My two lips stuck out and my clit was like a tiny little tongue, which shyly hid in-between them. I touched it. I ran my finger up along between my lips. It was very wet indeed and it wasn't from any bath water. My clit was slippery to the touch and wanted to be rubbed from side to side.

Once in my bed, I continued to molest myself. My clit

rose outwards to my self-pleasuring and my mind filled with images charged with sex. I couldn't, nor did I desire to rein in my sexual energy. I tried to turn my mind to Fez's playful gyrations on the dance floor, but I quickly lapsed into my hedonism and thoughts of MacLean's indiscretions with me instead: him assaulting my being, at once deeply frightening me and arousing me. Were my sexual imaginings now an effort to claim my own part in the debauched episode that my professor had with me on the dance floor? I could still feel his finger sliding into me.

My cunt was so bare, it was frightening. I burned with orgasm, one that I could guide from my swollen clit into the cave of my pussy, through and through, so hard that it spasmed into my anus too.

To sleep. It had been a long week. Yet even in my sleep, I could not escape my fantasies.

I dreamt about my professor. In the empty classroom, he was standing quietly behind me and he was accusing me of being very wet in-between my legs. Whispering close to my ear he was saying that I was a bad girl, that I liked being a dirty girl and that I wanted him to touch my pussy. He said he knew my cunt was so naked because I had shaved it bare. I was a bad enough girl that I wanted to feel my own underwear rub against my shaved pussy underneath, he accused me.

'Show me,' he ordered, as I was standing at his desk. 'Pull your pants down,' he said sternly.

In my dream, I couldn't tell what happened next, but my pants were somehow pulled down. In-between my legs I was feeling my soft, hairless sex in front of him. Slowly, and without a breath, I pulled my cunt lips away just enough for him to see my clit. Without a word, he flicked it with his finger and then spanked my naked pussy three times while I stood there. Next he drew me onto his knee. I was sitting on his lap without any panties on and I was bad – so bad, so dirty, he told me – for shaving my cunt. He spanked it several times while he made me lean back into his arms.

His fingers slithered condemningly along my cunt. Yes, I was indeed wet. His voice was telling me so, reprimanding me, as only a professor's could.

3

I woke to the phone ringing. It was Bee. 'I wanted to know that you're OK. Kind of a weird night, eh? But fun. Did Fez behave himself when he took you home?' She spilled her questions out.

'He's here right now,' I replied playfully. Then I said, 'No he's not, but he could have been if he'd wanted to.'

'They've gone fishing, so let's f-off to the mall,' she suggested.

'I turned him off. And that was why he didn't come in,' I said sullenly, suddenly concerned about Fez and real life.

'It was late, too late. They set off at sunrise. They planned this camping trip weeks ago, so don't worry about it. Joey didn't stay at my place either. So, you into it? Come with me.'

'Why didn't he tell me about the camping trip?' It tortured me.

'Don't worry, he's hot for you,' she said. 'Now, I'm coming by to pick you up,' she said.

'Sure. I'll put the coffee on before I jump into the shower. Use your key if I can't get to the door when you come,' I said and hung up.

I loved Saturdays. I checked the clock. Nine-thirty. In the bathroom I looked in the mirror for a moment. At first I chortled to myself in a friendly way. Then I shook my head and looked at myself very earnestly. 'What kind of girl are you?" I asked the image in the mirror, and for God's sake, it smiled back at me. Devilish thing.

When I stripped, I looked with some chagrin at the

shave I'd given myself the night before. As I continued to eye it, I said to my pussy, 'Well, I hope you have time to grow back before Fez might find out what a horny bitch you really are. That is, if he ever cares to find out, which he will, won't he, you sleazy creature?' And truly, I couldn't possibly wait that long – like, long enough for my pubic hair to grow back before I could sleep with Fez. That would be too agonising.

Clean yourself up, girl, was my next thought.

I luxuriated under the jets of steaming water for more than a half hour. Hot tides of it coursed through my hair and pulsed down the back of my neck. I could stay in the shower for ever, like a seductive mermaid under a waterfall.

Later, Bee and I were in the mall. In one of the many identical stores, I picked out two short skirts. They were gauzy and light and I idly wondered how it would feel to wear to them without any underwear in class; in my class with MacLean. Bee interrupted my scandalous thoughts as if she knew all about them. 'Gonna model those for your mystery man?' she asked.

I laughed. 'What do you mean?' My, how I liked being bad. It was like leading a double life. One sacred, one profane. One Fez, one MacLean.

Fez. I simply, deeply wanted to fuck him.

'Did I totally fuck it up with Fez on the dance floor? Say it's not true, Bee!'

'Fez saw you were a knock-out, my dear. Volatile, perhaps, but I think he found you exciting. But do you think he would like those skirts on you? Pretty sleazy, girl! And I know you. You wouldn't wear a slip, would you?'

'Pretty see-through, I'll wager.'

'Did Fez really feel you up on the dance floor?' she asked again, obviously intrigued by what had happened.

'I can't tell any more, Bee, it was probably all in my mind,' I said evasively.

'Either you felt it or you didn't, Santa,' she argued.

'I think we were both just getting carried away. I'm such a flirt on the dance floor, it could have just been some jerk feeling me up,' I said trying to close the subject.

'Why the hell can't a girl have fun on a dance floor? Really, this society makes us feel so guilty about our sexuality,' Bee complained. 'Don't you dare feel that way, Santa,' she insisted.

'You're absolutely right,' I agreed with her. In principle, I did concur, but if it had been MacLean that had secretly violated me, I guiltily knew how long I'd been provoking such an incident with him. And a girl may want to have her deviant fun too.

'C'mon, I'm going to get these.' I nodded at her and started making my way up to the front of the store with the two skirts.

'I can't believe you're going to buy those,' Bee commented with a slight laugh as she followed behind me.

'I think they're like angel's wings.'

'You know full well that the last thing they are is innocent,' she remarked.

'No way,' I said and smiled to myself.

'Just don't wear them to class.'

'Crime and Enforcement!' we said in unison, both tittering at the thought of the lecherous professor.

After I paid for the skirts, I offered to buy us both lunch.

We went to the restaurant in the mall. It was a mid-range joint and it wasn't crowded. At the table next to us was a native couple who sat waiting for service with their menus closed in front of them. As the waitress was bringing us our menus, I saw the man raise his finger to try to get her attention. The waitress didn't seem to take notice and continued towards our table.

'G'day,' she greeted us pleasantly. 'Can I bring you a beverage to start?'

'Just a couple of coffees, right, Bee?' I told the woman as I looked over at the two waiting for her at the next table.

'Right away,' she said and turned to move off for our coffees. The native man put his hand up again to signal her but the waitress walked right by without so much as looking at them. I felt irritated by this. Why would she ignore them? I mean, we'd just got there; we could have ordered our coffees in a minute or two. By the look on this couple's faces, I could tell they'd been waiting a while.

'Santa, what are you going to order?' Bee asked, and I looked down to read my menu.

'Something nutty and light,' I said hopefully, 'but at this place, it should probably be pizza.'

'Well, they seem to have a few salads with nuts and cheese in them.'

I read the selection and I said, 'Actually, spinach and warmed goat's cheese on toast sounds fabulous. What do you want?'

'Maybe pasta or something,' she said indecisively.

The waitress was back to set down our steaming coffees. She stood there, smiling at us and asked if we were ready to order.

With a frown, I looked up at her. 'No, we haven't decided, but I think those people over there are waiting for you to take their order,' I informed her as I discreetly pointed to the couple beside our table. 'They've been trying to wave you down. Haven't you noticed?' I asked her, making it plain that I was annoyed. She looked over at the couple and shrugged her shoulders, smiling imp-ishly back at Bee and me.

'Oh, yes,' she tried to say casually. When she went over to them and took their order, I thought that I could overhear her being short with them. Being outright rude. Bee noticed this too.

'Dumb bitch,' Bee said quietly to me about the waitress.

'No kidding. They shouldn't put up with that. I'd ask for the manager. Racist bitch. She probably thinks they have no money or something,' I guessed angrily.

'Let's not tip her,' Bee suggested.

'Darn straights,' I confirmed.

After we had eaten, Bee announced some surprise plans she had for us. 'You and I are going to find the boys. After lunch, let's go searching for our rugged men!'

I sensed there was no time to waste and we were pumped for it; we wanted to be with those boys. Adventure awaited. Bee proposed a camping trip to find the boys somewhere in the bush, but I wondered if she really knew how to find them. She was no tracker.

I asked for the bill. I wasn't going to tip the waitress and when she brought me my visa card back I explained why I wasn't going to give her a gratuity. 'I'm not leaving you a tip and you need to know why,' I said. 'You treated those people incredibly rudely and I find that obscene, do you understand me? You should be very much ashamed of yourself.' With that, Bee and I left. We felt righteous and proud and we smiled at the couple and they smiled back at us, though they were none the wiser about the discussion we'd just had with the waitress.

Off to go camping! I wasn't at all sure of how our reception would be. Plus, I had this shaven pussy now, which I hadn't yet fessed up to Bee. Fez might find out what a horny slut I was if he were to discover such a thing so early on in our relationship. That would be too much. I paled at the thought of his possible reaction.

29

Some guys, I guessed, could get turned off by that sort of thing. I was on the verge of telling Bee that I wanted to forget the whole thing, but then I realised how badly I wanted to see Fez again. He was so good looking. And I wanted to make up for shoving him for no apparent reason on the dance floor last night by giving him a blow-job tonight.

Bee and I left with the two-person tent she had stored in the trunk of her car and we went to hit the big road that would take us north and up to the Canadian Shield. It was about a two-hour drive. I offered to take the wheel, while she was to navigate.

'We're never going to find them, Bee,' I argued, and laughed as the countryside whizzed by. I didn't want to find them, in point of fact – not with my bare pussy syndrome.

'Not so, my sweet friend, they're actually expecting us. I know their exact coordinates,' Bee finally disclosed. Count on Bee; full of surprises.

'They're expecting us? I asked. 'Why on earth didn't you tell me this was all planned?'

'Because it's an adventure!' she laughed.

'And all day I was worried Fez may not appreciate our intrusion on their camping trip. You're a twisted bitch is what you are,' I said. 'So he wants to see me tonight, then?'

Bee laughed. 'Of course, and he's lucky that you want to see him again, is all I have to say.'

I smiled. 'You're sweet to say that, Bee. But you're a total wench for leaving me in the dark like that.'

She laughed at me. 'Aha!' she said, and she'd got me good. I loved Bee. She was as twisted as me in her own way.

God, what was I going to do about my admittedly perverse-looking pussy with Fez tonight? I could always tell him I never sleep with a man right away. Yeah right.

Point of no return was the situation for me and my shaved cunt. So there was nothing else to do but calm myself down. Well, take it or leave it, Fez, if you think I'm screwy for having a shaved pussy, you may be right to think that, but tough luck for you. I looked over at Bee as she checked the map that would guide us to the boys and whatever else the fates might have in store.

'Stay on number one for the next hour or so,' she told me.

We sailed on through the changing landscape. For a while we were quiet in our own thoughts. At one point I looked over at Bee and saw that my navigator was napping. I continued driving.

I wondered if she had such deviant sexual tendencies as I did. She'd told me once that she and Joey liked to talk about kinky sex, and would relate some of their more iffy past sexual encounters to each other. But they were probably healthier than any of mine tended to be, no doubt.

While I drove on down the highway, I recalled one of the first strange experiences I'd had, which had irretrievably shaped my sexual nature. This same experience would serve to set me on my future course of strange liaisons with men. It was an event that shaped me into the woman that I was now. A woman with unusual erotic propensities.

I have always been unbearably easily sexually excited. Maybe one would go so far as to say that my libido was a tad over-active. Obviously, I had slept with a good many men by the time I was in my early twenties, but it was pretty conventional sex, so to speak.

My fantasies, however, had never been anything but of the most perverse nature; forbidden and strange imaginings involving risky encounters. Once, when I just turned twenty, I met someone who also had debauched fantasies, and when we came into contact, he chose to act on them.

I was to go for an appointment to see my doctor, for my annual physical exam. But as my doctor had broken his leg, I was to see his partner at the clinic. I only ever spied this dark-haired, white-coated doctor from a distance while he attended to his own patients, though he did always seem to be looking over at me when I was in the waiting room and he gave me the strangest of feelings.

As I said, on this particular occasion I was to see the peculiar Dr Bird.

Once I was shown into the examination room by the medical secretary, I had to wait about five minutes for the doctor to finish up with another patient. The office was obviously busy, but in short order Dr Bird entered, nodded hello to me and set about looking at my medical file. 'I see,' I was to hear him say mostly to himself, and then he cleared his throat and quietly wrote a few things down.

I'd always had a slightly strange relationship with my own doctor.

God knows what he had written in my file about my high libido and his likely suspicions of my promiscuous ways, but when Dr Bird looked up at me he seemed perturbed and he spoke to me sternly. 'Tell me about yourself, Santa.'

'What do you want to know?' I asked. 'I mean, I have no health complaints, I'm just here for my annual physical.'

'It's been over a year, yes. I gather from your file you've been sexually active since you were quite young. You've been on the pill from the age of fifteen. Are you still taking oral contraceptives?'

I felt he was being presumptuous in drawing that sort of conclusion about my early behaviour, so I replied,

'Oh, no, I had terrible cramps as a teenager, and the pill helped, that's all. Still does. Yes, I'm on the pill, if that's what you're asking.'

He looked at me amusedly; he clearly didn't believe that was the only reason. His eyes wandered down to look at my chest. He registered that I wasn't wearing a bra and disapproval was the expression that crossed his face.

His terrible look made my pussy tingle slightly. I couldn't help but feel I might be in for the most unusual physical exam at his hands. In fact, I dirtily hoped I was in for a little fondling by him. It promised to be scientific in its execution.

At any rate, I never wore a bra; the doctor could go to the devil if he was to judge me on that. I'd heard bras were bad for you. Anyway, I was small, so why should I? Even if I was big, why should I have to wear one? Unless, of course, I was more comfortable. No. Overall, I resented it that one was expected to wear a bra. How dare he look at me and condemn!

'Put on the gown,' the strange Dr Bird now ordered.

Now, ordinarily the doctor leaves the room while the patient makes ready for the examination. But Dr Bird had no intention of leaving and so I had to change out of my clothes into the gown right in front of him. I could have objected; it would have been totally within my rights, but part of me wanted him to see me undress. His penetrating eyes were turning me on and he watched me the whole time as I took off my clothes. He then referred soberly to my file. I tried to be discreet, I tried not to look at him, but when I did, I could see him growing more stern and reproving as I slowly shed my clothes. He asked me questions: 'How many men do you have regular intercourse with? I'm sure you've heard of STDs?'

'Umm...' I wasn't sure if I should answer that, or

how I might answer that. He was trying to be a moralising bastard was all. God, this whole thing was sexy and he was going to examine me on a whole other level as soon as I was undressed.

'Do you have a boyfriend?' he asked me and now I was completely undressed and trying with some difficulty to put on the gown. To do such a simple thing as put on the robe was, of course, more awkward than I'd ever before experienced.

'I don't have a boyfriend right now,' I answered, still trying to figure out how the examination gown worked.

'Hmm,' he responded, clearly not believing me about my not having a boyfriend. 'Get up on the table,' he ordered gruffly as he stood up from his chair.

I was still trying to secure the gown. I had it on now and was beginning to tie the strings at the back as he approached me. I felt utterly shocked when he gave my fidgeting hands a slight tap and said, 'Don't bother with it.'

He was standing behind me. 'Lie down now,' came Dr Bird's voice. That was all I needed. The tenor of his voice caused me to fumble nervously and my pussy gushed forth with wetness. Disobediently, I continued to try and tie the damn robe, while at the same time climb onto the high bench. Naturally I found that I could not do both at once. The gown was therefore left untied, and the doctor was soon guiding me up onto the bench. The folds of the gown opened during this process and my ass was admittedly exposed as I climbed onto his examination table.

As if he were expanding the wings of a bird, the doctor pulled my gown away from my hips and, in so doing, completely exposed my lower parts. 'Don't get caught. There, there,' he said gently to me as I knelt on his table.

Get caught? What did he mean? Ostensibly, he must

have meant that my gown might catch me up. Now he put his one hand on the back of my neck and the other on the region that was between both my breasts and pressed down so as to make me lie back. The examination table felt cold and hard as I lay down. My position was still not to his specifications and he further adjusted my body on the table by placing each of his hands underneath my gown, under my naked buttocks; and then he raised and lowered me into place. Clearly this move was meant to establish control, as I ended up in the very same position as before.

He proceeded to lift up my gown, all the way up from my thighs and right up past my breasts so as to completely expose my naked body up to my neck. As I said before, my examination gown was not caught up under me, or under my buttocks in any way. It was easily pulled off my entire torso. Dr Bird scrutinised my now nude body in the most satisfied and self-assured of ways. 'What's your boyfriend's name?' He smiled. I involuntarily squeezed my thighs together with the somewhat unwelcome pleasure I seemed to be experiencing at all this. Of course, he did take note of this, and his smile disappeared into an expression of severity.

'I don't have a boyfriend,' I answered. This was actually the truth, because, of course, I had not one, but many boyfriends at the time.

He shook his head like he was correcting me in my answer. His eyes grazed once again all along my naked lower parts. 'That's not true. Yes you do,' he insisted. 'Spread your legs a little for the doctor.' And he helped me to do so by parting my knees gently, and then when he met my slight resistance, he pressed more firmly and spread my legs apart so fully that not only were my knees pushed right back, but my bum was raised also. 'Are you letting this boy have intercourse with you?' he asked. From his position at the end of the exam table, I saw him peer in at the private place between my thighs and I could feel his eyes stroke the sight of my vulgar openness.

'No,' I said weakly. My body parts twitched; more specifically my pussy pulsed nervously. No doubt this was visible to his scientific eyes. In fact, I was certain my pussy was wet now, and somehow, in his eyes, this was reflected. My guilt and my pleasure were registered.

'I can tell, you know. I can tell if you've had sex. Are you a dirty girl? Do you let all the boys touch you?' He then smoothly and expertly slid his finger into my pussy and probed deeply. 'Oh yes, you like being touched by boys; touched all the way down to here.' In a circle he felt around my innermost spot and I couldn't help but rise to the occasion, so to speak. That is to raise that so highly-charged, ignoble pussy of mine, so innocently burning and helplessly wanting this touching. Pussy o' mine. It was starting to sound like a song. Whatever the music of it all was, my cunt just simply felt moved to the point of unendurable pleasure. My, he was expert in his touch. He almost had me orgasming. I couldn't bear it as he probed with his fingers, digging into me so sensually.

'You're very wet,' he admonished. How could I help it? I squirmed with embarrassment as the doctor vigorously stroked my cunt lips. I thought of how I might try to resist his urgings. And of how I might not. His fingers plunged softly and insistently in and out of me, in and out of me. I was growing ever more wet and his finger slid more and more easily now, as I was increasingly becoming wetter in-between my folds.

'Put your heels together,' he ordered as he finally released my knees. There was no hope for it, and as I put my heels together my sex spread out and opened in a new and different way and was exposed to its widest extent. As he looked down on it, an idea seemed to cross his mind and he went over to his desk. I lay there, hearing him opening a drawer while he continued with his verbal condemnation.

'Do you not know never to let boys touch you?' he fairly snarled. 'You bad girl.' Momentarily, he was back at my side.

What he did next was so strange that later I wasn't sure it had even happened. I lay there with my heels together and he was holding what I guessed was a tongue-depressor over my nude pussy. He then proceeded to tap my moist cunt with this flat wooden stick, hitting my clit and all regions around it. With each little blow of the tongue depressor, I squirmed, for it gave me delicious, slight stings and I let out more juices all the terrible time. Throughout, he expertly fingered me with his free hand and I must confess, though I tried to hide it from him, I was having mini orgasms every so often throughout the exam. I didn't doubt it would perturb him even more to know such a thing and only bring on a lecture.

'Stop it and lay still for the doctor, you bad, bad girl,' he demanded. He put down his tool, spread open my cunt lips with his fingers, and pressed down on my exposed clit.

'You could get pregnant, or contract dirty diseases.' He gave me a particularly hard tap on my clit with his hand. He looked up at me and placed his attentions on my hardened dark, nipples. Moving up closer to my breasts, he took it upon himself to pinch them both sternly and he continued to squeeze them that way for more than a half a minute, saying, 'Do you understand me?'

This marked the beginning of the breast exam and he began to run the palms of his hands over my hard, protruding nipples. I secretly touched my pussy while he did this. It felt red-hot and wet inside and out, God help me. Well, he was going to put an end to that; the female patient wasn't about to be allowed to orgasm. 'Turn over,' he ordered, and he helped me go onto my stomach in the most manipulative of ways. In no time, I was placed on my belly. My robe, completely off, had now fallen to the floor. There I lay before him, my naked bum exposed for him to punish. Once he had me in place, he backed off and moved over to his desk again, glancing back every so often to see my tensed, naked, waiting ass. I turned my head to see him opening a different drawer from before, from whence he'd produced his punishing tongue depressor. Ensuring that he wasn't looking, I couldn't help but for a moment press my cunt down onto the hard, cold bench, to grind it with pleasure. Soon, I felt his hand sharply slap my ass and, following that, he spread my cheeks, almost to the point of pain, and found my asshole with his searching fingers. Next, a cool-feeling instrument was being inserted into my asshole. A gasp was released from my mouth. Something small but unmentionable happened and he had to wipe me up. He seemed to expect it, as he had a cloth all ready to wipe me up and said, 'You're just a baby, aren't you?' And he expertly wiped my ass, then spanked me hard on my bare bottom till it burned all over. I would never know if he'd detected how at that moment I was massively orgasming, in my favourite position, on my belly. Of course he could see that I was helplessly grinding down on the bench. He knew what a naughty thing I was indeed.

The doctor had gone through the examination, he said, to check that my promiscuous ways hadn't caused me any consequential physical problems. Dirty doctor.

In the car, I looked over and Bee was still asleep in the passenger-bucket-seat beside me. I had been occasionally touching myself through my jeans, thinking about Dr Bird and our escapades while I drove on.

Aphrodite help me, I prayed, as I loved every moment of my interaction with Dr Bird. And so, two years later, I continued to fantasise and refantasise about the sexual episodes with my doctor that day. Me, a mature law student, a terribly turned-on university student who loved her secret memories of Dr Bird.

And how simply, too, did I become so easily aroused by the mere act or thought of buying sexy clothes for myself, like, for example, the gauzy skirts I'd bought that morning with Bee. I imagined all the places I might wear them, not only without a slip, but sans underwear, for that matter.

4

Bee and I had been travelling northbound for about two hours on the Manitoba highway. When we reached Canadian Shield country, we had the unfortunate timing of meeting one of those occasional spring thunderstorms that raged over one's head, threatening all kinds of miseries, from lightning striking you to huge hailstones that might bounce off your head and knock you right out. We had to wait in the car until the tempest blew itself out. The rain drummed madly on the car windows. This fabulous pulsing weather naturally brought me to think of MacLean and all the energy that seemed to be pent up in him. How exciting it was to experience the forces of nature working through us, I thought. And when it came to MacLean and I, our particular passion was powerful decadence of the highest order. It was quite the storm we were churning up!

How I was like the storm outside our own car. And dirty MacLean, too. The great tall trees waved in sensuous wet circles over our car. In the gusty wind, the leaves throbbed with the rainfall. Only once all was washed clean did the storm subside.

When the weather cleared, we were not too far from our destination, and after some map-reading Bee gave me directions for the final leg of the journey. As she'd said, she knew where they were all along.

We left the car parked under a big tree and went out in search of the boys. Our legs were getting wet from the long rain-drenched grasses and it made us giggle as we headed for the far side of Caribou Lake. The sun was coming back out for its last hoorah of the day, then it slowly disappeared into twilight and lit the way to a small campsite where we found Fez and Joey, who had toughed out the storm in the way one inevitably does, as camping forces you to do. The two of them appeared in the distance and, as we were coming up on them, they struck me like wild-looking bushmen – scary, savage-looking creatures, really. Or so I was terribly excited to think.

Up closer, they in fact looked rugged and devilishly handsome. They were wearing wet, sloppy hats and colourless, dripping raincoats. Those good and hardy boys were waiting for us. And they were so especially cute because they hadn't shaved that day and there they were, camping out with the bears. They were sexy and grisly in appearance. How I loved that! How I wanted to feel Fez's fuzzy male face and his chest. I longed to touch his broad, lovely chest. To kiss his manly hair there and everywhere else on his body too. It was to enough to make me melt! He looked delicious.

Fez and Joey were glad to see us. At first I felt a little shy around Fez. Although he behaved with a proprietorial air, this was so magnetic that in only a few moments I felt at home with him. We set up the extra tent together, wordlessly claiming the night to come. I was excited and worried about what he might discover about me, my shaved pussy especially. Overall, though, I was ready to settle into his arms and, as it turned out, I didn't have to wait long for his affections. Early in the evening, we wandered away from the other pair and ended up with warm kisses to exchange in the seemingly uninhabited woods. This was just as the sun finally set and the woods were beautifully lit. Later this new relationship would be consummated. But not before the bizarre and unexpected fireside story-telling night that was to take place first between the four of us.

Around the roaring fire, we each, it was decided, had to tell our most secret story. The rules were that it had to be based on a true situation, but one might embellish as one needed to make it the most exciting and forbidden of tales. What stories had I to tell? If I related any that were even remotely true, let alone heighten it with more deviant fantasy, I would be outcast before you could say Jehovah. The others surely didn't have such controversial stories as I, nor could match my perverse imagination. Or so I thought, but, as it turned out, they had plenty of their own secrets to tell.

Who came up with this game anyway? It was Bee, of course. She avowed that she and Joey played it all the time. And that no detail in the stories must go unmentioned, and that all poetic license in our stories should be richly seized upon.

So Bee began. She described her encounter with a much older man. 'He was a storeowner. Peter was his name, and this was a job I'd taken between university sessions. I had almost finished my first year law. Anyway, he and his son, about my age, were always harassing me, offering me things, pulling at my skirts, copping a feel whenever they could. The father was much more overt, being more experienced at harassing young women. The son, Paul, however, was slightly more menacing, plotting and dangerous. I knew he wanted to possess me in a distinctly different way than his father, who just wanted a quick dirty little romp with a younger woman, preferably a young, female employee whom he could dominate. Paul and all his friends with their muscle cars would stand around gawking at me all the time and it made me think that not only did he want me, but he wanted to share me with his friends. It was like I was a piece of merchandise in his father's store. Paul took every opportunity to lift my skirts up in front of his friends. It was like a power thing with him to take liberties with me in front of his gawking friends. They would try to corner me and I would scarcely get away with my purity intact. I would never put up with that now, I assure you. And I doubly assure you that I would never do what it is that I'm about to tell you that I did.

'So anyway, these silly games were going on for some time and I guess the whole thing was also giving me a cheap thrill too in a way. All this sexual nuance, this odd foreplay with both the father and son – it was turning me on, I must confess. So one day, I –' Bee cleared her throat and paused momentarily, '– now do remember I was a little wild in those days,' she continued.

I laughed at her remark and interjected, 'What's with the past tense in that last sentence, girly?'

Joey grunted at me. He was looking at her with a mixture of horniness and disapproval.

'Shall I continue? Or maybe we should stop this little game?'

'Go on,' Joey urged her and lightly pinched her thigh.

'Alright, then,' she said as she cuddled up closer to him and resumed her storytelling. 'I got very daring, you see, and one day I decided not to wear any underwear beneath my indecently short skirt.'

Oh, my God, Bee was just like me. Is she still? I squealed with shock at her great nerve.

'I thought I'd give them a real thrill,' she explained giddily. 'So there I was swishing around the place in my short skirt and the owner, Peter, thought he'd caught a glimpse or two of something he hadn't seen before with me. But he hadn't quite figured it out yet. At any rate, I was mightily amused when I had to go out back and haul in a shipping order where Paul and his muscle-car friends were always hanging out. So out behind the store, I was naturally bending over to inspect all the incoming goods. I was fully leaning over, and perfectly exposed if anyone cared to take a look. My, how very breezy it was inside my skirt. At first, these boys weren't at all certain they were truly seeing what I was showing them so matter-of-factly, so boldly. I brought in the first load of boxes and, of course, once inside, I was shaking with I don't know what! This was so unbelievably nervy of me, what I was doing in front of this horny group of young men. Well, out back I went again. I pretended to ignore them, and bent over to pick up another box. But they still weren't quite certain of what they truly were seeing beneath my short, short skirt. Oh, I showed them everything. And I shouldn't forget to add, it was windy that day. Swirly whirly skirts were mine! It was funny because these fools seemed to suddenly become shy and intimidated, what with my boldness and all.'

Bee lit a cigarette and inhaled satisfyingly.

'They were sort of pushing each other,' she continued, 'daring each other to accost me, but no one had the guts. I do admit it excited me that I was actually showing them my bare naked pussy. But their reaction ... hilarious, no? They didn't know what to do with a girl putting herself on show, them with their big, overblown cocks. They'd lost control of their own game and I couldn't help but laugh inside. So I finished taking the last load of boxes into the store,' Bee explained amusedly.

We all laughed. Though I didn't know Joey or Fez too well at this point, it seemed we all shared in the eroticism of a young woman and her private parts on view in front of a group of supposedly unbridled studs. And what a great joke Bee had on those guys!

'And so when I went inside the store to continue on with my working day where more intrigues were waiting to occur for the 'clerk without panties,' continued Bee, giggling at herself, 'the store owner, as always, was always, was watching me intimately. And he saw what was to be seen when I bent over for him and I saw him turn all red with desire. Ha!'

We all laughed at this.

Bee carried on with her story. 'He was looking at me with a new intensity. And I felt a good deal more nervous than I did with his son and his stupid friends, who were my own age, because I knew this seasoned old pervert intended to make me from the get-go, like he decided he would when he first hired me. Something was going to happen and he was hatching his plan. Well, after a short time, and after a few exposures on my part that same day, he asked me to come into the stock room to help him put away all the new merchandise that I'd carried in from out back. Now, this was not my usual job, really, as he had always been in control of the stock-checking. But today, I, sans panties, was to stock the shelves with Peter. Lo and behold, what was to happen?

'Well, I went into the small cramped stock-room and he followed behind me and shut the door. He handed me the box he was holding and he chuckled, 'Set it down in front of that shelf,' and then he pulled at my skirt playfully. So I turned to set the box down, giving him another view of my pussy, but this time, up close. "Without panties ... you aren't wearing any panties, I see." He then lifted my skirts right up and said to me, "Look, look, you're bare naked! I should I fire you. What are you doing in my store like that?" He then chuckled and began to toy with my wet pussy while I struggled to get away, but I was backed against the shelf in the very small room. There was no getting away for this girl. So he felt me up freely and he rummaged around my cunt until I finally pushed him away. As any girl would do! It was my employer that was doing this to me, after all! God, how he set me on fire, though. Excuse the expression,' Bee chortled as she turned a log on the fire. 'But truly, how I pulsed when he touched my down there, what with his obvious power over me, I was utterly caught up in this. And so Peter was now standing against the opposite wall and I watched as he tasted his fingers that had my juices on them.'

Bee continued to tell her story as if magically possessed. 'As I watched him lick his fingers, I slowly lifted my skirt and I showed him my naked cunt and touched it right in front of him. I drew apart the folds of my sex for him to see my clit. And the deviant man from his corner watched for a few moments. He came out shortly from his recess and rather swooped down onto my crotch area. He knelt in front of me and proceeded to bring his mouth near to my cunt and then swirled his tongue around the lips. All around my clit he did swish and swirl and he seemed to thoroughly enjoy this so that he was groaning as he relished the taste of me. So slowly did his tongue circle my lips, it felt amazing and so dirty. I knew I was totally wet and so helpless to his appetite.'

Bee stopped for a moment to look at each of us for our reactions. I was certainly beaming at her. She was so beautiful and told her story so bravely and well. Fireside Joe was taking off his shirt at this point. Guess he was heating up, I thought, even in the cool of a springtime night. What was he planning to do?

I looked at Fez. He was dead sexy, I thought, as he looked back at me with his glowing, dark eyes. God, we hadn't even made love yet. How exciting was that prospect?

But for now, I did want to hear the rest of Bee's story. I watched as Joey snuggled up more to Bee as she carried on her tale of sexual torment.

'Then my naughty boss stood up and unzipped his pants,' she continued. 'I saw him dig inside his pants with his hand and squeeze and pull gently at his dick. He eventually exposed his raw member for me to see. All the while that he unzipped his pants he was looking me directly in the eye. And he also steadily eyed my sorrowful nude cunt as I continued to hold up my skirt and show him my bareness. With his pants now down, he rubbed his cock at length and patted my pussy with his free hand; his finger tilled my cunt up and down along the folds. Next he guided my hand over his long, hard cock. It was red and hot and pulsing. I drew closer to it, pushing on it with my bare belly. Along my torso, he guided his cock upwards while he pushed down on my shoulders until I was squatting before him and me and his cock met at my dirty, hungry mouth that so wanted to suck it and suck it. And so I did. I sucked his blood-filled cock that I wanted to relieve from its apparent pressure, for, as I took it in my mouth, I felt it was wanting to burst. I ran my hand slowly along his engorged member as I took him in my mouth with my tongue circling its tip. Next I softly sucked on it. In but a few short moments he spilt his come all over my face.'

We all laughed, approving of Bee's story. I loved it. And now I also knew a little more about the rules of this game. Count on Bee to set the bar so high. One thing I knew for certain was that I shouldn't talk about any present tense weirdness as I was most ashamed of the thoughts I invariably had of my professor. And at my age too, when I should be over that stuff. I was no longer a young adult, but a perverse, maturing and excitable woman.

I could talk to the fireside group about the restaurant owner that I'd once worked for – that was safe – and he was slimy and repulsive enough to amuse my friends. Or I could talk about one of my doctor encounters, perhaps, which were still in some way curiously innocent. Someone taking advantage of you, touching your wild pussy out of control and the good, harmless fun to be had in that – that was truly exciting, was it not? That was, if you loved that sort of thing, which I did. But weren't my doctor stories far too perverse? What with all the special instruments used in creative, sexual ways?

My professor, well ... that was way worse, because it was definitely present day. It was within my current fantasies. I was a bad girl, and all too ready to admit that I was looking forward to a future experience in relenting to authority, an experience that he seemed to want to provide me.

Well, for now I was anxious to hear the boys' stories and listen to what they came up with first.

Joey straightened up; it was his turn. He smiled at Bee. 'My, my,' he said. 'I certainly can't top that, nor would any self-respecting person want to.'

There was more laughter. Bee looked abashed, but she'd established herself as a hard act to follow. And what a supreme story she'd told!

'Let me begin my confession,' he said, 'with the open admission that I've had sexual relations with my friend's older sister and we were caught at it. At the time I was living with this friend of mine, who had this lovely older sister.' Joey laughed, remembering. 'So, in order to find an opportunity, a quiet, private space to make some moves on his provocative sister, I had to be quite creative. I mean, she was a seductress of the first order. She hung out with us quite a bit, and made herself well known in our crowd among the guys. Anyways, I knew she had a thing for me.

'My friend and I were altogether too terribly excited to be around her and her pretty female companions. They were just slightly older than us, and what beautiful girls, but unfortunately their boyfriends sometimes hung out too, but that's another story, for another time.

'Anyway, my friend and I were feeling our proverbial oats and we wanted a girl. We were roommates at the time, as I said, and he made it clear he wouldn't like it if his sister and I became an item. That was a problem as I was unattached at the time, as was she, and we were both hot for each other.

'So I was in first year at university and I didn't own a car, which would have well afforded me the opportunity of having a private space to make it with her. She and I had to find a place to meet so we came up with something crazy. I called her up on a weekend afternoon, which was not so crazy, of course, but we really had nowhere to go. And we hadn't been anywhere alone up until that hot, sweet summer afternoon.'

'Sounds like you loved her,' Bee said jealously about the older sister. 'Was she so gorgeous?'

'Well, I did lust after her, it's true. And we got up to no good, oh yes. And just you wait.'

We all giggled except for Bee.

'Bee, you are my true sweetie. This was a couple of years ago, OK? This is the story I'm trying to tell. Do you want to hear this, or not?' Joey asked her.

'OK, OK,' she said.

'So anyway,' he continued, 'we went for a walk around my old neighbourhood where I'd grown up and we happened upon this big old tree. I had climbed this tree many times as a kid and I remembered how a long time ago I'd played doctor up there with a girl who lived down the street.

'You little devil,' remarked Fez. Bee and I laughed appreciatively.

Joey went on with his story. 'So of course I asked her if she wanted to climb a tree,' Joey said in the most beguiling of ways. 'It was the biggest tree in the neighbourhood, but this didn't seem to daunt her. I could see up her skirt while she scrambled up the trunk. She was wearing those silk drawers, you know, the loose ones? I could see something of her pussy underneath those drawers. My, how she was a good tree climber! It even made me wonder if this was a regular thing for her. The dirty thing! I loved it! Well, I can tell you, without any trouble at all, we were both up that tree in no time. Quite hospitable too was the crotch of the tree!' Joey excitedly told his story.

He continued, 'Well at first we sat with our legs just sort of intertwined together while we looked down below and all around us. No one would take any notice of us, we said to each other. They wouldn't see us at all, why would they? We were surrounded by leaves, and if we were very quiet ... The only way we could be seen was if someone were to deliberately look up while they walked right under our tree.

'I started to raise her skirt and touch her pussy through her satin shorts. Then I reached up inside them and she spread her legs and pulled her loose underwear aside. I unbuttoned her shirt as well. Her beautiful tits were all goosebumpy and her nipples were hard. We managed to take off her panties completely and she arched her pelvis to the afternoon sun that was filtering through the trees. Up along the semi-awkward tree trunk, she moved her body upwards.

'Her pussy was right at face-level to me. So I started licking her cunt. This I did with my tongue deep in her hole, as deep as I could stretch it, I moved it, in and out. She moved her pussy up and down in rhythm with my long tongue. We stopped. We heard some people talking as they came walking up the street. This further aroused her and she gasped and spread her legs even more and I was also excited by this new dimension to the scene.

That is, by the strangers walking up the street that might possibly seeing her naked cunt. I sucked her clit briefly again and then looked down on the on-comers once more. I pulled down my own pants and started to whack off while I was eating her out. The people were almost right under us by now and she moaned audibly. Below us, the pedestrians were walking past under the tree and I rubbed my cock even faster. And as I was stroking my cock, the rhythm of my tongue on her clit increased as well, as I made circles around her most sensitive place. The pedestrians below walked right on by under us, they didn't have a clue. I laughed and breathed gustily on her cunt while the strollers moved off and turned the corner at the end of the street.

'Up in the tree, I moved my body along hers and I guided my cock into her mouth. I held each side of her head with my hands while I gently moved my hard dick in and out of her mouth. We now heard some other people coming down the street and, along with their voices, we could hear the clitter-clatter of a dog's paw nails on the pavement.

'I removed my cock from her mouth and moved it back down along her body. Just when I was getting ready to enter her, we heard that same damn dog barking. I'd almost entered her but I stopped to look down and this little mongrel was right below us with his loud barking muzzle pointed right up at us. An older couple could be now seen coming into view below us and naturally they looked up at what their dog was barking at. Their faces totally contorted with shock at the sight they got. They pulled on their dog's leash and hurried away.

'From our tree-top view, we continued to watch them hurry down the street and we giggled nervously. We saw them reach the end of the road and look back up at us and then, they each turned to the other, and took each other by the hand and kissed. The old couple finally disappeared from our view.' Joey paused and laughed. 'My girlfriend and I thought we'd given them some good ideas.'

'Ha, you probably did!' said Fez mightily amused.

So that was Joey's daring story and I loved it! Bee and Joey were good at this. I didn't know what to think any more, or what story I might risk telling.

It was Fez next. I was terribly intrigued. What tale did he have in store for us?

'Last summer,' he began a little self-consciously, 'I was staying with my mother for the weekend while my dad was away on business. She gets nervous alone, you see, so I was sleeping over at the house,' Fez explained as he changed position and now lay on his side. 'Now, my mother has a very good friend, younger than her by quite a few years; she was around fifty, I guess. She was over a lot at that particular time as she was going through a nasty divorce. Her name was Rhoda.

'To me, she always had this strong sexual energy lurking beneath her surface appearance. Since she had been going through this rotten divorce, though, she was even more charged up. She hadn't had a man in months. And me, my mother's son, I mean she *watched* me, I could tell. It was hard not to be attracted to her, beautiful and sexy she was. Well, she and my ma were having a few drinks one night, and Rhoda didn't want to drive home. I offered to drive her, but she said it was simpler if she just stayed over. She was going to sleep in the guest room.

'Some time later in the evening we were upstairs and she passed me, or rather brushed against me, as she made her way down the hall to the bathroom. She left the door slightly open and I heard the shower being turned on. Curious as hell, I quietly went towards the bathroom. I saw her head turned slightly to the side as I peered in, like she knew I was in the doorway watching and, with her back to me, she let her robe drop to her feet. Her ass was very shapely and I could see from behind that she was touching her breasts as she climbed into the shower.

'I got a very delicious idea and that was to hide myself in the guest room closet and perhaps watch her go to bed. Maybe she would do certain things at bedtime that I could enjoy watching. My penis stiffened at the prospect and I snuck back down the hall, entered the guest room and made my way towards the closet. I would be well-hidden in the there and, once inside, I stroked my cock for a short while until I heard the shower being turned off. She would be coming down the hall any second and I had to be quiet now.

'Through the slats of the closet door, I watched her enter the room; her robe was loosely on and more or less open. I had a perfect view.

'I lightly caressed my cock, now sticking out of my fly. I held my breath as she slid the robe off and proceeded to lie down nude on the bed. She squirmed a bit, then her fingers lightly tickled her nipples and she caressed her breasts, so slowly, and she watched her hands as she did so. With a little of her own saliva on her delicate finger, she wet her dark, tender nipples. Next, she sat up and seemed to look directly at the point in the closet where my eyes were, and she smiled while she leaned back onto her elbows and spread her legs wide open. The whole time she was looking straight at the closet door. With one hand, she parted the lips of her pussy and she fingered herself slowly, especially the area around her clit. Then she turned over, raised her ass in the air, reached in from behind to slide her finger in and out of her pussy and played around with her asshole in the same way; at first tentatively, then almost savagely, she plunged her fingers in and out, in and out.' Fez paused in his story and licked his lips.

Listening to Fez's story, and how he told it, I was feeling undeniably aroused. I could hardly wait to sleep with him.

Fez continued. 'I knew this woman was reaching the heights of pleasure. Join in, I thought to myself. What she wanted was at the end of my own fingertips, so to speak, so I came skulking out of the closet and prepared myself for touching her pretty pussy, given her grandly open position. I was holding my cock in my hand and I was slowly stroking it and I stood there a few minutes, just watching her moan and finger herself from behind. All too soon, I was almost coming and in my heat I inserted my finger, alternating with hers, in and out of her asshole and her pussy. I did not want to astonish her too terribly – that is, I wasn't going to introduce my cock just yet. And it seemed at first that she didn't even notice my fingers, so great was her self-pleasuring.

'Without missing a beat, she then flipped over onto her back, her eyes closed the whole time and I was standing there, still jacking off and preparing to guide my cock into her open pussy. She looked even more beautiful than ever. With my hard, hot cock, which had taken on the shape of a powerful snake, as I had never seen it so long before, I nudged at her open wet cunt. Then I couldn't resist it any more; I plunged in. My balls knocked against her inner thighs, and I banged her harder as she lifted herself up in response to me. I took her by the hips and moved her in motion with my thrusts, and she looked at me as she grinded her groin as if she loved having my hard, hard snake in her. I could bear it no longer and came deliriously. It was such a hard come, man, so powerful I thought I might faint. But she wasn't finished, so she roused me and guided my mouth down to her pussy, which I slowly licked – all regions, from her anus, and all along her folds and finally up to her clit and shortly, I could feel her spasm wildly with orgasm.'

Everyone was silent around the fire while Fez continued. 'We were well spent and fell asleep together afterwards. This was quite foolish because, in the morning, my mother came and knocked on the guest room door and forthwith brought some coffee in for her good friend. When she saw this scene, her son in bed with her best friend, she was in great and understandable shock and dropped the tray with the coffee and it spilt everywhere. Immediately, her friend screamed as if she'd no idea why I was in her bed and I started to claim I had been sleepwalking and acted as though I was terribly embarrassed. I apologised profusely.

'Wanting to cover up too, my mother quickly recalled how, as a kid, I did have this tendency and that I was indeed a sleepwalker and would be found in the strangest of places some mornings,' Fez said, ending his story.

I laughed, well amused and excited by Fez's story. He'd had some adventures too. Just like me, just like us all. Did he still, I wondered?

I realised suddenly that it was my turn to go. Now I knew why it was worst to go last. I had to top all their stories. Then I remembered a story I could tell about my travels in Europe, and Bee had been there with me, so, if I got sketchy on the details, she could always bail me out. I straightened up, and they all looked at me expectantly.

'Well, I have the unfortunate tendency to experience things from time to time with an intensity quite disproportionate to the situation,' I began, and they all laughed at my hi-faluting choice of words for what was going to a very dirty story. 'Anyway, I was an au-pair in France for a few months and I wanted to take the opportunity to see more of Europe. So my dear Bee here came over to join up with me for some travelling. To the south of us was Spain and we decided to start our exploring there.'

I coughed a little nervously and cleared my throat. 'It was late one night and Bee and I were on a train en route to the south of Spain. There were all these military guys travelling from post to post throughout the country, many of them extremely well built and good looking. Remember Bee?'

'I do indeed,' she said.

'Well, we were travelling overnight on this train and Bee here had come upon this gypsy woman who was going to read her fortune. So, Bee was up in the corridor of the train for most of the night, talking to this strange, strange woman. What did she tell you, Bee?'

'That I would meet Joey,' Bee said shyly.

Joey smiled. 'Is that so?'

'But she also had a warning too, right, Santa?' Bee aptly added.

'Precisely. And it was just about to happen to me, this warning. What were her words of caution, Bee?'

In a Spanish accent Bee obliged, 'Be careful of those bad boys.'

I chuckled and continued the story. 'These supposed bad boys were the same guys who were in my compartment with me. They were having a great gas of it, singing and playing on my guitar, flamenco style. I don't know why I brought my guitar with me around Europe, I didn't play well or anything, but I was so glad because these guys were absolutely amazing musicians and singers. It was quite something, riveting, in fact; they were like a choir of angels. But angels they were not. Anyway, you must understand first that the Spanish women don't ever travel alone. Only Spanish sluts do, according to the soldiers' way of thinking or, of course, North Americans. The men absolutely take it carte blanche to make sexual advances if you're a foreigner from the west travelling without a man, and they constantly made these weird snaky sounds at Bee and I and uttered lewd suggestions in their native tongue, which I could kind of understand sometimes. They even offered money on a regular basis. It had the unfortunate effect of turning me on, though, especially if a handsome militia man went as far as to cop a feel, which often happened. All this sexual energy, all these dark, tall, handsome, muscular men in uniform that would talk amongst themselves about me in a foreign language that I could barely understand ... well, it made me cream my pants, I'm afraid to say. Didn't it you, Bee? '

Bee laughed, 'I suppose it did too.'

Fez looked at me hungrily and possessively.

'Anyway, I'm in this train car with several of these military guys. They were literally each taking turns at trying to kiss me and touch me. I resisted, like a decent girl would, but by God, I was getting worked up, it couldn't be helped. I have to confess, I even chose to ignore what they were doing sometimes, especially with two of them in particular who were incredibly good-looking. Super-fit, tall, dark-haired soldiers. They had this horrible knowing in their eyes; a knowing about me and what they might be able to do with me. And I would let them rub my breasts a little here and there and I wasn't wearing a bra either. The others knew I preferred these two to the rest, though they all still attempted to caress me and kiss me when they could. If I wished, I could have always left the compartment to find Bee, but I simply wanted to stay there and endure more of their overtures towards me. They were calling me beautiful in Spanish, and made other remarks about me in their tongue that I could not really understand. A word here and there, a couple of essential phrases, sort of thing, was the best I could do.'

'*Bella senorita Americano,*' Fez said appreciatively. He had quite the accent. Well, I supposed he knew the cousin language to Spanish, being Italian.

I continued on, encouraged: 'So these Spanish guys were talking to each other and in the undertone of their conversation, it sounded to me like they were making some plans and I strongly sensed they were talking about me. Then they set to playing another song on my guitar, this time much more loudly than before. And I'm telling you, their music and their voices, well, they all knew the songs – such beautiful melodies, it just filled the train car to the brim, and it felt like it was pulsing through me. The effect was trance-like. At last, when their songs were done, they all began to leave the compartment. All but one soldier, the most handsome of Spaniards. He was looking at me with the most intense smile on his face as the others emptied out of the train car. I looked back at him in the most innocent and indifferent of ways.

' "Si, si," he said earnestly, trying to dispel any concern I might have that we were now alone in the train car.

'I made as if I was going to also leave the compartment too, like the rest had, and I said to him, '*donde amigo?*' I was trying to explain to him that I wanted to find my friend, Bee. But he wasn't going to let me get past him. Instead he put his arm around me as I tried to get by his big physical presence. With his other hand, he began to fondle my tits, as I'd let him do earlier. At first I tried to move away, but he gently pulled me back in close to him and rubbed them. I couldn't help but moan and, with that, I arched my back and raised myself upwards to receive his caresses. Now, as he was reaching under my shirt, I opened my eyes and saw that, outside the compartment, one of the other Spanish guys was standing with his back to the door. While I let this powerful soldier feel my bare tits, I wondered if this other fellow was planning to watch, or even come in. The Spaniard started to kiss me, his tongue licking the inside of my mouth, and my pussy twitched and became wet. He stopped kissing me, looked down at his hand under my shirt and proceeded to lift it up; and I closed my eyes again and vaguely wondered whether any of the other Spaniards were trying to watch us and observe how their compatriot was fondling the North American girl's naked breasts so that they too could have a little thrill from outside the compartment window.

'The soldier was now sucking my nipple, lightly squeezing it with his teeth. With his hands, he was feeling my pussy and ass through my pants. His mouth moved back up to mine, while he expertly unbuttoned my jeans and unzipped my zipper. I could feel his stiffened cock as he pressed against my thigh. He was looking at me as he finished unzipping my pants and slipped his hand in to feel my naked pussy. He fingered my wetness and moaned with pleasure at finding it. He was making me move back towards the bench and stopped momentarily to pull my pants half-way down. His fingers fluttered in my cunt as he lay me down on the bench. Momentarily, I resisted him, nervous that those other guys might see, uneasy with what I was allowing him to do to me, but I soon submitted to him again and lay down along the bench. Kneeling beside me, he put his tongue in my mouth while his finger went slowly in and out of my cunt. It felt thick, slippery and wet. I was squirming with pleasure, moving my groin upwards to receive his probing, allowing his tongue to stretch as far as it could down my throat. My private parts were actually facing the window to the outside corridor of the train but as the compartment wasn't that well lit, I trusted no one could really see inside at what we were doing. And yet, I knew I was very naughty to feel excited at the thought that someone could see what this stranger, this soldier, was doing to my bare-naked pussy. The soldier looked me up and down and then back up into my face. I opened and closed my eyes, sometimes looking at him as he smoothly stroked me, sometimes looking past him out the compartment window where I thought I could see vague silhouetted shapes. While he was tilling the folds around my clit, the Spaniard looked at me with intensity. His eyes travelled down to my moist cunt and he wet his lips a little. He lowered his mouth down onto my clit and started sucking on it. I had a mini spasm that went throughout my core and made me grow wetter yet. We moved together, bad girl that I was.

'And as I moved with him and his dirty ways, I looked up at the compartment window, in order to see who might be watching. My terrible soldier now gently thrust his tongue slowly in and out of my pussy as he used his hands to push my knees further apart. He was so soothing, it felt so good and endlessly, slitheringly smooth.

'But outside, I could see that there were, without a doubt, three or four figures plainly turned on and looking in through the window of our compartment of sex. I was so blatantly nude in front of them and I moaned and raised my naked pelvis up and down while my soldier probed. But at the same time, I was truly trying to get away at this point. There was no way out of this, though. We were love-making and past the point of return. I was highly excited by what this horny guy was doing to me, this soldier that I'd aroused on a train in Spain. Oh, the Spanish men ... don't rile them, let me tell you.

'And the next thing I knew, I heard the compartment

door open. It was the other handsome soldier that had decided to join us and in the back of my mind I thought it was entirely possible that the two had planned this all the while. The second Spaniard came over to me and was now kneeling at my side. He felt up my breasts, as I'd allowed him to do earlier, and then he kissed me on the mouth with urgent, wet kisses. He was unzipping his pants and I was wet with anticipation at what might be revealed. Then I felt his cock against my lips as I looked up at him and obediently opened my mouth and sucked the tip of it. He moved it slowly in and out and I felt my sex begin to wave with orgasm while the other Spaniard licked around and around my clit. I spasmed and burned down below, and then the first soldier actually got his cock inside me.'

I paused and then said, 'And what happened next, Bee?'

Bee replied, 'I don't know, but when I came in, the three of them were zipping up their pants.'

'And thankfully, it was the end of the line, the train had arrived at its final destination and everyone was getting off. I was glad to move in to the crowds on the platform and out from view of those Spanish guys,' I said, panting nervously for effect. Fez and Joey laughed at this.

'They were following you, you horny thing,' Bee exclaimed.

'Just for a little ways, thank God,' I said, shaking my head.

With the last story told, our fireside game ended and we set into discussion about the virtues of each other's stories. They all said mine had the utmost daring, though I didn't know what kind of honour this could be, but it had certainly been fun to hear about all their adventures. Shortly afterwards, we all retired for the night to our own tents. And Fez and I made love at last.

'*Bella senorita*, you do have a dirty mind!' Fez said gustily as he undressed me in a playful, rough sort of way.

'No, *bruto*,' I protested softly.

'I bet that entire story of yours was true,' he said knowingly.

'C'mon, I thought we were all embellishing for creative license,' I said. Fez started to pull down my pants. I didn't want him to see my cheap Brazilian, and it was already dark, but he could easily feel it. It had no class, it was too much. I couldn't let him see and I wriggled away.

'Don't be shy, you're not shy, I know,' he said, amused by my timid behaviour.

'I made a little mistake with my razor the other night,' I said, still holding up my pants.

'You made a mistake?' He pulled down my pants with the curiosity of a doctor. 'What, you shaved it all off?' he asked, smiling.

'Kind of. I've never done it before, it was an accident, I got carried away and then had to do a fix up, and then, before I knew it, I'd shaved it clean,' I explained awkwardly.

'Ha, ha, let me see closer.'

'No.'

'Let me see,' he said. The hint of authority in his voice moved me to obey and I let him pull down my pants. He looked closely at my nakedness.

Next his hands found my ever-so-naked parts and he patted my pussy softly and then dug his finger deep into my moist cunt. I heard him gasp raspily as he touched me and he seemed turned on by my hairlessness. It felt incredibly sensitive, my cunt without any hair, as he massaged it with his fingertips. My folds were full and firm under his touch, warm and wet as he stroked my pussy lips and in-between them.

His raw penis was now rubbing against my hairless pussy; it was gliding along my slippery clit, unfolding my folds – flesh to flesh, like I'd never felt before. He was licking my nipples and pushing my own hand down between us so that I could further tease my clit and his penis too. I wanted to take his cock into my mouth, but suddenly it was slithering inside me. So powerful his thrusts, so slippery our bodies; sweetly fucking we were.

Afterwards we giggled together, teasing each other about our secret, secret tales and recalling our friends' most colourful stories from that night. We decided that we were all truly depraved, but in good company with each other.

But neither Fez nor anyone else would ever really know how true my story was. Those Spaniards were such horny, hunky bastards. Bee, Joey and Fez's stories were probably also more true than not, for that matter. While they all thought mine was the naughtiest, it didn't even come close to the deviance I liked to explore in my current and degenerate fantasies about my professor.

Next morning the four of us went for a walk through the woods. On the Canadian Shield the high, rising rock seemed to grow out from the land. These huge boulders had been planted there from the last ice age and from between them tall pines rose up to make a canopy above us. It was glorious as the sun streaked down from above and cast its streams of light along the mossy forest floor under our feet. Here and there, spider webs fanned out between the branches of trees, and the spiders in them were phenomenally huge. Fez and I would stop to admire the webs at length, seeing how the gossamer threads glimmered in the sunlight. Fez put his arm around me as we marvelled at the intricate workmanship of the spider. He told me that we would be up to our knees in insects, if it weren't for spiders, and that made me feel more comfortable with them around. It was so good to talk to him; I was so glad to be with him. Bless Bee for introducing us.

We started to get real hungry by the afternoon, but neither Bee nor I had had the foresight to pack any food, and the boys were clean out of provisions too. So there really was only one thing for it – to strike camp and head back to town.

I really could love Fez, I thought, on the drive back home. I knew I already did. But there was still this nagging element tugging at my deepest core. Despite all the fun and tenderness I'd experienced with Fez, my terrible mind got to thinking what I could do next to get a rise out of a certain professor. I was so very sure that I could not escape MacLean, neither in fantasy nor in reality, as it was to turn out.

5

In class, I secretly scrutinised MacLean – his large hands, his stained teeth and his dark eyes that didn't miss the slightest movement of my legs underneath my desk. He was ultimately debauched, I could tell, by the habits, and the degenerate forces at work underneath his faculty-of-law appearance. The edges of his nails were manicured but when you got deeper into the nitty gritty, how dirty he was! And the more depraved he appeared, the more alluring he was to me. I imagined his dirty nails scratching my private folds.

I swung my legs to a new position under my desk and his eyes followed my slender limbs while his mouth hammered on about sentences and incarcerations. My genitals twitched helplessly at his penetrating and close observance of my every move. I wanted him to incarcerate me in his crime and punishment course! This urge was spurred on by my sense of revolt against his inherent power, plus plain revulsion and yet desire for him. I was thrown into confusion every time I saw him. I needed a cigarette or a drink or anything to calm my nerves. I diligently took down notes while he droned on. I was noticing his lips; they were dry, too dry. My mind began to wander further. And so my hands followed my naughty thoughts, for what was I doing right out in front of him during his lecture?

What I was doing was giving him little peeks of my bare, shaved pussy. I was so slyly showing it to him all through the last bit of class, in fact. He couldn't really see, but oh I did expose myself to him, I did! And the only way he could have spied my nasty activities was if he were to sit down at his desk, then his eyes could see right through to underneath my front row desk. But he always lectured standing in front of his desk. So I noted that well.

So secretly, so exquisitely slowly, I did unveil my cunt to him. My hairless pussy, smooth and slippery. Just a little at first. The prospect of him seeing was in itself exciting enough, for it was terrible behaviour for his student to pull her skirt a little away from between her legs and show her bare cunt, even if it was just a tiny bit. Only the edge of it was exposed, mind you. But there it was in plain view. I was showing him a tiny bit of my cunt. I pulled my skirt back further still and I felt my clit, running my finger up and down along it. Oooh, it felt good. Look at it, professor. Sit down. Look down. See my wanting, pulsing cunt. Spank it. I'd pulled my underwear further away from myself. Spank it. Spank it hard. Hard! I was such a bad girl.

I was out in public and so I had to be sure to be careful and discreet, but my raw pussy loved the cool air on it. My hot liquids were rising inside me and burning under the possibility of him seeing what I was doing. He could sense what I was doing, I could tell, and he seemed to become agitated as he lectured to the class.

I'd executed the next move in such a way that was nice and creative and discreet. First, I reached for a pencil from on top of my desk and, once I'd taken it up, I then rested my docile hand upon my little lap. With the tip of the pencil I lifted my skirt ever so slightly away so that my underwear was showing and then I sat quietly again for a few moments. I leant forwards and jotted down some notes like the rest of the students. In short order, I subsequently positioned my naughty pencil back down in the vicinity of my panties, and, with the tip of it, I pushed aside my underwear and touched my clit with the eraser of the pencil. Oh, what a good student she was. Terrible me.

This made my wet clit pulse unbearably as I slid the pencil along the folds of my pussy. It was hungry and unsatisfied. It was wanting MacLean to see; it was wishing the professor would touch it someday. Will he sit down at his desk so he can see me masturbate for him, please?

I looked around; everybody was writing down notes. Nobody seemed to have noticed my personal fingerings. My professor couldn't see, but surely . . .

To increase the possibility, I opened my legs a little more and my skirt parted and exposed the dirty, dirty thing that was my pussy. I hunched over my notebook and wrote, 'Professor, look at my wet clit. I want you to touch it. Suck on it, professor.' I chuckled silently at what I'd written.

Sneakily, my hand went back down to find my clit. I pushed my underwear aside again and squeezed my cunt so that my clit stood out amongst my folds. Now I saw MacLean go to stand behind his desk, which wasn't his usual pattern. I mean, he never wrote anything out on the chalkboard or anything but, for some reason, today he was going to. He looked at me from the front of the class and, though I was sure he couldn't see what I was doing, I casually stopped my misbehaviour. Idly, he continued to look in my direction and went on with his lecture, turning to write something on the chalkboard.

I would touch your cock, I said to him in my head. I would suck on your professorial cock for a long time and would choke on it happily if you were to drive it deep into my mouth.

With his back to me I started once again to secretly touch myself and, this time, I was definitely being more risky. At any moment he could turn around to the class and merely lean over ever so slightly to put his chalk down and take a good look under my desk and see what I was doing. At the chalkboard, he turned to address the class, and, though I did stop fingering myself, I was still exposing my goods. I held the crotch of my underwear aside and dearly wanted him to see my nude cunt – the one he'd already touched on the dance floor just this Friday last. He would love to see me do this; that I certainly knew. If he were to sit at his desk, he would get a full view. But instead MacLean pretended to drop his piece of chalk on the floor, and he squatted down to pick it up. He looked right under my desk and I didn't flinch for a good few seconds while I showed him a good eyeful. He straightened up, turned back to the chalkboard and cleared his throat as he went on lecturing.

My God, I couldn't believe I'd just done that. But I knew all too well that he saw me showing him my nude pussy in his class. He had seen my shaved mound. I was in serious trouble now.

Naturally, for the last part of class, I became very civilised with my skirt again, as if nothing of the sort could have happened. It was ten minutes to the end of the lecture and I had to clean up the notes I'd scribbled down so hurriedly.

No longer was my professor's regard towards me one of intense curiosity; it was now a decided look. He'd determined what I was, which was a very bad girl indeed, and for this I couldn't look at him. I was in certain trouble now. By the end of class, he was staring steadily at me. Maybe I should feign to faint, I thought. See what he does then! Would he take me to his office to recover? He would probably think he could do whatever he wanted with me.

Believe it or not, I decided I would. I had to get out of the trouble I was in at any rate, and in reality I couldn't bear to have him keep me after class and confront me for masturbating in public. So, que sera, I rose from my seat along with the other students and I pretended to faint in class. I was impressed with my performance as I made my own body fall under me and I floated like a feather to the floor and I made no sound as I hit the ground. I'd executed it so well. He could have me right there and then. He could explore the gateway to my inner being and undo me with his slithering fingers right up my skirt.

Soon my classmates were gathering me back up and trying to help me stand. But I acted as limp as can be and so they set me in my chair and told me to put my head between my knees and breathe slowly. I watched MacLean hasten to leave the lecture hall telling everyone he was going to fetch the campus nurse. God, I had actually pretended to faint right there in the lecture hall. I had fallen across the aisle from my desk. Good and naughty girl! But this wasn't working out the way I'd planned. MacLean was supposed to take me to his office to spank me for my misbehaviour.

The campus nurse was a little bewildered but determined that I must have low blood sugar. Ostensibly that made sense – I was rather thin and I allowed that I hadn't eaten much that day. In fact, all I'd had was a glass of water at lunch and an orange for breakfast. I loved to graze; I told the nurse that was why I was so slender. Little food and lots of liquids of any kind. I loved that, I informed the nurse.

Now all I knew was that I was stuck in nursey's room and needed to get out of there and not be under anyone's scrutiny, unless it was the professor's, of course. I suddenly felt very foolish and dearly wanted to have a cigarette. But, before I could go, the nurse wanted me to eat and made me phone Bee to bring me something. God! What a tangled web I'd woven.

Not only Bee came, but Fez and Joey too. They were all so worried! The whole thing was absurd and I was in a gnarly state of mind by now. There everybody was, come to nosily speculate on my mysterious collapse. Bee, Fez and Joey crowded in the small university nurse's quarters and regarded me in what was supposed to be my shaky condition. I felt a true fool. Why hadn't MacLean just caught the frail, swooning maid and brought her into his office to molest her? That wasn't how it turned out and, at that moment, I hated everyone and was angry with myself for pulling such a poorly engineered job. Moreover, I was paranoid that everyone knew all about my thoughts, deviant and impure.

Fez stayed the longest; even after my best friend Bee had left, he remained at my bedside. I was fine, of course, and only wanted to go home. Plus I did not want to look weak in front of him. But he loved this because it made him feel happy to be strong for his light-headed wench.

Fez invited me to come stay with him and convalesce at his place. As if I needed to. Though I wasn't sure what he thought of me any more; I certainly knew that I didn't want his pity. I wanted to be back at my own apartment and cease to seem so silly and female. I was a fake!

His pity was the last thing I was going to get, in fact. Quite the contrary, his reaction was disconcertingly stern and reproachful. I felt like I might be sent to my room, and so this pose of his only served to anguish me further. Though I kept quiet about my true reactions, I could feel resentment lurking beneath my surface.

'I won't let you go without eating enough, which is why you fainted, you silly girl, you.' Fez said as he pressed my hand firmly into his own. 'What are you doing to yourself?' he demanded to know. I smiled and tried to pull my hand from his grip, but he wouldn't let me go.

'Yes, I just have to eat better,' I replied and placed my hands on his great chest, suddenly feeling like I wanted to be encircled in his strong arms as I'd figured the best thing to do was to take this distressed maiden act a little further. Why not? I wondered, while he now was hugging me so warmly in the nurse's room.

'Look, Santa,' he said. 'I have a surprise for you.'

'Oh, what is it, Fez?' I asked, looking up at my dear, strong boy who was so handsome. He pushed me gently away and looked into my eyes momentarily while he bent down and kissed me softly on the lips. I touched his dark smooth hair. He reached into his pants pocket and, as he rummaged inside them, I wondered what he had in mind. Was he aroused? Was his surprise a hard-on for me right here in the nurse's room? Such was how my mind tended to work. I would have to do something about that in the future, with these thoughts of mine, wouldn't I? For pity's sake, here was a man about to profess his love and I could only think about my horny cunt. That was part of why I was in the outrageous position I found myself in. My pussy. Shouldn't she calm down a little? My sex-thoughts were taking me over!

I was growing tired of all these pretences of mine, and so I shifted away from Fez and looked deeply into his eyes. I wanted to have something real with him. And this had nothing to do with our bodies; instead it was a fountain of expression that took place between our eyes and I was silent while he put his finger to his lips as if to confirm our love. It was in our silence together that I knew I loved him.

From his pants pocket, he drew out a perfectly beautiful little box made out of pewter.

'Guess what it is,' he teased and extended his lustral gift to me.

I didn't dare guess what it was. With the tip of my finger I felt the box's surface. What was inside it? Certainly it wasn't an engagement ring. God, we'd only just met. What an ego I had! As if he was ready to propose to me. On second thoughts, why not? Sometimes that's how life happens.

Though every moment with Fez had been up to now awash with delight, I was nowhere near ready for any kind of commitment. How could *he* be? Men are usually slower to warm to making pledges of the heart, those giving-over-to-a-life feelings where the ends were all neatly tucked in. Though when he gazed upon me, then, I did feel love radiating from his being to mine.

'I don't want to guess,' I said, embarrassed.

'C'mon,' he said to me.

'All right, it's your first condom on a string?' I laughed heartily and he joined in.

'Brat,' he said and stroked my cheek tenderly.

'I know I am,' I said shyly. He smiled at me and it seemed undeniable how endeared he really seemed to be to me. Me and my shaved pussy and all, and I laughed quietly to myself at how well he seemed to accept me. There is no better gift than that, I thought.

I ran my fingers over the splendid round little pewter box that had an ivy design in relief all over it, not daring to open it.

'Guess what it is,' he urged me.

Just then the nurse appeared with a tray of food. 'Here's a little extra,' she told me. 'I know your friend brought you something to eat, but I thought I'd best round it out with some soup too. It's from the cafeteria, but at least it's hot.' She came round the side of the bed where Fez was sitting to set down the tray.

'How are you feeling now?' she asked.

'A little tired, I guess,' I replied, playing the part.

'Well, you won't let yourself get so run down again, now will you, my dear girl?' the nurse admonished gently. 'I see it all the time,' she continued, 'students that study around the clock, forgetting to eat and just not getting the rest they need. Tsk, tsk . . .'

'We won't allow it,' Fez assured her.

'Good that you have such a caring friend,' the nurse said, smiling.

"He is very caring,' I said as I looked warmly at Fez. 'But I can take care of myself, naturally,' I added. The nurse smiled at us and left the room. I toyed with the box. Fez gently took it from me and offered me the soup the nurse had brought.

'First eat, you can open it after,' he suggested.

I stiffened a little and took the food. I wasn't even hungry and I felt unnerved by Fez's patrician pose. For him, he was happy being the knight in shining armour, but what he didn't realise was that he couldn't save me from my terrible obsession with Professor MacLean. Did he know what a crazy fraud I was? No. He didn't know the truth behind why I'd wound up here, like this. He was right, I was a brat! And underneath I was enjoying all this more than I cared to admit. I sipped my soup. It was surprisingly good.

Though my mind rebelled against such a thing, I knew it was my perverted professor who had full mastery over me at this point and that's why I was in this strange situation. My loins directed my mind around such matters. If Freud had me on his couch, he would find enough in my cranium to fill a whole filing cabinet. God help me!

After I finished the soup, Fez gave me back the mysterious box.

'Such a pretty box for the sick and ailing,' I joked. What I was expecting, I didn't know. Surely not this gorgeous long chain, gold and fine. It might reach down to my navel once I'd put it on, I thought. At the end of it I saw that there hung a key.

'How beautiful, Fez!'

'Do you see the key?'

'What's it for?' I dared not guess.

'To my heart.'

'Do you always give your heart away so quickly? Especially to a swooning wench like me?' I laughed.

'When I saw the chain in the store, I thought I had to give it to you,' he explained sweetly.

'I love it, Fez, thank you,' I said to him and pulled him close and kissed him lightly on the lips.

'Put it on, *mia bella*,' he said afterwards.

I felt a little guilty and undeserving. 'You know, you shouldn't have done this. I mean, we only really just met and there are many sides to me you don't know about,' I confessed to him.

'Like the one that pushes a man away when he gets fresh?' he asked teasingly. Which brought me to think about the night MacLean felt me up on the dance floor. I still hoped to unravel the mystery of that event.

'Yeah, like that, I guess. Did you think you were being too forward that first night?' I asked.

He grinned. 'I was intoxicated with you, how you moved, your eyes, your dress; I got carried away and was certainly pressing the old groin a little, now wasn't I? I deserved to be rebuffed by a woman of virtue. Though I know I sulked a little afterwards.'

'But that was all, right? I mean, you danced a bit close, perhaps, but nothing more than that, right?' I badly wanted the intrigue of MacLean to continue; that he had been the one who perpetrated the act of violation against me and my body. Someone had felt my soft cunt that night and it wasn't Fez who had fondled me, oh no, it couldn't have been him. No, Fez had an entirely different style. Professor MacLean, though? I could still feel his fingers scratching at me from behind. Those nails of his. Ha! He'd felt my raw sex that night; he'd touched it and sucked my wetness off his very own devilish fingers! My exposing myself to him during his lecture was just the next move in our little game.

'What do you mean, what did you think happened?' Fez asked with some tension in his voice.

This startled me. I needed to cover my tracks as best I could and assured him. 'I don't know, I guess I was a little loaded.' How weak.

'You're trying to conceal something from me,' Fez pressed me. 'You are protecting someone. Someone touched you and I demand to know who it was.'

Of course he demanded. This made me feel protected in a distressed maiden kind of way. But I wasn't a maiden in distress, was I? Although I played the part so well. The depth of my naughtiness was becoming more known to me as it took on the added dimension of now relishing the prospect of making Fez jealous. I saw fire in him, and I liked that very much.

'Tell me about your family,' I said, trying to change the subject.

'You don't want to know.' Then he rose impatiently.

'Yes I do.'

'You're not listening to me,' he replied.

'OK.'

He finally said, 'What happened on Friday?' He was trying to be so smooth, but I could see his anger mounting. My, how handsome he was!

'I really don't know. There was nothing that happened,' I protested.

'Who was it? I think you know,' he insisted.

'No one really.' I was so much more a slut and a liar than he could ever imagine. I didn't deserve him. But this was OK too. One day I would tell him everything

75

about me, perhaps. That is, once I trusted him and once I'd gotten this demon out of my system. Hopefully I wouldn't destroy everything in my wake as I'd done with so many relationships before.

'I'm so glad about you and me,' I told him happily.

'I want to know you, everything about you,' he said.

Pleased with myself and him, I felt the edges of the coarse metal rounded box he'd presented me. Then I said, 'Sometimes I wonder if that's at all possible ... to really know another.'

'You are a strange one, Santa. You intrigue me so much. That's why you have the key to my heart, and to my apartment, I might add. I want you to feel at home with me.'

'Bet you say that to all the girls. But how wonderful to hear it, nonetheless.' I looked down and studied the key at the end of the chain.

'I don't say that to all the girls,' he corrected me sternly.

It was the key to his apartment. He had a spacious loft right downtown, between what was called Little Italy and the university. Gosh, he was giving me his key.

What about Professor MacLean? I wondered wickedly. Where did he live? Did he know where I lived? He could easily find out. What was it in me that I had to have the most excitement possible? I was altogether too willing for dirty fun. What if Fez knew? I would lose him, surely. He must never know about me and my ways. Or would he still love me anyway? I was still confused by what my terrible mind threw up into my consciousness.

My Fez was everything you could want. Rugged, handsome, a little rough, a little gentle. He was smart, but a little too dumb when it came to females. Forwards and backwards: he was everything a girl could hope for. But it seemed to me that I didn't want to be possessed by any man entirely, and that was the whole thing. Wasn't that what I wanted to get away from?

But it was so ironic, for I was running towards the very thing I needed to repel: Professor MacLean and the actualisation of my fantasy. God, I was like a soppy young girl hoping the boy would like me. In this case a dirty old man. And thus, in my world, to collide with Professor MacLean would at once satisfy my lust and quite possibly destroy all hopes of my happiness with Fez. Or would Fez ultimately understand? Understand that I was a horny girl. Oh my God, I exposed my naked pussy to MacLean in the lecture hall. How could I have done such a thing? It couldn't be! It shouldn't be!

I looked up hopefully at Fez.

'Let's spend more time together, maybe after a few more months we could...' he cut himself off, apparently unwilling at this time to finish expressing his thought. He played with the key at the end of my new chain, but he couldn't bring himself to utter his true desire, his plan. Though I did know what he'd meant to say, and I knew he didn't want to scare me away, or even scare himself, for that matter. How could he be so sure of what he might have wanted to express to me at that time? I could be certain, though, that he was clearer about his feelings than I was at that point. I was so full of deceit, and he had this pretty picture all dreamt up for us. He had wanted to say that he would love to see us live together.

I looked up at him, my hero, and I heard my inner voice name him thus. How wonderful. Then the other part of me screamed out: where was MacLean and why did he not come visit me in the nurse's office and molest me?

Why did I allow my world to be so dominated by men?

I was a woman so on my own. I could love Fez, at

least the better part of me could, but I liked my own place; I needed, loved, my own space. It was a space for more rebellion to happen. Bee could come over anytime; have coffee, joints, wine even. As if I wanted to be watched twenty-four hours a day. Bee didn't live with her man. Why should I?

'Perhaps someday . . .' I dared to echo Fez's unfinished thoughts.

'Santa.' He whispered and kissed me again, this time a little more urgently.

Santa. Such a funny name for me really. Who was Santa Pertog? Santa, my mother's name, an Italian name. It sounded so pure, even saintly, but I wasn't saintly at all; in fact, quite au-contraire. I liked my name, though, especially when Fez said it the way he did.

Fez told me I should rest awhile and that he'd be back after his class. With that he left me alone.

I closed my eyes. What a day it had been so far! I was totally depraved according to any society's standard of behaviour. It was just who I was, though. The world stimulated me in all ways, including my sexuality. As a woman, I was sexy enough, but too strangely unattainable and mysterious to be a typically attractive female to men. God, what a curse that was, but how it geared me up, for I was a plainly sexual being. Men – left, right and centre – gave me concern, presenting themselves at every turn. I had a lot of sexual energy to release, which came to the surface as men propositioned me relatively often. Men made my head veritably spin and I seriously had to ask myself each time: shall I go or not go with them? So many tantalising possibilities. Maybe I should compare notes with Bee, as she was so beautiful, far more so than I. But all this lusty energy; it simply surged through me, and it wasn't normal, nor fair, because it was forbidden fruit. And for good reason, I supposed. I could end up diseased or pregnant, as my doctor had once warned me. The evil things of the night.

I was raised a Catholic. Therefore sex was dirty. It was for shame; it was the tree of knowledge. I would have preferred not to know too much about the tree of knowledge because I was made to fear it. But alas, it was the loss of innocence, an experience from which none would be spared. From a young age the world of men had assaulted my innocence like a wave repeatedly unfurling itself on the deck of a ship; and my ship was navigating tidal waters.

It was weird to be lying in the nurse's campus bed. The door was semi-shut and I could see people passing by in the hall outside. I lay there and thought how shocking it was that MacLean had actually seen what I was doing in class. I reached down under my covers and touched myself comfortingly.

MacLean could fuck me now; he should come visit his poor light-headed little student. Or I could sit on his knee on his professor's chair while he touched and fucked me. He could be sleazy and secretive with me – the dirty girl who must be disciplined, must be touched.

I was all worked up and getting bored lying in the nurse's office and so I went on to fantasise about MacLean.

He has returned my paper to me with a note indicating I am to meet him at his office at such and such an appointed time. Is he going to accuse me of exposing my naked pussy in his class? I dread the prospect as I arrive at the scheduled time and knock tentatively on his door. It opens and there he is in the dark doorway, casting his long shadow, marking the path I am to follow into the room. It is an ominous road. I hold my breath as I move past him into his dark office and I hear him click the door shut behind me.

I am standing in his office. 'Sit down.' His voice is practically inaudible, yet it echoes in my head. This worries me intensely, as I feel far too attuned to him. If I pretend not to hear this voice of his, I may be able to get out of this dangerous situation, but it hypnotises me. I am stung with the realisation that upon the shutting of that door I have gone beyond the point of return. We both know perfectly well why I am here; he is going to confront me with my inappropriate, indecent behaviour and punish me.

I am terribly menaced – by my own desires and by him. And an awful burning inner awareness is deep in the pit of me. It is the beast, the one that smells of the aroused animal, the adrenaline pumping through me, the fear. All the while my professor is trying his best to send a chill down my spine. He tells me to sit down and I try to act cool, like I don't know which chair he means for me to take, for example, even though there are only two seats to choose from, and his own chair seems apparent, given its position by his desk. I then go on to further experience the great indignity of fumbling with the goddamned chair I do finally take. I don't quite sit in it right and I manage to hurt my inner thigh on the metal arm. The room is dark like an animal's den as there is only a small window set high in the wall which barely casts any light in the room at all. I finally settle in the chair.

'Did you hurt yourself?' he asks, studying me solemnly. I shake my head. He smiles, knowing I had probably bruised the inside of my upper leg.

I'm holding my failed paper in my hand and I calmly ask why I had received such a low mark. He takes the paper from me and regards it with suspicion. I look down at his shifty hands and back up into his eyes. The professor's dark eyes slide down to regard the document in his hand, then they linger at length on the hem of my short skirt. I cross my legs. He smiles so secretly, but I can see the grimace on his face. He may as well be holding my soiled underwear in his hands, because I am not wearing any anyway. As I remember this rude fact, panic suddenly seizes me. Is my mind as transparent as my skirt? What am I doing going around dressed like this? I squirm nervously in my seat as MacLean reaches over to turn on his desk lamp.

'What were you doing in class?' he asks me amusedly.

'What do you mean?' I try my best to sound innocent but my throat is dry and my face is flushed as he is confronting me with this terrible question.

'You know precisely what I mean. Show me, show me what you were doing in my classroom,' he insists.

There is a painful, uncomfortable pause.

'Show me,' he presses. He slowly lifts my skirt with the corner of my academic paper. The more I squirm, the more he can see of my shy bare pussy, my hairless cunt. The more I wriggle, the juicier I become, as his eyes feast on me. Next he comes in closer and begins to part my legs and touch me. I try to remove myself, to rise.

In the nurse's bed, I was raising my pelvis up under the covers and was almost orgasming right there and then while I fantasised away. But before I could reach climax, the nurse came in the room. She was none the wiser.

'How are we feeling now?' she asks.

'Better, thanks. I think I'm ready to leave.'

'Fine. Well your friend's back too,' she said moving aside in the doorway so Fez could peer in.

'I'll take you home, OK, Santa?'

'That would be great, Fez,' I said gratefully as I pushed the covers away and stood up.

Back at home, I felt relieved I wouldn't have to go back to class for a while because of my supposed fainting spell. Actually I began to ponder whether I should drop MacLean's course altogether; my behaviour was so inappropriate and I was playing with fire by giving him far too much power. But that would draw weird attention and raise questions about my relationship with him and, of course, undermine my serious career intentions. And what about my serious pursuit of a law degree? Enough of this game-playing, girl!

But then, what could I do about the fact that I would have liked to have fainted right in MacLean's arms? And how I hoped my professor would take advantage of my frailty at the time and do unspeakable things to me? Would he give me a good mark afterwards? I needed to accept what a foul a creature I truly was.

Would I rather have fainted in Fez's loving arms? He would take me. Take me as a woman that would lovingly cleave to him. And he would love me and me alone. Something pure was in my reach.

And something profane. The old professor, he meant to touch my womanhood and punish the bad girl. Pretty lame really, but how it excited me and made me much more open to suggestion. It stemmed from something delicious that my doctor had once done to me ... and others too. It was my fatal flaw, my deviant sexual nature. My professor didn't need to work hard to find it if he wanted, and I didn't mind waiting; that was half the fun. If MacLean was clever enough, he may earn the rewards of his intrepid efforts.

I would let myself fall, fall for ever into his arms. And he would call up his men in arms to encircle me, to gangbang me. That would be fine with me, truth be known. I would take on the entire faculty of law, so big was my crotch. Ha! Let them all at me, all at once. I shuddered to think of it. And, of course, I grew with pleasure, contemplating all of these debauched thoughts.

6

That evening I called Bee and, when there was no answer, I remembered that Wednesday nights Bee had MacLean's class until nine. I wanted to show her Fez's gift to me. In the directory I found the pizza joint I always used down the street to order a delivery. Shortly after I hung up, the phone rang and I presumed the pizza people were calling me back to confirm my order. When I answered, there was a long pause and after I said hello for the third time, the party calling hung up, in a sort of slam the phone down manner. Perplexed, I looked up the number and called the pizza place back. But it hadn't been them calling. Ah well, I thought, no doubt some jerk had the wrong number. I hate it when people don't apologise when they dial wrong, otherwise it unnerves a person. Or, what about the stimulating possibility that the good professor was on a break and might be using the phone to sexually plague me. Perhaps to see how his ailing student was doing. Silly girl, I thought, it was just a wrong number.

With my pizza, I had a glass of red wine. Meantime, I should have been setting the night aside to study. But I told myself: Relax, girl, you've had a hectic day. So I ate on the couch, put my feet up on the coffee table and listened to some jazz on the radio. They were playing the jazz master, Stephane Grappelli, fantastic stuff. I wondered if Fez liked jazz too.

An hour later, I heard Bee's familiar rapping at my door. I always knew when it was Bee.

'Guess who was asking about you?' she teased as I

poured us both some red. I spilt a little. 'Hey, girlie, are you still shaky from your fainting spell? How many have you had tonight anyway? You've eaten, haven't you?'

'Yes, I have eaten and don't start policing me, my dear woman!' I mock admonished her. We clinked glasses. Then I inquired in an affected, high-class tone of voice, 'Who asked after me, then? Pray tell.'

Bee tossed her beautiful dark curls. 'Well, only your great admirer, MacLean!'

'Well, and so he should,' I brushed off. 'It was his deadly dull lectures that caused me to escape in any way that I could. Isn't he such a droner? Rather inventive of me to faint, don't you think?' I said, self-satisfied.

'Don't make a regular practice of it. You could have just met me for our legendary smoke,' she scolded. 'At any rate, we know full well that's not why you fainted, silly girl.'

'Fez gave me this.' I showed Bee the excellently long chain.

'Gorgeous, must have done him some serious financial damage,' Bee said admiringly. 'What's this, though?'

'Key to his place. I think he was hinting that we should shack up together.'

'My my, that's rather quick. You sure got to his heart fast, my friend. Told you so. And so?'

'Too soon and he knows it too. Don't even know if it's at all wise anyway.' I shrugged. 'Probably the same reason you haven't moved in with Joey, after what is it now, a year or more?'

'Almost a year and he's never asked me.' She frowned. 'And now with this news for you, I feel utterly pissed off.'

I pulled at one of Bee's finely carved curls and gently inquired, 'What would you do if he did ask?'

'In his dreams,' she said with wry indifference and

we both shortly fell into laughter. 'Suddenly life would become so très ennuyant, and he so tiresome.'

'You love him, you wench,' I told her, admiring her ability with French. 'So why, really, why would you not move in with him? I mean, Fez is making this gesture solely out of pity. He wants to watch over me, so to speak. How appealing or how appalling for me, don't you think?'

'No. Not really. Do you know how many girls he can choose from here? It's you, Santa, you! He's handsome, smart, wealthy. Don't be a fool!'

'What a pile of bull that is. I have to be ready to live with someone and I'd never go for a man just for his money. I'm surprised to hear you say that!' I said this knowing we'd discussed men and money many times before. There was a moment of silence while we stared at each other.

'How wealthy?' I asked her, and we both burst into laughter. I couldn't stop. I was giddy as hell. We laughed until Bee could laugh no more. Our lives were ahead of us. So much promise awaited us.

We were both from the same background, more or less, with the same values, give or take. She had told me about her parents. Intellectuals both, her father was a painter, originating from Belgium and her mother, a French literature professor at some small university in the States. They didn't have much money, but they had tons of culture. Her father's paintings were marvellous, though perhaps the kind that would only find their true value after his death. He sells the odd one for large sums of money, but his main income was from being an art dealer. It surprised me that Bee chose the field of law, given her background. My father, for example, was a lawyer himself, now a judge, so the world of law was a frequent topic of discussion around my family's dinner table. It seemed natural for me to go into the field.

So my marks had better pick up!

Bee, I was to discover, was much consumed by the notion of Joey not having asked her to live with him, particularly since Fez had hinted at such a set-up with us. I knew it would make better economic sense for Bee to share the rent with someone.

She felt she loved Joey more than he loved her. In spite of herself, the proud Bee wanted more from him. And so it began. My putting off Fez caused Bee to unreasonably criticise me for rejecting that which she herself wanted, and we were bickering about it while we were at my place the next night, waiting for the boys to come over.

'But you see, Santa, if you did move in with Fez, then it might occur to Joey to ask me.' She'd said this to me already several times, but I remained firm in my position.

'Look, girlie, you can't expect me to move in with Fez for your sake. It just doesn't work that way.' I shook my head, my eyes widening in disbelief at her. She looked down and sulked.

'Why don't *you* just ask Joey to live with you?' I finally said impatiently to her.

'He will have to beg me to live with him! But he won't because he simply isn't as dedicated to this relationship as I am,' she complained and sighed unhappily.

'You're both just students. These are the years to be independent, whatever, not to be so terribly tied down. I'd feel like a bird in a cage. I mean, I'm flattered at Fez's rather indirect offer, but I'm not altogether sure what's behind it.' I took her wrist and looked at her watch.

'They're overdue,' I remarked. 'Geez, we should just get them to stay in tonight, I don't feel like going to this rally.'

'Don't you bloody care about bringing down the corrupt powers that virtually fuck people's lives up all over the western or whatever world? It's beyond our small world! OK? What's your problem?'

'It's just that the last time we almost got arrested, hello?'

'We all have to make sacrifices. God, Santa.'

Bee was being more than a little cranky.

'What's up your ass?' I asked her. 'Look, you go out with Fez, then. God knows I don't deserve him, anyway,' I sputtered.

'Santa! What are you talking about?'

Of course, I didn't want this, and nor did Bee want to take Fez from me. I knew we were getting carried away. 'Let's forget it,' I said to her.

'OK, sorry.'

There was silence and I plugged in the kettle.

'Why are you doing that? We're going out in a few minutes, dearie,' she reminded me.

'Do we have to?'

'You betcha.'

I unplugged the kettle with a sigh. The fact was that I didn't want to go to the rally because I still hadn't returned to MacLean's class and I feared I'd run into the lewd professor there. He was at the last demonstration. I dreaded seeing him again. I'd behaved so outrageously. Of course, off I went again with my inner contradictions because, underneath, I badly wanted to see him. I needed to like an addict had to have a fix. I was like a moth to his hungry flame yet I needed to wean off these imaginings of mine that so distracted me from Fez and the serious relationship I wanted to pursue with him.

The guys were knocking at the door. Bee went to answer it when she realised I was going to be passive-aggressive and not get the door. Before she left the room, she said brightly, 'Hey, you and me, let's you and me move in together, hey? Maybe that will make him notice,' said Bee referring to Joey.

'Let's talk about it later,' I offered.

The gentlemen callers arrived and nothing I said could discourage them from their need to publicly rail against the world in the form of an organised protest against the power holders. All for a good cause, I supposed, and we were going, I had to resign myself to that. I went into bathroom to powder my nose. If I ran into MacLean, I wanted to look pulled together; now I *was* hoping he would show up. God, what a bitch I was. What a sucker for self-inflicted punishment. Sure, I was off to the protest against authority – his most of all. He was the nearest authority at hand. I was spurred on. For me, it was a rally against MacLean.

He *was* there, as it turned out. MacLean spied me right away in the mass of protesters and he moved to a remote position from which he could watch me. I noticed this from the corner of my eye and he was staring, this I unerringly knew. I ignored him as best I could.

The legislature grounds were crowded with people holding banners that read, 'World Trade Organisation Run by Oligarchs', and 'Secret Societies Violate Human Rights', and 'Bring Down Corrupt Powers'. Protest organisers were making people march in a circle around the government buildings. As I followed the group, I looked up at the smooth copper dome at the top of the main legislative building. The oxidised copper had turned green from the forces of time. Changed by the elements. How beautifully it reminded me of my own tarnished soul. I was bizarrely oversexed, but I was elegantly corrupt.

'Are you better, then?' MacLean asked, letting the question hang in the air as he was suddenly by my side.

'Um, I haven't been to class,' I stated lamely with a note of apology in my voice.

I know,' he said. 'You must attend.' His voice was low and intense.

Officials were now arriving in long stretch limos that stopped in front of the main steps that led into the building. Everyone around us had now ceased marching to observe security and police surround the V.I.P. cars as they discharged their cargo, the politicians.

I tried to smile and acknowledge my professor's point that I shouldn't miss his lectures but I could barely meet his gaze. He knew I'd masturbated in his class and I found myself once again desperately looking up at the copper roof of the government building. There were flags at each corner of the supporting level below the curved dome and they flicked lazily in the wind, like a girl with her naughty skirts. I looked at him, feeling guilty, and noticed that his eyes were trained on me the whole time and that he was doubtlessly reading my dirty thoughts.

MacLean accommodated the pressing front row crowd and moved in closer to me. He was right beside me, almost facing me, and I felt my visage growing very red. Then there were his long fingers, which he pointed at me, only inches away from my chest, and as he spoke to me he made circles in the air, as if he was encircling my nipples. He told me about all the work I was missing, but, while he did so, he did not avert his eyes from my breasts the whole time.

My nipples were erect and showing through my shirt, and I was growing intensely uneasy. The experience was so strange and unnerving that I actually came to believe that he was touching my breasts and nipples. Like the flags above us, lifting under the force of the insistent wind, my very shirt felt lifted. This my professor did with such casual indifference that no one could reasonably detect the mischief. It was as if he knew how to get under my skin, oh how well he knew, and that was precisely what he was doing. Like he somehow had ownership of the female anatomy – more precisely, mine – that he touched so uninvited.

And so I was in complete shock and also so fully aroused. The wind picked up a little, and from over our heads I heard the sharp snapping of the flags of the Commonwealth; it sounded like the spanking I wanted him to give me.

MacLean said, 'You must come and see me about the work you've missed; we don't want your marks to be affected, now, do we? Then there's the matter of your behaviour in class.' He disappeared abruptly. It was like he had everything calculated.

I realised my marks may well realistically be at stake, as he'd threatened. I always had been terribly conscious of the undoubted power he had over me. Where does he live? I wanted to know suddenly. He had such power over my destiny I thought I should go and kill him. I seethed with angry blood and lust and I exulted in how I despised him and how I loved him.

After the rally, we all went back at my apartment. 'So what did MacLean have to say for himself? Fez inquired. 'I saw him talking to you at some length.'

'He's concerned that I'm missing classes, the dumb bastard,' I replied and laughed offhandedly.

Bee said, 'You're just recovering. What's so surprising that you're resting up a little? Tell him I said so!'

Fez was slightly heated. Actually I sensed he was set off to blast. He seemed suspicious of MacLean and a part of me loved the tension. 'I can get some friends to come by and bring home the point to him, if you wish,' Fez added.

'What, sir, do you mean? What friends?' I asked, intrigued. 'What friends do you have, then?'

'Never you mind. Just don't let him cause you any kind of grief,' he said, as he wagged his finger seriously at me. 'Another beer, Joey?' he asked.

'Thanks.' Joey nodded.

Fez rose and went into the kitchen.

So I could get Fez's mob to squash MacLean for me. What kind of associations did Fez's family have? OK, get a grip over your crazy mind, girl, I thought.

It was quite a job to keep up with my spinning-out-of-control imagination. I had to fuck MacLean, was all I knew, or he had to make love to me. It was all wrapped up in the idea of who had the power.

But my poor work; well, I could manage to stop worrying about it so much if I just hunkered down to my studies. I could simply return to class, work hard and pursue my honest dreams and goals. Forget all this weird intrigue. But how? How long could this go on? We were both of us caught up, my professor and I, and I knew I couldn't trust MacLean to be a gentleman. Or could I? Could I give him half a chance and see what he might do if the opportunity presented itself? Like, if he wanted to discuss my marks. Like, if I fainted in his arms.

The next morning, I rose early to copy out Bee's notes for the 'Crime and Enforcement' classes I'd missed. Photocopying may have been faster, but this way I could commit the work to memory by writing it out. I wanted be a lawyer, and I believed I could be a damn good one, so it was high time for me to get back to my classes. MacLean could be given no opportunity to negatively scrutinise my academic efforts. I would press on with my work and be up to speed in no time with the rest of my classmates. I would be beyond reproach and it was time to take his power away. I wanted to commit myself to the deserving and wonderful Fez and stop being such a naughty thing.

Bee and I later resolved to save the partying for the weekends and to be study partners through the week-nights. We were total party girls whenever she was over, which was often.

Though my apartment was small, Bee's was smaller. We decided it would be a good and sound idea to move in together soon, both at my place. This I thought would solve both the issue of Fez's intention to get me to move in with him, and Bee's strong desire to live with some-body. We both decided to remain independent while our studies remained paramount because, if we lived with our boyfriends, then the whole playing field would change. Live with our boyfriends? We couldn't do that while at college! What were we thinking? Laundry, dishes, cooking ... with guys in the house! Just imagine. Well, we agreed quite categorically in a moment of prac-ticality and inspiration that neither of us felt that taking care of a male was what we needed in our lives right now, and we were convinced that this would be exactly what would be in store for us if we moved in with any male, be it Fez or Joey or anyone. So that was that.

I was meeting Fez at his place at nine-thirty in the morning. He wanted to serve me espresso and bagels. This is when I would break the news.

How sweet he was to me. I was well aware that he was making damn sure I ate a proper breakfast every morning, so much was his worry about my weight and my fainting spell. Bagels, coffee, pears and cheese. How could I resist his good care?

'Why didn't you use your key?' he asked, after open-ing the door.

'Good morning,' I said as I walked in past him. He followed me into the kitchen. I couldn't help but notice his elaborate new counter-top espresso machine.

'That's amazing,' I said.

'I will prepare you the finest of coffees. Now, if this doesn't entice you to move in with me, well then, I give up!' He laughed. I laughed too. The magnificent machine took up a whole counter and was glistening new, made of brass and untarnished. Unlike myself. How sweet a coffee would be produced from that, I thought. I would enjoy this as a guest, but never as a roommate. My coffee at home came from the worst of the boiled-over-too-many-times percolator. Same as the fantasies that ran over and over again in my fevered brain. They were sour, bitter to the last taste and served quite the punch.

'Fez,' I said to him in his kitchen, 'you need to give up on our moving in together for now. Trust me, it's better that way.'

'I'll be the judge of that,' he interrupted.

'I have some news. And also, by the way, I won't use the key to simply walk into your place. I'll keep it for you. It's always good to have someone trusted to keep a spare key for you. Plus it will remind me of your wonderful offer, but for now ...'

'Why is it so important that you remain so totally independent of me,' he sulked. 'I want you in my life, OK? I said it, OK?'

'I am in your life,' I said.

'Not as much as I would like.'

He turned his back to me and started up the espresso machine. 'A double?' he inquired sulkily.

'Great. So Bee and I are moving in together,' I continued. I think it will be a very good arrangement. We can study together, save some money, you know?' I said, rushing out the words.

Fez stopped his activity around the coffee making. He faced me once again. His countenance was perturbed and rather hurt. 'I will pay the rent here for both of us.'

'I wouldn't expect that.'

'I would love to do it. I can afford it,' he insisted.

'There is so much we don't know about each other, Fez. I don't even know how you can pay for this big place, that espresso machine...'

'I told you, I work for my father here and there.' He smiled mysteriously.

'And there's lots you don't know about me,' I advised playfully. 'Let's just take it slow, as they say.'

'What, my dear, do you hide from me? Is there another man?' His eyes turned to dark slits. I could see here how it might be unwise to arouse his anger. And how exciting it was too. I couldn't hold his gaze for long. I looked down and denied that I was trying to conceal anything. It wasn't as though there really was anything to hide, anyway. Liar, liar, pants on fire, Santa loves her professire.

'I want you to meet my family this weekend, would that be all right?' Fez asked, as he stroked my hair and put my bagel and coffee down before me.

'I'd love it.' I would be happy to finally meet these rather mysterious sounding people.

'Good. We'll go to my father's restaurant, then, say Saturday?'

'Great,' I said. I took another bite into my bagel. 'This is great too,' I gushed. What was I going to wear to meet his family? I would have to have Bee over for a clothes consult.

Thereafter, I set off to MacLean's class, determined to simply join the lecture like any other student, and not one whose grades were suffering; not one who had strange sexual yearnings for her disgusting professor. Nor one who had masturbated in front of him in class. All of this can be ignored. I was going to simply forget all about it.

Once at my seat, I did not as much as glance up at MacLean. My head was decidedly down, my pen fever-ishly scribbling notes, listening as attentively as I could to his broken language. God, he was hard to listen to. When my hand momentarily tired from writing, out the same old window I gazed, my eyes settling on the small pond in the university grounds. My innocence was like a memory, like the water shimmering, reflecting light back towards the empty, indifferent universe. But it was late spring, a chance for renewal. Sensuous melting liquid, I could feel it course all over my body. Stop!

Quickly, I set back to my work. When MacLean posed questions to the general class, I raised my hand several times, knowing the answer, but throughout that class he never did call on me, and I wasn't about to care either. I was going to be the best student with or without his attention. It wasn't until he announced at the end of the lecture, out loud and to the class at large, that he wanted me to remain behind to speak to him, that I became painfully self-conscious, trembling in my poor skinny legs. At my desk, I crossed my legs protectively and then realised how upsettingly involuntary a reaction this had become for me: I was trying to hide my private parts, which I felt sure he could see. But it was too late for that, wasn't it, for had I not secretly exposed my naked pussy to him during class already?

The same situation wherein I pretended to faint? He'd already seen me in the most intimate of ways. First my breasts in the library and then he went ahead and touched my cunt on the dance floor, and then again where I was so shamelessly touching myself during that fateful class. What was I thinking? What did he want? And whatever it might be, there was no hope of my remaining in proper possession of myself under the circumstances. Was he going to spank the bad girl now? I so deserved it.

All the students exited; it seemed that the rest of the class had vanished, in fact. As MacLean sorted out his papers, he looked up at me every so often as I waited at my desk. His expression was dark and serious as he straightened a few sheets of paper by tapping them sharply on the top of his table. Several times he repeated this with other stacks of paper. It was sheer torture.

I realised how much I needed and longed for my professor to confront me, to finally release the demons in me. Was I up for it? Had I had enough to eat that day? Of course, Fez fed me well at breakfast, and it wasn't even noon yet. I looked up at him, all the while putting up a veil of confidence on the exterior.

'Your participation during lectures contributes to your overall grade, did you know?' he casually informed me from across the room.

'Oh, I know,' I mumbled. 'You didn't see that I'd raised my hand?'

'Speak up!'

'I said I tried to participate. You called on the other students, so far as I could tell. You didn't seem to notice me.' I realised I may be sounding cocky with what I said, but it was true.

'No, I didn't see you raise your hand. Are you feeling well? I know you're prone to fainting spells. Perhaps it isn't good for you to raise your arm above your head.' And he trailed off, seeming to be detached from his own words, apparently thinking of something else at that moment.

'I'm fine. Much better. I don't faint.' I looked at him, miffed and yet feeling such self-doubt. Had I not raised my hand? I truly wondered now if I had.

He moved away from his position behind his desk and came over to mine holding a thick stack of documents. 'I have a special case for you to study. Since you have missed so many classes, this will give you a chance to catch up with the rest of the students. This year is a very strong group. It'll require some effort on your part to match the talents of the rest. This is a very interesting historic case,' he assured me, smiling and finally looking me in the eye. 'Prepare a defence for Yvonne Dupres. She went against the church. She caused a storm amongst French society in her time. It was a famous case from the eighteenth century.' He dumped a set of photocopied documents onto my desk. Rather, he dropped it so as to cause my hair to be carried upward in the breeze of his ill-intent, or so I interpreted it.

I opened the first page, dutifully, like good student. It was called: *The Legal Battle between Father Paul-Baptiste and Yvonne Dupres.* 'Have a defence prepared before the end of the term. That's in two weeks,' he reminded me patronisingly. 'Don't forget about the other assignments and then you should be right up to speed with the rest of the class.'

'Of course,' I replied, perplexed. I looked down at the stack of documents and felt his presence move away from me. 'Thank you, sir,' my voice croaked as his form disappeared from the room. What was he trying to do, give me an extra chance or undo me completely? I decided for the former, a far healthier view, until I came to read through the strange, strange case of Yvonne Dupres documented in 1729 in Reims, France.

I went home and shut my door. I had a heavy assignment from my law professor. To my amazement it turned out to be the case of a person in authority taking advantage, or rather, fully sexually exploiting a subordinate. Not that Yvonne Dupres, the female protagonist under the care and guidance of father Paul-Baptiste Lemartre, was an innocent. But she was a character so completely open to suggestion, and was ultimately fully under the influence of the powerful, much older priest. The imbalance of power was all too clear. And so the implication of this case was menacing to me, insofar as MacLean would assign to me such a study. What was he suggesting by this?

I stayed up late into the night to review it and review it again. I found myself shaking my head repeatedly at what an incredibly curious thing it was that MacLean chose this case for me to dissect. The story was an echo of him and me, in its twisted, student-teacher, seduction-provocation dynamic. In the court case drama, the priest was so corrupt and the young woman so willing to participate to gain her own particular ends.

I surrendered to this new fascinating scenario my professor seemed to have so slyly introduced into my own fantasies. He appeared to be implying, in his assignment, that he knew full well about my deviance; about my skewed sexual nature. Unfortunately, it was an undeniable, living part of my being.

It was only after I'd inevitably imagined myself as Yvonne, and MacLean as Father Paul-Baptiste Lemartre, with his lewd flame burning for her and her seemingly innocent willingness to fall so completely under his power, that I could finally put down this fascinating reading for the night.

I gave over to this multiplicity of character, as I was to newly regard it. I also sounded my muted call to that similarly deviant part of my professor. We were now to share in the same fantasy. Things between us had moved to a whole new level of badness.

To the bad man I called. To the bad girl, also. I subscribed ever more to the awful unlawful; to the arousing dirty, debauched thoughts of interplay that might occur between us. In my imagination I was myself with MacLean, only inside the story of the historic case of Yvonne Dupres and Father Paul-Baptiste. I was helplessly pulled in. Time for bed.

I masturbated, unfolding the repeated scenario slowly in my mind of a young religious girl seeking sainthood, and an opportunist priest who bewitched her. She was a fraud of the first order and the Jesuit priest knew it all along. In Father Lemartre's self-appointed way, he divulged to her the ways to purity through repentance and the promise that she was to be his prodigy. As she so keenly desired, he would lead her to perfection, telling her that she should not be disturbed by what happens to her body; that she needed to banish her scruples, her fears and doubts and allow him to master her completely. At first, so subtly, he breathed on her neck. Then his lips brushed her skin there, then his tongue, all the while telling her to be obedient to him. His hand slid slowly down into her shirt, until it found her soft breasts that he lightly stroked. The other hand unbuttoned her blouse to finally expose her breasts, where his stroking continued unimpeded across both her nipples. 'God is well pleased with you,' he whispered into her ear.

I didn't need to go much further in my imaginings before I experienced the release I sought. The orgasm rippled through me, pleasure akin to pain. Only then did I finally yield to slumber. Sleep, to sleep ... it was three-thirty a.m. and I knew I wouldn't make my morning class with MacLean. And so the plot thickens, I thought. So the pattern of my misbehaviour would go on and gain even more momentum as I defiantly missed another class.

The phone rang at nine thirty the next morning. I didn't answer and the machine picked up and it was Fez's voice asking where I was and that he had breakfast all ready for me. Loving man. 'You're probably on your way ...' Click. With no intention of calling him back, I rolled over and went back to sleep. Oh, how good it felt to go back to that quiet, warm place, even though I knew I owed Fez the courtesy of calling to tell him I wasn't coming. He'd understand, and I'd make it up to him sometime.

Needless to say, for the rest of the week, I tried to make it to most of my classes. By now, I was in denial as to how many lectures I was actually missing. Fez insisted I visit him daily and eat with him. I couldn't face going to MacLean's class, as the very sight of him would possibly cause me to pretend to faint again. I was so under the spell of our little play, and, against my better judgement, I wanted to provoke his anger further by not coming to his lectures. I would simply complete the assigned work, hand in this crazy defence case and then resume my normal student status in the class. Working from Bee's notes would serve to keep me up with the rest of the group.

7

Bee just didn't understand the extra work I had been assigned, or my change of heart with regards to our plans to move in together.

'It's just that I have to go day and night with this assignment now,' I explained. 'I need my full space, my own hours. I mean, it was a great idea, all of it, being roommates, studying together, everything, but now I'm on a completely different track,' I explained, running at the mouth.

'But I'll help you!' she insisted.

'I don't know. Let me talk to you tomorrow. Meet you for a smoke in the first fifteen?' I offered.

We hung up. I was beset with this whole thing and, once again, I was swept away by my compulsive thoughts about MacLean. Bee shouldn't know too much about me and my inner workings. No one should. Not until I could work this out of my system somehow. But how?

Must I go through with the unspeakable act of allowing my professor to seduce me? He was already doing this, so passively and covertly and insidiously. His method was to unnerve me, to make me question my perception. Absurdly, I knew how to play along, until the moment where I would give over my power entirely.

It was near to supper time. I ate lightly and made some tea before I resumed my study of the historic case.

Yvonne Dupres was plainly neurotic. It was her great aim to become a saint, and she was determined to have Father Lemartre beatify her. In order to prove her holiness to Father Jean-Baptiste Lemartre, she behaved as if possessed, manifesting nervous prostration, convulsions, epileptic hysteria, hallucinations and traces of insanity. Of this, the priest took full advantage, particularly when she succumbed to regular fainting spells only to wake up again to find herself partially undressed and being fondled by her confessor. His explanation to her was, in his own words, 'It was God's will that you experience humiliation in order to proceed to perfection.' God help her, I thought to myself, and laughed aloud. Did she fake her fainting spells?

I took off my sweater and long pants; I was feeling overheated. I looked down at my very bare, shaven, trouble-making cunt and then continued to examine the case. I fondled it with my teasing fingers. So nude it was. I loved to touch it.

Yvonne Dupres had fallen in love Father Paul-Baptiste Lemartre.

He received special dispensation from the abbess to visit the young woman in her room, where he would spend hours alone with her, encouraging her spiritual quest. There, she would go into trances and have visions of a bleeding heart. It was her fond hope that Father Lemartre would become convinced of her sainthood.

But when he ultimately expressed doubts about her sainthood, she accused him of witchcraft and of putting her under his spell and bewitching and seducing her.

The phone rang and disrupted this most spellbinding story. When I answered it, there was silence on the other end. Moments after I'd hung up, the phone sounded again. There was no one. Again. I hung up, and resentfully went back to my studies. The phone pierced the room again with its shriek. I answered and it was calming to hear Fez's voice.

'Oh, did you just call a moment ago?' I asked.

'No, why?' he said.

'Someone hung up, I guess.'

'Has that happened before?' he inquired.

I replied, 'No, not really.'

'What do you mean? Either it's happened before, or it hasn't. Is someone bothering you?'

I laughed. 'Don't be silly. Someone just dialled wrong.'

'Idiots. Let me know if it happens again.'

'Yeah, yeah, it's OK,' I said, trying to brush it off.

'Did you get to class today? I was looking for you this afternoon.'

I coughed briefly, buying time, wondering whether I should lie. 'No, I didn't go. I'm so bogged down with this extra work for MacLean's class that it isn't funny. Bee is taking notes for me. It's going to be a busy weekend. Some fun.'

'You're not forgetting Saturday night at my father's restaurant? We're meeting them at seven.'

'No, that's great, Fez. I can't wait.'

'You want me to come by and give you a kiss good-night?' he asked sweetly.

I made kissing sounds to him over the phone. 'I won't be going to sleep for hours yet, dear heart.'

'Shall I, then?'

'I hate how much work I have,' I explained.

'Fine, then.' There was a long pause. Then, 'But I'll have breakfast ready for you tomorrow. And please take care, my love. I know you're not getting enough sleep.' He sounded so genuine. 'And if you don't mind my saying, I think you should attend class tomorrow. It's the end of the week, and you need to make an appearance and ensure MacLean's not assigning your class different work than he is to Bee's.'

I agreed and said, 'You're probably right.'

'I hate MacLean,' he averred.

'OK, Fez, I've heard it all before.'

'I'll walk you to the campus after we eat.'

'See you tomorrow, then. And thanks. Oh, and I'll bring some grapefruit for the table.'

'Got some already. Goodnight, my beauty queen.'

'Bye.'

I poured myself another cup of tea. Stupid bitch, I thought to myself. Tea always kept me up for hours. Anger began to rise in me. With each sip of tea, the fire of fury was stoked even higher. MacLean was ruining everything – driving me to insomnia, even; working round the clock with his unrealistic demands on his student. I finally hurled the papers across the room and ran into the bathroom and looked in the mirror.

Though I looked tired I still looked beautiful, I thought. I was all too alive. MacLean, he wasn't so dangerous to me. If he went too far I could make allegations of harassment against him. That could be the case I was building. I narrowed my eyes and effected a dangerous expression in the mirror. But who was I kidding? I asked my reflection, as I stared wide-eyed at the mirror. Almost innocent, I looked, and I chuckled to myself. There I was, silly Santa, who simply loved two men at once. One was a romantic love, the other, a dirty and depraved affair about to happen.

There was the final rub, though. This whole perverse situation with MacLean was just as much my fault. I was just as liable when it came down to me and my professor's antics. It was so like the many other strange cases one heard reported in the paper. The same twisted stories that took place where both parties were entirely enmeshed with the other and neither were truly at fault and yet both were to blame. Such was the case of Yvonne Dupres and Father Lemartre, and such was the situation with MacLean and me. I wanted to be his law student prodigy. I wanted to be adored and exploited; literally washed over by his weird sexuality – in the same way as Father Lemartre had done with the young and beautiful Yvonne. I went back to studying her story. I was coming closer to an understanding of it.

Yvonne, the young religious girl, was to ultimately accuse her spiritual father of sorcery. She took her case all the way to the highest of the French courts. But the good father was never to burn at the stake. Even though that was surely the style of the times – a good old roasting at the stake was a routine public diversion. Like going to the movies today. Well, perhaps that was going a little far, but still . . .

The trial spanned two years and the case surely excited the society of the times. Their strange drama conjured up a great deal in the minds of the people, even though they were a repressed society and must have been uptight and terrified about sex. In this historic case, the final outcome was that, after the lengthy trial, the two protagonists were both sent home packing. Even in such superstitious times, the powers that be could see the difference between what was termed witchcraft, the spiritual fear of the times, and two people trying to get off with each other.

Perhaps I loved Professor MacLean as Yvonne Dupres had loved Father Lemartre. A confused love generated by his power over her and her complete repulsion and fatal attraction for him. A gross love.

I decided that the following day I would submit a draft of my argument for Yvonne Dupres in the historic legal case against the very lecherous Father Lemartre. And this case, this character, would in no way be construed to mirror me or my obsession with my law professor! I'd have to be very careful about that in my report.

The case was cut and dried to any law student. Yvonne Dupres was out to become something of a celebrity of her time. Sainthood was her goal. Visions, apparitions; she even claimed to be a vessel for the spirits of other saints, and she came to express by her self-mortification. It was all ripe fields for Father Lemartre. He, alone with her for hours in her dark chambers, guiding her prayer, helped her ask forgiveness for her human weaknesses, for her very sexual form, for her very being. The dirty father seemed to have authority over her spirit and body, and both, of course, needed forgiveness. He would ask her to be in her most vulnerable state. To undress and take her position of prayer, leaning over her bed with her backside nude for him to gaze on. He said to her that she needn't be disturbed by being in God's sight in such a way; that He needed to see her in all her perfection and sin. Lemartre would then strap her with thin braided leather strings across her bare bottom while she would recite a prayer that would help her to transcend what was happening to her body. She admitted to feeling all wet between her innocent legs: this was reported in the arraignments from the late eighteenth century and was now provided by Professor MacLean for me to study. I would have to take her side and argue against Lemartre's accusations that she was a fraud.

It took place at a time when the church, the state and the individual were polarised and when a woman could be caught up and tossed about by the divergent and corrupt powers that were at work. Rotten patriarchal authority was all around, from one's father to the local priest. Yet Yvonne Dupres was not so helpless, and it was this that made my sexual imagination catch fire. She would bring them down and fuck them – the church, the priest, whoever. In that way, I could relate to this Yvonne character. She was trying to bring down the establishment in her own screwed-up way. And that was orgasmic for me in and of itself. Railing against authority was my big turn-on.

In my research I surmised that Father Lemartre was a kind of lone wolf in terms of the establishment. The bottom line was that the Jesuit was in serious moral question. He was trying to get away with all kinds of shit and Dupres knew it and even, to a degree, controlled his manipulations over her. By the seeming innocence of her own sexuality, she did such a thing – which couldn't have been all that hard. Maybe she had shown her naked, shaven cunt to him, like I'd done, and pretended to be innocent by fake-fainting.

MacLean was an opportunist as much as the Jesuit. He was ready to get his own thing going with me, as Lemartre had done. And the veiled young Yvonne gave him some definite openings. Just as I had.

But how could I possibly present this kind of analysis to he who'd seen me touch myself, expose myself. I would be accusing my professor of the very same misdeeds as Father Lemartre had committed, and admitting to my own sexual misdemeanours around him. In doubt of my paper, therefore, I would have to stay up all night working it out; and once again I would be in no shape for tomorrow. I was going to make Fez mad if I missed another one of his breakfasts. But what about my laboured-over paper? I would have to make it ready. Perhaps I could get Bee to hand it in for me. But no, it could be entrusted to no one.

In the best of worlds, I made myself believe that the next day would be a fine day, with a fine start with Fez and his espresso and bagels. How sweet he was in his true love for me. And he would walk me to class, and I will think only of him, and my future with him, and the way to the future is hard study and keeping my eyes fixed on the brightest of horizons.

Next day, wrong. For there I was in class, trying to keep my composure while MacLean's eyes burned into me, right through my clothes, my skin, my bones. My paper wasn't near ready to hand in. I wondered if it ever would be, or even if I had the courage to submit my personal thoughts on such a bizarre case. As I exited to meet Bee for a smoke in the first fifteen, I wondered if he would actually follow me this time, lean me over and spank me in a bathroom cubicle. And so my exit wasn't smooth, given these thoughts. I bumped into the furniture as a bad actor would. I shouldn't have called such attention on myself, but I did. I felt trailed by him as I made my way to this lawless date with Bee in the campus washrooms. I looked over my shoulder in the corridor, but of course he wasn't following. As if he could, nutty girl, he was in the middle of a lecture! The same place I should be right now.

'You look like shit,' Bee observed. 'What's going on with you, for heaven's sake? Now you're not even moving in with me any more.'

'Do I? Damn. I'm not sleeping great. I don't know. Do I really look crappy?' I whined.

'C'mon Santa, you're beautiful, but what's up with you?'

'I don't know. I'm fucking up. I'm fucking up in school. And you're way more beautiful than me,' I said.

Suddenly the bathroom door swung open hard. There we were smoking our rude cigarettes and being caught at it, and this wasn't the first time. What a couple of rebellious brats we truly were. We even had the audacity to giggle as we were led out by the 'authorities'. At first we were told to wait outside the dean's office for further instructions and we still couldn't contain our nervous, tittering selves. Shortly thereafter, we were both hanging our two heads before the stern university administrators. There, Professor MacLean and the dean and some security man addressed the problem formally and collectively in the dean's office.

I looked at MacLean. Clearly it had been he who alerted security that there was smoking going on in the downstairs women's room. He knew exactly where I was going when I took my exit from his class. He thought he was so smart. So powerful. He believed I needed civilising, and he wanted to conquer me. I caught myself looking very cockily at him. He was staring back at me, assured of his undeniable authority. I thought to myself that he really had no power unless I gave it to him.

This all took place during a break between a busy day of classes for the faculty, and so they gave us short shrift. They'd had enough of us, in truth. This time, the dean pronounced, 'You are suspended for the remainder of the day and don't let us see this repeated.'

Afterwards, Bee and I made plans to get together this welcome Friday night, intending to giggle away this particular day. But first I had to return to MacLean's lecture hall to collect my things. And out of deliberate antagonism, I ended up taking my seat and staying for the rest of the lecture. It was as boring as ever. MacLean so didn't care about the class he was teaching. But he had it in for me, and the whole time he looked at me like a snake ready to strike.

After class MacLean came to sudden life as he blocked my way out of the lecture hall, and his eyes lit up in their dazzling way. I was made to stay. The recurring urge to faint in his arms took me over. It was so strong that I actually persuaded myself that I was feeling dizzy. It must have been the same thing that Yvonne Dupres had experienced when the Jesuit priest was alone around her.

MacLean was standing close to me and he said, 'Sit back down.' So I went back to my desk. 'Why did you remain in my class when you'd been suspended for the day?' he demanded to know as I took my seat.

'I just thought it would be more of a disruption if I

came in and left right away again. I was trying to be considerate of the others,' I explained, pleased with the steady timbre of my voice.

'You're not well today, are you?' he probed.

'Oh well, I'm fine, you know,' I said, wondering what the hell he was trying to suggest.

'No, no, I don't. Tell me, are you feeling faint? You seem a little pale to me,' he suggested.

'Do I?' I asked.

There was silence.

'At any rate, it's not acceptable to leave my lectures to smoke cigarettes in the building, not in the least. There are consequences,' he warned.

I responded, 'Yes, I know I'm suspended for the remainder of the day.'

He meandered over to me and inquired, 'How is the case you're preparing? Are you finding it interesting?'

I badly wanted to ask why he had chosen that particular case but I sat in silence.

'I can't hear you,' he said. So he leant in close and I felt his breath on my neck. I swallowed, thinking of how Father Lemartre claimed he was hard of hearing and had to lean in closely to hear his prodigy whenever she spoke, which was seldom. And how, when he breathed on her the first time, she was transported by love for him.

'Ummm,' I answered weakly. I felt like I was breaking out in a sweat and I closed my eyes momentarily.

'Do you want a spanking?' I could barely hear him whisper in my ear. Is that what he said? It couldn't be!

'Pardon me?' my voice barely uttered.

'I was asking about the legal battle between Yvonne Dupres and Father Lemartre. All of France,' he continued as he strode back to his desk, 'was captivated by their dramatic case in the late eighteenth century. What did you think of the verdict?'

'I've not quite finished it. I feel so hot, I...' I swallowed, unable to finish what I was saying. What a fool I was! I was letting him in!

'What's wrong? Let me take you to my office, I have a chaise-longue where you can rest,' he offered.

'I have another class, I just need a minute,' I stammered.

He interrupted: 'Nonsense. You're suspended, remember? You're not to go to any other classes today. You need to come with me. My next lecture is in ten minutes. If you're not feeling stable by then, you may remain in my office as long as you need.'

I looked up at him, but his face did not betray any malice. In fact, he was being surprisingly fatherly about the whole thing as he nodded at me, closing his eyes reassuringly, indicating he would take care of it all. Surely I'd imagined him speaking so menacingly in my ear – and what he had said.

'Thank you,' I said and rose numbly. My legs were a little wobbly and I held on to the corner of my desk. Then he came around behind me and put his hand on the lower part of my back. It felt like fire, with his hand just above my ass. I couldn't bear it. And I gradually weakened under his touch because, whatever was happening to me, I wanted it to happen.

'Come, I'll help you.' He fairly whispered his words.

We made our way down the corridors that led to his office. There were few people around and along the way we didn't speak a word to each other, although my shoes seemed to echo really loudly as I walked beside him. We reached his door.

Soon, he had me sitting in his chaise-longue and had covered me with a small blanket. It all seemed very caring, really, except for the strange, slight smile on his face.

'Close your eyes,' he told me gently and then said,

'I'm sorry you're not feeling well.' He brought me water, and I took it with a shaky hand.

'You're shaking,' he observed, then turned off the lights and went to his next lecture. Maybe, I pondered, I had misjudged him terribly. It was so dark in the room that I wasn't sure where I should set the glass back down, but how comfortable was his chaise-longue. And how disappointed I was he hadn't taken this obvious opportunity to molest me. Was he waiting for me to fall asleep? Did he plan to return then?

And so, willingly playing out my part of the game, I closed my eyes and pretended to fall asleep there and then in his office. Daydreams of MacLean returning to find me in my slumber-like state haunted me. I slid my hands under the blanket and I rubbed myself lightly through my pants. Wait. Did I hear the door? Silence. I ceased my masturbating and listened for a spell. There definitely was a presence in the room. Vaguely, I could see the shape of my professor approach me. I rolled my head to the side, as if in sleep and kept my eyes shut.

MacLean was kneeling beside the chaise-longue where I lay so still and waiting. He was breathing ever so quietly. Did he really believe I was asleep? Whatever the case, he was certainly willing to play the dirty professor and next, imperceptibly, so that I almost couldn't feel it, he was lifting my shirt up and sliding my top up underneath to expose my small breasts. He did this in small stages. His eyes feasted at first; not touching yet, not wanting to wake me. And then, yes, it was exquisite to feel him lightly run the palms of his hands over my nipples. He then backed off from feeling my breasts, so as to make sure he wouldn't rouse me to what he was doing. But not being able to contain himself, he was fixed back at my breasts, finally cupping both mounds and putting his breath near them. Then his tongue quickly circled each nipple. There was nothing for it; what he was doing to me was pure pleasure, and I involuntarily let out a slight groan.

'Are you asleep?' I heard him ask in a whisper. 'No you're not,' he snickered. 'This is what Father Lemartre did to her, isn't it, Santa?' I continued to pretend to be asleep and then I felt him twitch my nipples. He continued, 'To Yvonne Dupres. She was a foolish girl too. Are you a foolish girl? I saw what you were doing in class. You naughty girl. And I shall teach you, you wretched girl, that in order to study the case, you must understand Yvonne's experience, moment by moment.' He said it all in the most seductive way. I wanted to raise my arms to put around him, but I didn't dare reveal I was truly awake. 'Ssssh,' he whispered as he sensed I might respond, and then he silently and swiftly exited the room. I opened my eyes and looked out into the dark. I was alone. He'd left my breasts exposed and I touched my still wet, hardened nipples.

Slowly, I pulled my top back down and sat up. I became aware then of the moistness between my thighs and suddenly felt I must flee the scene.

Thank God nothing more had happened, I thought to myself. This had already gone too far. Although I felt deliciously dirty and admittedly excited by my encounter with MacLean and couldn't deny I wished he'd stroked my wet cunt too. Maybe next time.

I needed a swim and made straight for the campus pool.

After I'd done twenty-five laps I left the pool for home. I checked the time and saw it was four-thirty. Bee and I were meeting at my place in a half an hour and I still needed to pick some stuff up for dinner. Thinking I'd better call her and tell her I may be a little overdue, I searched in my purse for my mobile. But it wasn't in there, nor was it in my back-sack. Did I leave it in the locker at the pool?

Bloody hell, I had to go back and find it. Now I couldn't even call Bee to tell her I was going to be late.

Soon I discovered my lost mobile wasn't to be found at the pool either. How maddening. But frustration was soon replaced with fear, as I realised the other place it could be was in MacLean's office. Wait, no need to panic yet ... I'd check the classroom first. With all the lectures finished for the day, no one would be there.

The mobile was not there either, which meant it was probably in MacLean's office, damn it. I suspected it had dropped out of my bag and onto his floor. It was a long shot, but I was counting on the remote possibility that MacLean may have left for the day and had forgotten to lock his office door before the weekend. I had to go check, as fruitless or dangerous an effort it may prove to be.

The last thing I wanted was for MacLean to have my personal mobile. I could just imagine the tricks he would play on me then. Like, what about when Fez calls me on it? I had now arrived at my professor's office door and it was closed. If I lent an ear, maybe I could hear if he was inside. Not a sound. I nervously thought that I might as well try the doorknob. I mean, what if it was open after all? I could just check.

The door opened. My heart raced as I peeked in. Was he in there? It was a lucky break for me this time and I stole quickly into the empty office. Without daring to put on the lights, I knelt down onto the floor to feel for my phone. I checked the chaise-longue too. Still not found. Shit, oh shit! It was time to get out of there. I was worried that I had ransacked the place a bit in my frenzied search. The blanket he'd placed on me earlier that day was on the floor. I felt it during my searching and I guiltily folded it up and placed it as nicely as I could on the chaise-longue. Then I was so out of there.

As I snuck away, I wondered where my phone could

be. On my way home I scanned the ground hopelessly for it. I'd have to cancel it right away when I got home. I was now late for my rendezvous with Bee, who was no doubt standing at my apartment door waiting for me, if she was even still there.

What a bloody mess. I started this dangerous game with my professor a long time ago and today I pretended to be light-headed in class. It was all part of our little play. He took the signal and led me to his lair where I pretended to go into a sleep-like state. His next move was to sneak a feel of my breasts. No matter how much I wished to deny it, in the back of my mind the strange affair with MacLean had truly now begun. And not only that, but it looked like he had stolen my mobile phone.

8

I desperately wanted to get home, to check if I perhaps had left my mobile at the apartment. Bee wasn't there, but on my door was a note from her telling me she got tired of waiting and so went home. I entered my apartment and made a bee-line to the phone and rang her straight away. When she picked up, I could tell she was annoyed with me.

'Yeah, I waited about forty-five minutes. What held you up?' she asked.

'Oh, I am sorry. It's just that I lost my blasted mobile en route home and it took for ever to retrace my steps and then I never did find the damn thing. I'm really upset about it.'

She didn't say anything.

'Hey, if I'd found it, I would have been able to call you and say I was going to be late. Ha!' She didn't laugh along.

'I lost my goddamn mobile phone, Bee!' I spelt it out for her.

'OK, sorry, that's the shits. Do you want me to phone it? Maybe it's in your apartment someplace?'

'Hey, good idea. I can phone it from here,' I said hopefully. 'Look, call you right back.'

'Wait a minute, Santa . . . are we still getting together or what?'

'Yeah, yeah, sorry. I'm so distracted.'

'You sure are,' she interrupted me.

'Why don't you head right over?'

'What do you want, red or white?'

'We're having yummy mussels. I'm going to make a wine sauce and we'll have crusty buns to dip.'

'Now I forgive you for not calling. I'll bring over the white wine I have chilling in the fridge,' she said enthusiastically. 'Be right over and hope you find your mobile.'

'OK, bye.'

I hung up and dialled my mobile. It rang and rang, but it wasn't ringing in my apartment. It was in some unknown location, probably MacLean's bloody briefcase. I got off the phone, went into the kitchen and heaved a great sigh and thought, well, at least I'd had a swim today and was feeling the good relaxation that swimming brings.

I lifted my shirt to look down at my breasts, thinking about how my professor had taken full possession of them earlier. My shrewd, lewd professor ... the fact that he was going to conquer me in such a really devious manner was unbearably erotic to me, for he was truly wicked. Though I knew I was naughty too, this mobile phone business was a bit much. It was really making me sweat bullets. 'You'll get it back from him,' I told myself reassuringly.

Bee knocked on my door and breezed in. 'Did you find it?' she asked me right away.

'No. I rang it and no answer. Pretty soon the battery will go dead, I suppose,' I said unhappily.

'Say, you know what we should do? We could take mine over to the campus and wander around trying to ring yours up,' she suggested.

'Well, I think someone's picked it up, frankly, because I went back and pretty much scoured the joint looking for it,' I explained to her. 'Besides, we can't get into the lecture hall or swimming pool tonight.'

'Guess not. Well, if you'd like we could go tomorrow, ask security to let us in.'

'As long as it's not the same security guy who knows we're suspended for smoking in the girl's,' I laughed. 'I doubt very much he'd help us out.'

Bee laughed. 'We're such little delinquents.'

'And pretty ones at that,' I added.

'I should say!' Bee said as she raised her glass of wine to mine. We toasted to that.

I prepared the sauce for the mussels while Bee talked about Joey. It was too bad she was so unhappy with him. She asked me how my work was going and when I might be clear of it. She said: 'I don't understand why he's given you this extra assignment, but anyway, I guess you can't do much about it. It seems to be stressing you out, which is too bad. Santa, I'm a little worried about you. You don't seem yourself these days. Is there something going on with MacLean that I should know about? If there is, I think you need to tell me, for your own sake. It's not just the extra work you have been loaded up with. It's just you kind of have this hunted look about you. Is he harassing you or something?'

Who was harassing who was the question that crossed my mind, too. I breathed in the steam from the boiling water for the mussels and closed my eyes. 'We all know he's a letch, but I can handle him, no problem, Bee.'

'Hey, let me try that,' Bee said coming over to the stove. We both steamed our faces and giggled as we did so, then patted our faces dry trying to clean the mascara off from under our eyes.

'Gently, gently, don't rub,' I advised. 'Stay young for ever.'

'I know, I know. Say, how's it going with you and Fez these days?' Bee asked me.

'Oh yeah, Bee! I almost forgot. Come and help me pick out my outfit for tomorrow. It's a pretty fancy restaurant his father owns.'

'It is. Joey took me there when we first started going out. It's very fine dining,' Bee acknowledged, as she followed me into the bedroom.

I stood facing my closet and looked at my clothes with dissatisfaction. 'Pretty slim pickings. Hmmm. This one? What do you think?' I showed her a black skirt and short jacket.

'Nice, but a bit uptight. I mean, you're not going for a job interview here,' Bee said. 'Maybe that's what's going on with you; you're taking everything too seriously.'

'Ha! Quite the opposite. I don't take anything seriously enough. I haven't taken school seriously enough, and that's why I'm in trouble with my marks; and, as far as Fez is concerned, I don't take him seriously enough either.'

'He's putting some pressure on, is he? He adores you. Wish I could say the same for Joey and myself,' she said forlornly.

'Joey adores you too. Fez's love is blind. Sometimes I think I don't deserve him. I'm so nervous about tomorrow night and I have nothing to wear,' I moaned.

'You look great in this one, and it's not over the top where first impressions are concerned.' Bee held up a knee-length black dress with slim straps over the shoulder and a silk mauve jacket.

'OK. That could be all right, I guess.'

'Gorgeous.' She smiled, satisfied, and then concern crossed her face. 'Santa, honey, you know you're not perfect. That's not an option when one is human. You realise that, I hope. And I know you do, you dumb bitch. But sometimes I wonder about the way you talk about yourself. It's like a perfectionism that borders on self-destruction, my friend. Why do you do it when you have every reason to feel supremely good about who you are?'

'Catholic conflict of the soul,' I chortled. 'Born sinner

and all that. I just can't get my soul to be comfortable in my body.'

'Really?'

'Yeah, well can you?'

'I'm not sure what you mean. Well, I'm not sure really,' she admitted.

'You know what I mean, don't you?'

I sunk into my thoughts. My ruling feeling was that I was completely astonished and freaked out by my body. It was the whole concept of my being a physical entity as well as a mind and a dubious spirit. I said to Bee, 'The body corrupts.' I confirmed to myself that this was the cause of my sexual deviancy. Suffer for sin, punish sin. I mean, wasn't that what I wanted? Wasn't that what Father Lemartre did to Yvonne, and wasn't that what she sought? It was some expression of that, anyway.

'How do you mean, the body corrupts?' Bee asked.

'When the physical body eclipses the light of the spirit with its orgasms and sweat,' I pronounced, trying to sound like a priest.

Bee giggled. 'You're funny,' she remarked.

'That's what it's like in the Catholic Church. Sex is only for procreation. Otherwise sex is akin to sin. I became convinced of that as I grew up. But the other part of me, the beast, the one that did discover sex, came to feel it was actually a celebration of life. And a dirty, fabulous one at that. I'm a total dichotomy in that respect – trying to be a good catholic girl, and then being such a slut. You know, the whore and the saint type thing,' I said as I burst into laughter, thinking of Yvonne Dupres.

Bee laughed along. 'I know all about you, you crazed thing with your wild spirit,' she joked.

Did she? Did she know I reached orgasms by re-enacting stories of people who seemed to capture the very essence of life's paradoxes? Like purity and sin, as was the case with Yvonne Dupres and Father Lemartre. It had to be cutting-edge stuff for me. As naughty as possible. It was rebellion, I liked to tip the balance of the whore and saint elements in me. God, I should go back to church.

'Anyway, this particular body is hungry and thirsty, so let's eat, drink and be merry,' Bee said, her mood much improved from earlier on. And so we returned to my small kitchen.

The dinner was grand and we were having a satisfying smoke afterwards. 'Remember the terrible look on the dean's face today. God, I felt like I was in grade six or something!' We laughed together. She and I were going to giggle the night away.

'You look wonderful, now stop being so nervous, they'll love you, absolutely love you.' Fez squeezed my shoulder reassuringly.

'You look handsome too,' I said. We pulled up to his father's fancy restaurant. It was called: Augusto's Fine Dining.

'Just be warned, my father is terribly weak when it comes to beautiful women like you. So don't let him disarm you if he seems to be drooling on your chest. And then there's my older brother, who I shall kill if he even looks twice at you, understand? So please don't be too charming.'

'Relax, my love, let's have fun,' I said, a little disconcerted at his macho stance. Now I wished I'd worn a turtleneck.

We walked into the restaurant and I said quietly to Fez, 'This is lavish as hell.' I had a slight nervous edge in my voice as we walked into the expansive reception area. There were life-sized Roman statues that circled a large fountain from which water poured out onto sparkly rocks, all of it beautifully set off by lush aquatic and tropical plants. On the walls were hung huge portraits by famous Italian artists; although, of course, they had to be reproductions.

An older woman suddenly came hustling up to us: presumably Fez's mother. She opened her arms, kissed and hugged Fez, after which he turned to introduce me. 'Mama, meet Santa Pertog,' he said grandly. Mrs Augusto extended her hand to me. She held my hand and seemed to look at me for ever and a day. In the course of which, she did smile at me warmly and she took my other hand into hers. She had a friendly and gentle way about her.

'Perhaps you are too pretty, but you have kind eyes,' Mrs Augusto said warmly.

'Thank you,' I replied sincerely. What the hell was I supposed to say?

'Come, papa's waiting.' And with that Mrs Augusto led us to our table in the corner of the large luxurious dining room.

'Bella!' was the first thing that came from Mr Augusto's lips when he saw me. I laughed aloud remembering Fez's warning about his father. Mr Augusto was a handsome man, with dark looks like his son. Though slightly shorter than Fez, he dominated a room. I was immediately charmed and invariably intimidated. Sitting beside him was Fez's older brother, Andrea. He was wearing a leather jacket that I could smell from where I stood and, with a sexy twinkle in his dark eyes, he rose slightly from his seat, took my hand and kissed it.

'Meet Andrea,' Fez said, somewhat reluctantly.

'A true pleasure,' Andrea said, looking me over like a hungry wolf.

'Santa, that's Italian!' Fez's father said merrily.

'My mother, yes. My father was Russian,' I explained.

'A dangerous and fascinating combination, my dear,' Mr Augusto commented.

'Why do you say that, papa?' Fez looked at me with an amused glint in his eye.

'Well, naturally, the result would be a deep thinker and a lively spirit; someone with much thought behind their passionate actions.'

'I wish I was that interesting. But I thank you.' I was surely warming up to this man. It was not in any weird way; I just immediately liked him. His brother, on the other hand, was looking me up and down too intensely. He was thinking dirty thoughts about me and I could feel Fez growing disturbed by this. I was glad to finally sit down on the beautiful round leather bench that encircled the large table.

It was just then that MacLean appeared on the scene. Unbelievable as it was, I couldn't help but stare at him. How does he do that? Present himself in my life like it was part of some normal routine of his? I must have looked perfectly flushed as I sat there in front of him at Fez's table. I felt like I might be melting. Where was the bathroom? For the lipstick just slipped right off my face.

Thoughts of all the dirty incidents that had occurred between us were fairly streaming through my head like devastatingly bad gossip. I was further scandalised by remembering the most recent incident of yesterday afternoon's private perversions with him in his office.

He was with a couple of men that I had seen before; they were a part of the academic world of the university and, in the group, MacLean stood out with a quiet confidence and with a certain kind of elegance too. Sweet Jesus, what was I thinking? He'd never been handsome before!

'Professor MacLean! How good to see you. Where is your lovely wife?' asked Mr Augusto.

'She is meeting with the coven. It's a monthly affair,' he replied. Laughter all around. So he had a wife! I felt almost jealous at that moment. But no, on second thoughts that made him more interesting. Fez touched my arm just then and whispered into my ear.

'Are you all right, you're all flushed?'

'I am?' I asked, whispering nervously back to him.

'I've always disliked him. Why does he make you so nervous?' Fez asked me discreetly.

'Allow me to introduce my son's lovely friend,' Mr Augusto went on.

'It's all right, we're already acquainted,' he said. She's my student.'

'Is she? And what kind of student is she?' Augusto inquired merrily.

'Oh well,' said MacLean, 'I may pass her.' And they all laughed again, myself included, fully knowing the deeper implications of his supposedly humorous statement. What a character he was, the bastard. Only yesterday afternoon he was twisting my mind and making love to me in his office. Maybe he had my mobile phone on him right now. I looked to see if I could perceive an outline of it in his jacket pocket but I couldn't detect anything. After what seemed like ages, he left to go to his reserved table.

Mrs Augusto said, 'Every Saturday he comes here. He's a good customer, your professor.' Fez's dad looked at me jovially, his mood was infectious, and even though I felt like there was a storm going on inside me, I couldn't help but feel my mood lighten as I smiled back at him.

'Let's order wine. My dear guest of honour, with whom we are so pleased to have acquaintance, you choose the wine tonight,' Mr Augusto offered, beaming at me. He made me feel so pretty in such an innocent way.

'Oh no, I couldn't,' I demurred and laughed.

'Of course you will,' Andrea said to me.

Fez sensed I was feeling a little self-conscious and said, 'Let's look at the menu together and decide.'

I smiled and looked down at the menu and Fez pointed out a wine to help me. But I knew wines more than I was willing to admit. I elbowed him gently and pointed to a nice, mid-priced Merlot. It happened to be their house wine and Fez nodded happily.

'I think this Merlot's great,' I said to his father.

Mr Augusto's eyes brightened and his brother studied me approvingly.

Fez's dad went on to say, 'That's our house wine. Not expensive, but it's very decent really. But at the same time we could order something even tastier perhaps, but you are too shy.' He was interrupted by the ringing of his mobile phone and the handsome Mr Augusto bowed graciously and excused himself from the table for a private call.

Hearing Mr Augusto's mobile ring gave me a sneaky idea. What if I was to excuse myself for a little moment and go use the payphone over by the cloakroom to call my lost mobile phone? Maybe I would discover it was not so very lost after all. Perhaps my mobile phone would start ringing at MacLean's table. Just perhaps.

A smartly dressed waiter came over to the table and I was compelled to order the wine. Fez approved of my choice and let me know with a sexy squeeze of my thigh. His brother smiled at me and asked, 'So, you are a student of law. What kind of lawyer will you become then?'

'Litigation,' I said with a nod to Andrea.

'She loves to argue,' Fez joked.

'That's good,' his mother assured me warmly.

'Thanks,' I said to her appreciatively.

His father returned to the table briefly to say there was some emergency and he had to attend to it. He seemed terribly sorry and said, 'It's been a great pleasure.' He smiled brightly at me. 'I am so sorry, but I know I will see you again. Fez rarely brings his girl-friends to meet us. I am pleased. Make no mistake, my beauty, we hope to see a lot of you.' Then he grandly came over to kiss my hand.

'You're too kind, thank you,' I said.

'Yes. My father is very ingratiating when he is in the presence of a beautiful woman,' said Andrea, looking at me wolfishly. It was almost like he was just short of licking his lips. I felt he could see through to the slut inside me; he was one of those men who picked up on it. It was a Steppenwolf phenomenon. He was like a werewolf, or a creature of the night. I could be like that too. But how could he know that about me, and what a bastard to think so. I decided I wouldn't care what he thought of me, as all females were probably sluts to him.

Fez grunted irritably in response to his brother's comment, and then he looked at me and I sensed he appreciated my quiet graciousness in the face of his obviously troublemaking brother. I simply thought it was too bad Andrea seemed to have a bit of a mean spirit when he was so handsome and all.

Mr Augusto checked his watch and then put both of his arms down to his side in a kind of salute and said grandly, 'Let's arrange another dinner for a week from today.' Fez nodded to his dad agreeably and I smiled at everyone in general, except Andrea who was making me feel uncomfortable.

I was duly charmed by Mr Augusto and, before he left, he kissed his tiny, lovely wife. If Fez was to age as gracefully as this man – and I suspected he would – how wonderful that would be.

I was endeared to Mr Augusto. There was nothing to dislike about the man. I mean, I didn't know his private business, but he was such a jolly, jolly man. It felt so good to be around him; he immediately made one feel at home. Fez had that effect on me too, but perhaps Mr Augusto had refined that gift as he'd grown older. I suspected it was something Fez could look forward to growing into in terms of his own character. I recognised that Fez definitely had that potential in him.

Where did Augusto have to go so urgently? I wondered. It was unsettling to me when I saw him stop at MacLean's table on his way out. He said something to him and they both looked over at me – Mr Augusto with a big smile, and MacLean with a narrow look in his eyes. Did Fez note that? I looked at him beside me but he was busy glaring at his brother.

Fez was so annoyed with his brother at this point that when the wine arrived he took it and purposely didn't pour any into Andrea's glass. This was a serious thing, let me tell you. And it would come up between the two brothers later, but thankfully Andrea didn't let it become a problem right then and took the bottle up and poured the rest of the wine into his own glass. Then, in the spirit of it all, he ordered another bottle. His mother looked disapprovingly at her oldest son, but he didn't care one iota. Oooh, he seemed like trouble.

At our table, Mrs Augusto was telling me cheerfully, 'I like your choice of wine, and of men.' And she touched Fez's shoulder and giggled like a young girl. Fez's parents seemed to like me, this much I sensed already. I didn't know why they took to me, but they simply did. It might have been in part because I liked them, and because I had Italian heritage.

But Andrea was a troublemaker. Fez and he had a serious rivalry going and Andrea studied me greedily, like I could be a spoil of war when it came to his brother's territory. The dynamics were so bizarre. And every time I looked over at MacLean, he seemed to be chuckling at something. This made me momentarily wonder if he was telling his cronies that I let him feel my tits yesterday in his office. No way!

It was high time to call my mobile, I thought.

I excused myself to go freshen up in the bathroom. It was located next to the cloakroom, and near to the payphones. I noted that they were positioned out of sight from the dining room, which was perfect.

Inside the bathroom, I reapplied my lipstick. I looked a little flushed, but overall I appeared reasonably composed. I planned what I might say if indeed MacLean was to answer when I rang my mobile.

Now inside the cloakroom, I plugged my coin into the payphone. My heart was pounding as I dialled my mobile. Soon, I heard it ring once in my ear, but then I froze as I listened to its distinct ring echoing from inside the dining room. Was MacLean going to pick up? Then the ringing seemed to becoming louder and by the fourth ring, I turned to find MacLean standing behind me, holding my ringing mobile out to me.

'I believe it's for you,' he said, looking at me evenly.

He grinned when I hung up the payphone and took my mobile from him. With a devilish glint in his eye, he turned and went back to his table without another word. I didn't move for a couple of minutes and I overheard laughter coming from the dining room. MacLean's laughter. Certain I was terribly red in the face I returned to the bathroom to check the mirror and take some deep, calming breaths. Well, I had got my mobile back and that was a relief. What a bugger, that MacLean! He hadn't seen the depth of my naughtiness yet, I vowed to myself in the mirror. He'd better watch out!

After dinner, we were supposed to join up with Bee and Joey at Seargent's Bar mid-evening. I was slightly troubled that Andrea decided to join us.

We said goodnight to his mother and promised to see her next week. She said insistently, 'I will make veal and pasta at the house next Saturday for you both.' Wasn't she lovely? Her sons both kissed her goodnight and then she embraced me too.

At the university bar I was watching Bee and Joey dance and I thought what a great couple they made; and the way he looked at her was with such intensity and dedication that there seemed no reason for Bee to feel insecure about him.

Andrea asked me to dance and I looked straightaway at Fez to see if this was going to bother him because it certainly might bother me, I thought. I appreciated that Fez was making a real effort to be easy-going and jovial when he nodded to me that it would be all right. I saw his father in him when he did this. But he couldn't conceal that this made him tense. It amused me to think that maybe his father once had an older brother too, and he may have had to kill him.

Taking me by my hand, Andrea led me onto the dance floor. At first it was all pretty harmless and we danced apart for a couple fast dances, but then the slow dance came and Andrea drew me near to him. I was coy and reluctant. Fez had now come on to the dance floor and he tapped Andrea on the shoulder from behind and gestured that he was going to dance with me, his girlfriend. Andrea said, 'I'm the older brother. You just wait your turn.' He turned back to me and tried to pull me up close to him but Fez grabbed his jacket and yanked it hard.

Suddenly enraged, Andrea struck Fez on the chin. He was caught off guard and suddenly Andrea had my Fez pinned to the floor.

'Don't you ever try to dishonour me again!' Andrea spat. You know what I mean, you shit-head brother, you!' I knew he was talking about the wine incident at the restaurant when Fez had rudely ignored his empty glass. It was a real dishonour; his brother was right.

Joey was standing by, ready to jump in, but Fez managed to push his brother off him and the two stood staring murderously at each other on the dance floor. Finally Andrea straightened his jacket and he turned to give me a nod and left the bar.

I stayed at Fez's place for the night. He was still seething with anger at what had happened.

'Are you attracted to him?' he asked me accusingly.

I groaned inwardly at this macho nonsense. I denied it completely, telling him, 'I just want to be with you.'

Fez was going to make hard love to me. I was past tired, but he was so sexy in this mood, really. I knew he was trying to firmly stake his claim; to place his flag of ownership on me, or rather, to plunge it into me.

Of course it couldn't be helped that I was super turned on by all the sexual tension that night. What a great slut I was! While Fez was kissing me, I thought about the way his brother looked at me. Though I'd never do such a thing, nor would Fez permit it, I thought about what fun it would be to pull my panties down in front of both of them and then Fez could take me into another room and spank me.

'I hate the way my brother was leering at you,' Fez said as he pulled my panties down roughly and gave me a little smack on my bare ass. He moved around behind me to unzip my dress which fell to the floor about my feet.

'Step out of your dress and panties, beautiful.' I lifted each foot and daintily stepped out of my panties and I was nude from the waist down. Fez was kneeling down as he'd held my panties so as to help me out of them and now he looked up at me and tugged on the bottom of my shirt.

'Take it off,' he ordered. And so I pulled off my shirt and my small breasts wobbled slightly as he continued. 'Sorry to be like this, but you are mine, never to be my asshole brother's!'

'Never!' I echoed him sincerely as I stood naked in front of him and he was looking up at me like an object of worship from down on his knees.

'The way he was looking at you, the bastard!' Fez started sliding his finger up between my legs.

'No way, he wasn't too,' I protested and pushed him playfully away. But it was true, his brother had been leering terribly at me all night; I could still smell the sharp, sweet odour of his fabulous leather jacket.

'Anyway, it doesn't matter, I'm so truly yours,' I assured him as he now stood up and pressed his clothed body up against my nudity. Secretly, I was hoping he'd get angrier and more jealous and maybe even spank my pussy. 'No doubt your brother is like that with all the girls,' I went on to say as I tried to squirm away.

'No. Not so. He's a shit. I hate him and he's not going to get anywhere near you,' Fez snarled and took me by the shoulders to guide me backwards towards his bed.

It was just then that I saw a dark form lurking by the closet and again I smelt it: the strong odour of leather swept through the room. It was Andrea! He was spying on us and I was completely undressed. Dare I say something to Fez? No, it would then be a murder-filled night. I couldn't alert him; it would be far too dangerous.

'Lie back down for me,' Fez suggested, but now I was feeling terribly shy, naturally. Then there was a long silence as he studied my body.

I laughed nervously. 'I'll get under the covers,' I told him as I proceeded to draw them back.

'What's the matter? No, no, just lay there, I want to see you.' So I lay back and Fez smiled approvingly.

'That's it,' he said, 'now spread your legs nice for me.'

It was unbearable, but I did it as I was terribly aroused by Fez and his commands, and by his voyeur brother. Fez unzipped his pants and pulled out his hardened cock. He looked down at it, then at my pussy, then at me.

'Oh, Santa, my Santa,' he uttered as he lay down next to me and took my hand, kissed it and place it around his penis. He showed me how he liked me to move it up and down along his shaft. Then he pinched my nipples and dug into my mouth with his hot tongue. 'Mm,' he moaned. I turned onto my side and put my legs around his hips, but he pushed me back and made me spread my legs again. Was his brother still watching? The aroma of leather was still strong, though I couldn't see.

'Ooh,' Fez groaned, as he now discovered with his middle finger how wet I was. 'You're so wet.' He pushed his finger in and out of me. Then he paused and looked me in the eye.

'Does he give you much trouble in class, that professor MacLean?' Fez asked, turning his jealousy to the subject of MacLean as he positioned himself on top of me and pressed his raw groin against my naked pussy.

'No. He mentioned I shouldn't miss too many lectures, that's all,' I allowed breathlessly as I tried to unbutton his shirt, for I wanted to feel his bare, strong chest against mine, but I only got it halfway undone before he poised his groin over me in order to thrust his cock into my open pussy.

I gasped – he was so full of force, like he was to punish me for being attractive to other men – and yet he felt so warm, so comforting, so powerful on top of me like that. He lay still inside me for a moment.

Then, I laughed aloud thinking about how I rang my

mobile in the restaurant and how the sinister MacLean answered. And to further heighten my erotic pleasure I thought about what my professor had done to me yesterday in his office. But why had I need to call up that memory when Fez's brother was still in the room? How horribly exciting was that? Fez started to move his cock hard inside me, hitting my innermost spot of pleasure and pain and just then he pulled out.

'Turn over,' he said hoarsely and I lay on my belly.

I gasped as he pulled my hips up so that I was on all fours and he entered me from behind with his naughty tongue which darted in and out of my oh too juicy pussy. He had his hands on my ass and was squeezing my cheeks roughly. Soon, he slid his body up along mine, his hands finding my breasts and squeezing them a little too hard. He penetrated me again, his furious cock like a warm stick inside me. He pulsed relentlessly inside me and then he came and I felt him and his fury explode inside me.

When he withdrew, he said, 'I'll be right back,' and he left the room. I heard him go into the kitchen just as his nasty brother emerged from his hiding place in the closet. I tried to cover up, but he whipped the sheet away from my body.

'Hello, beauty!' he greeted me as he approached the bed quietly, stealing glances behind him. What a terrific risk he was taking, for he lingered long enough to pat my bare ass and say, 'You liked that I was watching, didn't you?' Then he stole away. I was utterly speechless.

Soon, Fez returned to the room bearing a tray with two glasses of red wine and some lovely cheese and crackers, none the wiser to his brother's antics. I clasped my hands together, gleefully.

9

I left Fez's place for home early the next morning. I had to spend the day studying, writing about the famous French trial, of course.

I wrote that either Father Lemartre was guilty of immorality or Yvonne Dupres was guilty of perjury. Though my efforts were supposed to be towards the defence of Dupres, I couldn't just plainly fault the Jesuit priest. I needed to begin by putting forth what each side of the argument might be – the same arguments that would invariably be seized upon by the prosecution and defence. Any good lawyer would need to prepare for both sides of the debate in order to best serve a case.

Yvonne made the poor decision to be represented by her brother, who was just as much of a lunatic as his sister and had no understanding of a legal process. Lemartre, on the other hand, hired a lawyer, an independent agent, as he had no real support from the church.

Whether he molested her or not, he had ample opportunity to do so. He wrote her love letters and admitted to certain questionable actions. In her sobbing appeal to the court, she said: 'You see here before you a young girl of twenty-three years, plunged into an abyss of evils, but whose heart is still unsullied.' She went further to say she was justified in her claims against him, 'because, at the very least, she wanted to teach persons of her sex that they must be on guard against the appearance of piety.' In the description that followed, she related her experience of the strange spells he would put her under, telling her she must be punished for the sin she had committed by not freeing herself to him. This would all take place in her chambers while he had her nude and in a praying position over her bed. I decided not to add the compromising part where Yvonne admitted to the court that during these sessions with Lemartre she had felt all wet between her legs as he performed certain acts on her. Nor did I include the sections which revealed how Yvonne was transported by her love for him and that she consented to the Jesuit's erotic, sadistic flagellation of her and then how she got a ticklish feeling between her legs when he lightly fondled her body, kissing her everywhere he'd struck her, including every crevice of her sex, as she lay wide open on her bed for him. For, if I were to include these things, it would weaken my case in the defence of Yvonne, my position being that he exploited an innocent woman who believed he was bringing her closer to God. And in the undercurrent of my relationship with MacLean it would be too much like admitting to such thoughts about the destined reader of my final term paper – that is, MacLean.

I amused myself as the hours of study went by, imagining many of the possible scenes between Lemartre and Dupres. Such as the following fantasy:

Yvonne Dupres was leaning over her bed, bent in prayer, and Father Lemartre was standing behind her, eyeing her naked body. He'd undressed her himself, as was God's will. And now he held a heavy braided cord, and he was saying to her quietly, 'Do you wish to be cleansed again? Do you desire to find the road to spiritual perfection, Yvonne Dupres?' He'd already touched her breasts earlier that day in the confessional.

'Yes Father.' She was squirming and she gasped in anticipation of what he was about to do to her. She wanted to give herself over to her spiritual guide.

'Then pray,' he guided her.

Yvonne began to recite a prayer and, standing from behind, Lemartre looked down the nape of her neck while her head was dutifully bowed. His gaze strolled down lower to look upon her naked buttocks and he ran his fingers along the heavy-braided cord. She bravely continued to say her prayer aloud and he smartly struck her with the rope as her prayer became louder. He hit her with the cord a little more sharply and then he served her several more blows until her ass became red from the heat of the rope. Aroused, he placed his free hand on her fiery buttocks. 'It feels hot,' he says gustily. 'You are forgiven your sins.'

'Yes, Father,' she moaned, as he kissed her tender bottom and touched her now between her legs.

'Father, I had a vision!' she exclaimed. 'It was the Heavenly Mother!'

'See how God works through me to give you signs from his Kingdom,' he said to her.

She began to cry with joy as he inserted his finger into her wet crevice while still caressing her bottom with his lips.

'Turn over, Yvonne,' he ordered gently. She did so. 'Give yourself over to me and part your legs.' She did this and his eyes feasted on her body while he lightly slapped her between the legs with the braided cord. She groaned and moved her hips. 'Do you love me, Yvonne?' he asked, smiling down at her.

'I do,' she confessed.

He bent down and kissed her mound. 'Open up,' he said. And with her own fingers, she spread her cunt lips for him and he kissed between all her crevices. She was in ecstasy as he performed his unorthodox religious rites on her.

But her mood quickly changed when he said next, 'You don't really see the Heavenly Mother, do you Yvonne?' There was silence as he continued licking her cunt. At this, she released her juices, while he groaned, licking it up. 'You lie before me and God.'

'No, Father!'

'Yes, yes you do,' he insisted gently with his dark voice. He now probed her pussy a little more roughly, moving fingers in and out with lewd enthusiasm.

I found it most erotic to imagine the two characters at their play and I touched myself until I orgasmed. It took little time for me to satisfy myself, but, once I did, I could continue on with my work.

The Jesuit priest decided that Yvonne Dupres's signs of holiness were of dubious validity, I wrote. He did not believe she was a saint. So as a result she brought forth charges of sorcery against him. Her claim was that he bewitched and seduced her. She was more than a woman scorned. I hoped I was making a persuasive argument that Lemartre was the real perpetrator and not the foolish Yvonne.

I wondered then if I was going to get a good mark. Or if I might, on the other hand, have to submit to certain things to ensure my passing grade. Submit to MacLean. Did he not want me to? MacLean was leading me to the same transgressions as Lemartre, of that I was quite certain. Schemes filled my mind as to how another event might take place between the professor and me. How I might make it easier for him to molest me fully as Lemartre did Yvonne Dupres, and not just make the occasional grope of my breasts.

It was past lunch and I hadn't had anything to eat all day. I planned to make myself some toast with peanut butter but, when I went to the cupboard, I found I was out of bread. It was a good time for a break, so I decided I'd go to the store. I needed a little leg stretch anyway.

It was a beautiful spring day and the air smelt fresh. Down the street was a small grocery store I frequently patronised. The owner, George, always teased me. I once read that the British were the horniest men in the world; or, at least, their level of sexual activity was the highest. George was innocent enough, though. He had run a pub in London before he emigrated to Canada. And because he was always drinking too much with his customers and his mates, his wife thought it best to go into the business of operating a small corner store instead. Sonia didn't mind the way her sixty-year old husband flirted with me, and she seemed to look forward to my stopping in at the store.

George would always compliment my looks in the most amusing of ways. 'She just glows today,' he would say. 'You just are all aglow, wouldn't you say so, Sonia?' he'd say to his wife. 'Must be in love, must have had a little bit of something last night.' Sonia would nod and roll her eyes at me and we'd laugh.

So it felt good to go to their store and see them, especially after long periods of study alone in my apartment. Sometimes Sonia and I would have tea in the backroom and I'd enjoy some of her baking. I would bring flowers for her tea table and, once in a while, I'd buy the daily paper and we'd open up the crossword and fill it in together.

We also played chess occasionally. She was far better than I but it was a good contest nevertheless. I tried to match her chess skills and I didn't do so badly. But she always surprise-attacked me to win the game. Other times she'd ask how my studies were going and, when she heard my mixed reports, she'd encourage me to do better. She was a dear woman and motherly to me.

I walked home after having a short chat with her and George, because I didn't have time to stay today. But I did want to take the long way home. At times like this, I wished I could walk outdoors in the nude without anyone else seeing or, conversely, with everyone seeing because everyone walked around naked. And it would just be the breezy air against my skin.

I was four blocks from my apartment. The streets were lined with English Elms and gnarly, old oaks. They looked so grand, like they were stretching their limbs out into the endless universe to rejoice in the awakening of the sap under their rough bark. I wished I could wander anywhere I wished, all the day long. But I had little time to spare. It was back to work for this girl.

Back at the apartment I made my toast and tea and, while I sat eating, I glanced over my work. Happily I realised that I was not too far from being finished and that I could relax a little. After a break, it takes a while to get back into the work so I passed a little time fantasising about the day I was to hand in the report.

Even before he asks about my report, MacLean warn me about not repeating my usual misdemeanours those same activities for which I'd been previous caught and suspended. In the crowded university ha way, where he discovers me, he makes himself am clear.

'You're not planning to go to the women's fo smoke, now, are you, because I'll catch you again, I'll see to it myself that you are properly disciplined t time,' he warns. Then he informs me that I am expec to hand in my paper after class. He makes certain one else hears the sinister tone of his voice as he has, now, drawn me into a dark corner of the hall. 'The wo had better be more than satisfactory, Santa, as yo future as a student at this university hangs in th balance.' Thereafter, he walks away.

My stomach leaps into my mouth because my pape isn't ready at all and, not knowing what else to do, I go directly to the washroom for a smoke. I'm in no way worried that MacLean would come check for me inside the women's; he wouldn't dare! Then again, there was the vague, exciting possibility that he might.

Inside, it is empty and so into a cubicle I go to light a smoke in an attempt to calm myself. I hear the outer bathroom door opening. I think it best to extinguish my smoke, but I have to double check that it isn't Bee or another student before I sacrifice a precious cigarette. Peering through the crack of the door, I cannot see anyone, so I start to slide the lock open to check further. Suddenly the door flies open, narrowly missing my head. It is none other than the dreaded and angry Professor MacLean who has now appeared in the door of the cubicle. With fire in his eyes, he enters the small space – though I somehow quickly manage to extinguish the burning evidence of my bad deeds and flush it away down the toilet. Calmly, he shuts the door behind him and, once the door is closed, he bears in on me, pressing up against me and taking hold of me with his two hands about my hips. He pushes me firmly against the side wall, and proceeds to then quickly spin me around and bring me back into the centre of the small space. I am now facing the back wall with him standing close behind me.

My head is virtually spinning from his turning me around so fast. Besides that, echoing in my mind is his past warning that he would spank me if he were to catch me smoking in here again and that he was going to see to it that I was properly punished at his hands. No. He wouldn't. But should he? I hear him as he says it again: 'I am going to make your bare bottom sting, you disobedient girl.'

It is like a ride in an amusement park where I close my eyes and hope to survive. An amusement park which people go to wanting to scream; where their voices rise in the background of a wildly-fast moving set. Here, my carnival ride is on a roller-coaster driven by the sexual yearnings of an aggressive, unstoppable man. An unstoppable ride.

MacLean turns to slide the lock back in place to ensure we won't be disturbed. 'Lean over,' he whispers slowly to me. And so I do. As I hear his devilish voice command me, I have a ticklish feeling in my pussy and my underwear feels wet and sticky as I face the wall.

'Put your hands against the wall,' he next commands me and I have nowhere to lean forward but over the toilet and onto the wall.

'Lean over more, you bad girl.'

I am wetter now than I dare admit. I almost can't help myself from pulling down my panties and lifting up my skirt for him and him alone. Why I have that compulsion I'll never know; all I do know is that I want him to see my naked bum, my naked pussy, my open and wet crack. So that he could touch it and feel it. Of course, I could never act on such a desire.

Nor do I have need to. For as I lean over a little for him now, he discharges the questionable duty of lifting my skirt and sliding down my panties. Relieved of the confines of my underwear, I lean over yet more for him, offering the ultimate of views; my buttocks raised high in the air, my hidden folds now unhidden. Spreading myself open for him, I breathe heavily.

'Will you never learn the rules, you saucy girl.' He then proceeds to spank my naughty ass there and then, his hand often landing square on my flaming, wet opening that is calling out for him from between my cheeks. Without hesitation, his fingers take on a nasty life of their own and hone in on the wetness of my helpless cunt. I feel scared and excited as he fingers me. Heated, he speaks again.

'Legs further apart.'

I gasp and obey. And he presses his hard body against

mine as he leans over me, his hands rummaging quickly and roughly under my shirt. He finds my soft nipples and rubs me there momentarily. Next he pulls himself back and sharply slaps me on my ass again before he proceeds to gently drive his fingers into my ready openness and deep into my inner parts. He circles and probes my cunt and then next he drives one finger slowly into my asshole. Searching and searching some more. With his other hand, he touches my clit and repeatedly asks if the bad girl needed to pee. It is then that I have to let go; having no choice, I release with spasming orgasm and I wet into his hand.

With a hoarse whisper I plead, 'I'm sorry, professor!' But I continue squirting pee into his hand, and he collects it in his palm and rubs it slowly all over my pussy and asshole. My orgasm goes on violently and runs all along from my clit to my pussy to my asshole, that is, wherever he rubs me. Then, once it is over, he goes about the lengthy process of cleaning me up. He takes out his handkerchief with which to do so. 'Don't let me catch you again!' he warns, as he walks out of the cubicle without satisfying his own needs.

So went my fantasy. I would also see, in two days, what would truly transpire between us as events would unfold. But I wasn't going to be caught unprepared; I was going to hand in my paper, and a damn good one at that! MacLean would no doubt press me in more ways than one for the hard evidence and relevant testimony of the case. I was omitting a lot. So much of this crazy case was the stuff of pure wayward whimsy and hedonism. It was too concerned with her fanciful longings rather than hard facts; her wanting to go off on erotic reverie and imagined visitations. And yet in her sworn testimony, the admission of love from Yvonne to Father Lemartre was expressed right in front of the filled-to-the-brim courtroom. While Yvonne had admitted this was the case, she finally defined it as sorcery, swearing that she had been bewitched by Lemartre. He was lechery disguised as piety. That was how Yvonne characterised him finally. I said aloud to myself, 'What about a dirty old man disguised as an academic? What about a twenty-first century girl having to debase herself in front of her professor? What about getting an A on one's transcript?' I did so want that and I would seek that at any cost. In the same way as Dupres had wanted her aims met through Lemartre. It was my passive/active pursuit – this deviant game. I hoped for that occasion to arise soon.

But that occasion did not present itself in due course. MacLean was not going to let me be in control of this in any way; he was going to play the game his way. After I'd handed in the paper, which he received with such an indifferent air that he did not so much as look at me, he simply left the lecture hall. Now there were the two days through to Monday. The weekend lay ahead before I was to see him the following week. I was on pins and needles and I couldn't let myself be waylaid by these events, or, should I say, non-events.

10

It was in Fez that I sought distraction. More than willing to oblige, he took me to his parents' cabin for the weekend. As we drove along the highway that Friday evening, we were both quiet. I felt and looked tired. My mind was constantly detouring to thoughts of MacLean and I began to feel Fez looking at me out of the corner of his eye. Recognising his concern for me, I struck up a conversation about his father's restaurant.

'Maybe I could take a job waitressing there this summer.

Tips must be great in an upscale joint like that.' There was a pause.

'What do you think of my father?' Fez asked me earnestly.

'I think he's charming.'

'And my brother, Andrea?' he asked tensely.

Another pause.

'Well, I don't really know him, Fez. Maybe he seems a little intense, I don't know. He's hard to read, isn't he?'

'I'm going to tell you something now. I'm taking you into my confidence. My father can be an unscrupulous, even dangerous man. And my brother is worse.'

'How do you mean?' I asked.

'I don't want you spending any more time around my brother than is absolutely necessary,' he went on, ignoring my question.

'What about you?'

'What?' he said, sounding a little angry.

'Are you immoral and dangerous?'

He laughed a little. I nudged him playfully with my knee.

'I'm learning how to do business from my father. I'm expected to take over someday.'

Then he gave my leg such a tight squeeze that it made me squeal and then his hand moved up to my upper thigh until it found my crotch. He rubbed me so lightly it drove me wild, and it was all he and I needed for the next half hour. This went on as we passed through little towns, even when we stopped at red lights and pedestrians walked by in front of the car. This served to excite us both all the more. Admittedly, my mind occasionally went into its lusty MacLean portals, and how I delighted and rotted in my wicked ways. Eventually I lay my head across Fez's knee and he stroked my hair.

'Why doesn't Joey ask poor Bee to move in with him?' I asked him.

'Aren't you two still moving in together anyway?'

'I told her I wanted to wait until I was clear of my work,' I explained. 'Anyway, it'd be far better if she were to live with Joey, as that's really what she wants.'

'Then perhaps you and I should make the same arrangement.' He looked down at me smiling.

'For now, my dear, just answer my question,' I urged him.

'Well, I don't really know. Maybe he leads a secret life.' He trailed off.

'Is he seeing someone else, do you think?'

'Not to my knowledge. I think he really loves Bee. Maybe he wants to do the honourable thing and marry her first before they live together,' he said.

'That's romantic, I suppose. Doesn't make much sense to me, though. I think it's far better to live first with the person you intend to marry, then you find out if you're truly compatible.'

'I agree. So we think the same way about that, then, don't we?'

'At any rate, it's upsetting to her,' I told him.

'Why doesn't she just ask him?'

'Pride.'

Fez slowed the car as we passed through a smoky patch of highway. An oncoming car was travelling slowly by. Both cars came to a stop and rolled down their windows.

'Hey, Dom, what's up?' Fez asked as he greeted the older man.

Dom puffed on his cigar and smiled. 'The Johnson place burnt down to the ground.'

'Hmm, anything else?'

'Nope. Hey, who's the pretty girl beside you?' Dom asked, peering into our car.

'I'm sorry, how rude. Dom, meet Santa,' Fez said as he leant back so I could see. Dom smiled and nodded at me. I waved back.

'Have fun, you two.' He started to pull away, calling behind him, 'Say hi to your papa there, Fez.'

'Sure will.' Fez waved out the car window as we carried on down the highway.

'Wonder how it burnt down? Lightning?' I asked Fez as I looked through the trees to see the smouldering remains of someone's cottage.

'Some fires aren't so accidental,' he said mysteriously.

'What do you mean?'

'Dom's a pro, I don't know why else he'd be all the way out here.' Fez chuckled a little.

'Arson?' I said amazed.

'It's part of the insurance game.' He looked at me with a slight smile.

'My, you sure know all kinds of people. Sounds like a bit of a dangerous world, Fez,' I said worriedly.

'It's a world you're not getting near. Not to speak of either, to anyone,' he warned.

'Yes sir!' I replied cockily. He looked over at me with a stern expression on his handsome face. I couldn't help but giggle when I looked at him, and in response to this he wagged his finger sombrely at me. Soon we were both chuckling at ourselves and, with light hearts, we continued driving on down the highway.

The car pulled up to a glorious and substantial log cabin. When I got out of the car, I joked sarcastically to Fez that his dad must be very unscrupulous in his business affairs to be able to afford such a fabulous lakeside retreat. Fez rose to the occasion, (I think he was relieved that I understood about his dad), and he announced that we were going to very much enjoy the spoils of his father's dubious commerce and feast on food and wine for the whole weekend. Put some meat on my bones, finally, he said to me with undeniable earnest. He was right, too. I was perhaps a little thin.

It was a warm spring we were having that year and some time outdoors would be a remedy for any ailment of the soul. My cup was full of anguish mixed in with great happiness that I was with Fez. But he knew I needed something. Something, as it turned out, I had never expected to find in him.

Inside the cabin, Fez set down our bags. The main room was absolutely grand, its structure consisting of huge, beautiful glistening wood logs. Enormous beams buttressed the high ceiling and richly coloured tapestries hung down from high up the walls. Two full-sized cream-coloured couches gave the room a breezy feel and plush, centre rugs made it feel cosy. But the warmest place in the room was the sight of the hearth.

'Oh, can we sit by the fire tonight?' I asked Fez.

'Of course, but there's one rule,' he said with a twinkle in his eyes.

'A rule, eh?' I could guess what that might be.

'No clothes. It's just far too hot otherwise,' he joked.

'You're hot, baby,' I said, playfully pinching his ass.

I mixed us up some Tom Collins cocktails while Fez grilled massive steaks. Good thing, because soon the gin was going straight to my head. I needed food!

We were to dine out on the patio that overlooked the lake below. The view was utterly amazing. Down through the sloping pine forest, the deep lake majestically spread out before us in an inky blue. Islands were scattered around here and there in the magic lake which was framed by tall, rising rocks and evergreens. I longed to be in that water and swim from one island to another.

'I swam all the way to that island last summer,' Fez said as we sat down to eat. 'This summer we'll both go.'

'With an escort boat, of course,' I suggested. I wasn't sure how my endurance was in open water. It was one thing to swim laps in a pool, but in a choppy lake, quite another. 'So you love to swim too?' I said to him. I was well pleased with learning that.

'Late-night skinny dipping is something I love,' he said. 'A most exhilarating experience.' And his eyes shone at me.

'Gosh, I wish we could go tonight!' I said excitedly.

'Pretty frigid waters this time of year,' warned Fez. 'We could try ... but a warm fire might be nicer,' he offered.

'For sure.' I was so happy to be with this man. And I hadn't even thought of MacLean for hours. Oops. Banish him from your mind, girl, I thought. You are with your true love.

We were to spend the evening around the large hearth. The surround was constructed in different shapes of stone from the area. Someone had gone to a great deal of trouble to create such a beautiful fireplace. I learnt, in fact, that it was Mr Augusto, Fez and Andrea who were the stone masons. Men of many talents, apparently.

After Fez had built a roaring fire, he and I laid down some sleeping bags and he began to undress me. The fire was intense on my bare skin, and, with each item of clothing he removed, he would warm that part of my body in front of the hearth. If felt fantastically relaxing. I undressed him too, with the same ceremony, and finally and we were lying on the sleeping bags, spooning the other in front of the flames.

'Did you know that there are ghosts that haunt the Lake of the Woods?' he asked teasingly.

'You're just saying that so I cuddle up closer to you.' I giggled gleefully and snuggled into his warm embrace. I asked him to tell me some of his spooky tales. Some were actually pretty scary, others tragic and romantic. One story he told was particularly eerie and memorable for me.

'There was a couple that spent every summer here, for years upon years,' he began quietly. 'Their kids were grown up and they just loved coming out here together to their cabin and staying for all the warm weeks of the summer. They were known to be friendly people, although they kept mostly to themselves. The wife would often be seen swimming at all times of the day, or even at night, and she was reported to be quite beautiful. Now, this was at a time many years before my father had bought this place, of course, back in the fifties.

Anyway, so this woman loved to swim. On occasion, her husband would join her and swim too. He'd never go out as deep as her, though. She was known to swim quite far out from shore and she was a very good swimmer.

'Did she make any crossings over to any of the islands around here, like a marathon swimmer?' I asked.

'There was an island she liked to swim to and sometimes she'd make the crossing alone at night.'

'I love this woman,' I said. 'I love this couple.'

'I thought you might, because you love to swim too,' Fez said affectionately, looking down on me as I rested against him, my back to his warm hairy chest.

'Anyway, on hot summer days, her husband would sit on the shore and read his book and watch her do her beautiful swimming, until she swam out so far that he could see her no more. If she went all the way to her favourite island, she would appear like a speck on its far shore and wave to him from there. She'd then explore the island a little and finally swim back.' I could see that Fez was enjoying telling this story.

'It must have worried him horribly when she went out of sight during her crossing,' I ventured to say.

'Quite. But there was also something else that may have concerned him too. It was rumoured that she may have been meeting her lover there.' Fez's eyes twinkled at me as he went on. 'Her husband, of course, had never set foot on that island, and couldn't tell what she did while she was visiting there.

'One night his wife asked him if he'd like to go for a walk on the beach so she could swim in the lake. It was late in the season and a cool summer's evening and he said to her, "isn't it a little chilly in the water?" And asked if tonight she'd just stay home with him and they could sit in front of the fire together.

'Like me and you, right now,' Fez said, and took my hand and kissed it. This made me smile.

'But no, she said, the lake was calling to her that night and she wanted to go for a dip and the weather was fine. Besides, the water was bound to be warm because there was a storm earlier that day and the winds always warmed up the lake. He told her he was feeling tired and preferred to stay in that night. So she said she'd only be gone a short while and would come back to his side to watch the fire later with him. So, off she went to have her nightly swim.'

'Oh my God, what happened to her then? Did she go to see her lover across the lake, and he murdered her or something?' I asked, fearing the worst.

'Sshh. Well, a short while after she left, her husband lit a fire. But then the windows started rattling and he noticed that the wind had picked up a little outside. A storm was brewing from across the lake and he could see it coming up fast from the western part of the sky. This was the worst direction it could come from for this particular body of water. Some of the most violent storms would race across from the western prairie and sometimes they brought tornadoes that caused spouts on the lake. There were lots of reported drownings, swimmers that would be overcome by the waves only to sink down and perish at the bottom. This lake is littered with people who've drowned in it over the years; it's a dangerous and tricky lake. It takes less than a minute for a storm to brew up and this makes it especially treacherous for any swimmer or even a small watercraft,' Fez explained to me.

I loved hearing stories of wild, stormy lakes.

'On this particular night the wife by now was half-way across the lake in the water and her terrified husband planned to go and call her back in if he could. When he reached the edge of the shore, he saw what a devilish storm was churning up the waters and he could vaguely see her figure out in the distance and that she was trapped in the waves. Even though it was hopeless, he dived into the water to rescue her. Desperately he swam out, but by now she had completely disappeared; she had been swallowed up by her beloved lake. But he kept swimming out searching for her. Then, only a few yards away from shore, he too perished in the great waves,' Fez said sadly.

'How awful,' I said.

'And to this day their ghosts are seen haunting the lake on moonlit nights. This ghostly couple have been spotted strolling across the surface of the water and she is always a little ahead of him while he follows her, calling out to her to come back to him.'

'Oh, my dear God,' I said, truly spooked.

'Both my father and mother claim to have seen their ghosts,' Fez said as he held my hand and kissed it.

'I should like to see that, though I'd probably not sleep for nights.'

'Ha, ha,' comforted Fez, 'they won't hurt you.'

He turned me over to face him and started kissing me tenderly. Then, taking my hand, he placed it down onto my pussy and made me stroke myself. 'Keep touching yourself,' he instructed, as he rose up onto his knees. 'Get rid of your spooky feeling.' Whereupon, without preamble, he took his penis in his hand and made me watch him stroking himself to hardness. It didn't take long. Then he gently but insistently pushed it against my mouth until I opened up for him. He moved slowly in and out, so gently, and he groaned.

Then next he made me lie on my side, while he lay next to me – his hips at the same level as my head – and gently pushed the cock into my mouth again and, shortly, he thrust it in and out more urgently as he held my head in place with his hands. Just before he was about to climax, he pulled out of my mouth and moved down to enter me. In a few strokes he was spent. I hadn't had a chance to orgasm, but that didn't matter this time – his satisfaction was mine. We fell happily asleep in front of the fireplace.

Next morning, we woke early to take a walk in the

bright spring sunshine by the lake and dared each other to dive in. With our shoes off we tested the water; it was heart-attack cold and out of the question to dive into – although I would have loved to see Fez's tall muscular body plunge through the water. I wondered if I could beat him in a race. I bet he was a powerful swimmer but I should like to challenge him just for fun. Perhaps later that summer, I thought.

'Hey, this summer, let's swim out to the island in the ghost story,' I suggested excitedly.

'It's quite a ways. See, it's that one way out there.' He pointed to a small island south of the lake and it looked impossibly far for me.

'Have you ever?' I asked him.

'No, not yet, not that one.'

Later that afternoon, when we were lying in the spring sunshine on the patio, Fez started teasing me about my being attracted to other men. I said, 'oh sure', and foolishly even joked about MacLean. Fez did not find this funny in the least and I assured him I was totally kidding.

'Yes, because that's the vilest thing I've ever heard, you dirty girl. Are you a dirty girl?' he demanded to know. I tried to laugh it off.

'I've seen the way that nasty dog looks at you,' he added. 'Remember when he came into my family's restaurant ... he's weird. Like he is following you or something ... Anyway, what sort of things do you fantasise about your professor? That he gives you good marks in exchange for sex?'

Certain I was about to blush and therefore reveal myself, I started tickling his stomach and protesting loudly.

'Now just wait, you,' he said, grabbing my hands. 'If you want an A+ on your transcript, you must take off your top.' He pushed me away and leant back with a serious look on his face and I couldn't tell if he was putting me on or what. This game could be terribly exciting, I thought. I could even pretend he was Mac-Lean; he seemed open to playing along. Or was he trying to trap me into revealing my true desire?

'It's you who has fantasies!' I screeched to him.

'We all do, m'dear. Don't be shy, now.'

I didn't know what to do, but the prospects of playing out my fantasies about MacLean with Fez seemed rather like I could have my cake and eat it too. I mean, it couldn't go as far as pretending he was Father Lemartre with me as Yvonne, because that would require me revealing the strange assignment MacLean had given me and exposing how much mental energy I truly dedicated to such thoughts, stories and sub-plots. I had to admit that my fantasies about MacLean were all the more heightened and scintillating because of the story of Yvonne Dupres and Father Lemartre, the Jesuit priest.

As all these thoughts ran crazily in my mind. I didn't answer Fez right away and so he said, 'You're a highly sexual being, I know that. You're a naughty girl. But you're safe with me. Look, we have the run of the house; you've the run of me. Let's satisfy your thirst, so that you don't go astray from me. Like in that story last night of the woman swimming to her lover, right?' he reasoned, and he reasoned it well, although I couldn't quite envisage Fez having that sleazy older-man dynamic that I craved. All in all he was a young guy with a young guy's macho tendencies. MacLean was something else entirely. He was infuriatingly composed and authoritative, which drove me nuts, sexually.

It sounded from the story that the woman of the lake was a restless soul, alive or dead. I have always been restive as hell myself, and tempted to go astray from my men, which means I frequently seek to fulfil my deviant sexuality by having sudden, strange affairs. To touch something exciting and dangerous, like Professor MacLean. But Fez was dangerous too, as I was soon to discover.

'You go first,' I said, testing him, 'let's see how wild and sexually-charged your imagination is.'

'You don't trust me,' he concluded.

'I trust you, otherwise I wouldn't invite you to have your way with me,' I said readily. Of course, I didn't trust him ... with my secrets. I didn't know what he was going to do, or what he might have meant by his suggestion, but I did sense was that he intended to harness the wild mare in me, maybe hoping to break me in and eradicate my untamed nature.

This would be impossible. For there was no deciphering between action and thought, and that is my tainted sexual psychology. One was emotional, one was physical. He wanted to explore this in me, I knew. But did he know how much I liked danger? And could he handle it? Because of my psychological disposition, I was capable of a thrill-seeking excitement few dared to explore; the sort that touched on so many of my real and sordid experiences. So far, I'd had my doctor, another doctor, my employer, my landlord and now, at this particular time in my life, the beginning of my strange episodes with my professor.

'You don't trust me?' Fez asked and took my wrist.

'Oh, my dear,' I said, appealing to him. I was getting in to this suddenly.

'Come outside, I want to show you something.' By the wrist, he tugged me along through the cabin and pushed me outside into the great green setting. As the fresh air gushed into my excited lungs, I felt him pinch my buttocks hard, right near the very parting of my legs. He caught the edge of my sex too. I felt so full and ripe, so suddenly wet, that it was like I was wearing no panties. And, beyond it all, the landscape around us was budding with young green stems that showed themselves everywhere I looked, and I was part of it, ready to be plucked. Nature was heatedly alive.

'I know about your fantasies,' he charged. 'I know you're a very dirty, bad girl.' My panties grew wet and my head swirled with the scene. So far, Fez wasn't doing too badly with the game. I had the urge to take off my shirt, to show my breasts to the rest of nature, and to this dangerous animal beside me. I wasn't the only dirty one; it was he who also wanted to see to my nudity.

'Peel it off.' That was Fez's order. And so, breathless, I did. It was still light. There was a cottage in view next door, certainly too close for my liking, and I was all exposed to its windows and decks. Nevertheless my soft breasts were out in the warm spring evening, and the gentle, late sun was shining upon my hardening nipples. Fez felt them, sliding his hands up along my abdomen to my raisin-like nipples, relishing the experience of feeling my small hardening buds.

'You're going to show me now. Show me how you masturbate,' he insisted. I let out a breath. I knew I couldn't possibly. And surely he couldn't have meant for me to perform such an act out here for all to see.

'Let's go inside,' I suggested.

'No one can see but me,' he said, as he came around to face me. His hands deftly unzipped my fly and slid my pants down to my knees.

'Stop,' I urged.

'Let's get you started,' he said as he knelt before me. I could feel his breath on my pussy, then his tongue, which slowly drew itself along my wet cunt lips right up to my clit, and there slowly made circles and wet sounds. Next he looked up. 'You are a thing of beauty that all of creation should see.'

My pants fell to my ankles. 'Step out,' he urged. I stepped out of my underwear. Then he slipped my shirt back over my shoulders and said: 'Now, pretend I'm not here. You won't see me, just go into the woods and play with yourself.'

At this, I was quite certain my eyes betrayed my fear, or was it excitement? Fez swiftly disappeared back into the cabin and closed the door, locking it behind him. It was then I realised he'd taken my pants and underwear with him. So I was stuck with only a shirt on that hardly covered my ass. The wind blew at the bottom of my shirt and it swirled between my legs, gently, insistently.

I walked across the property towards the woods. Carefully my eyes combed the surroundings for any sign of human life. It seemed quiet and still and the sun was starting its descent in the sky. Warm rays of light streaked through the woods. It made a pattern along the smooth bark of a fallen birch tree I came upon. I knew I wanted to feel the penetrating sunlight glow on my wet cunt. Tentatively, for I had never done any such thing before out in the open, I leant with my stomach over the log and raised myself up. This exposed my anus and my pussy lips to the sun somewhat. But not fully. Urged on by the pleasure of the warmth, I raised my buttocks further up into the free air. Aahhh! It was at once such a comforting feeling, and a highly stimulating one. Sideways I rocked back and forth, luxuriating in the heat. As I made love to the sun, I made love to myself, my hand reaching behind, my finger slowly inserting itself in my crack.

Then I stopped. There was a sound. Was it a car door shutting, or was it Fez leaving the cabin? Abruptly, I changed position and was now sitting on the log and searching the forest around me with my nervous, darting eyes. No one. The log felt smooth underneath me so I straddled it and gently rubbed myself on it. I parted my shirt to expose my breasts and tickled my nipples with my excited fingertips. Leaning back, I saw how wet the region was on the log where I had rubbed myself against it like a wanton woodland creature. Dare I, I wondered? Was the coast clear? Was Fez near? Was anyone watching me? I couldn't detect a presence anywhere around me. And so, with my ears and eyes alert for any movement, I lay back on the log, fully exposed. The prospect of possibly being spied upon was incredibly arousing to me as I dirtily played with my clit, pulling back my lips so that it protruded noticeably.

Not only did I enjoy the notion of Fez spying on me, but possibly someone else, a stranger. Or, as my mind was so apt to wander, how sexy it would be if MacLean had been watching the bad girl in the woods? I heard twigs snapping, but I couldn't stop rubbing my clit at this point. I was close to orgasm. Someone was nearing. I could hear them, and I grew more and more excited. What came to me next were huge waves of physical pleasure that travelled from my clit, and throughout my cunt until my anus itself throbbed. I opened my eyes in the midst of my spasms and found Fez casting his shadow over me, his cock, long, painfully hard, red and pulsing between his hands. He slowly stroked it and brought himself nearer to me. He spread my legs with a nudge of his foot to insert himself between my folds, and then, within a few strokes, he pulled out and ejaculated all over my arching, reaching pussy. Great spats of white come were falling on top of me and I loved it – this feeling of being used in the woods. I was a wanton slut and I loved the attention; of making a man set upon me in the wilds, unable to contain himself.

We then both picked up our clothes and ran toward the house, laughing all the way.

I loved Fez. I was sorry the weekend had to come to an end. I reviewed in my contented mind the many indescribable moments that had taken place between us. Our friendship has deepened and our sexual relationship was more trusting and intimate than ever. I never had such a friend in a lover before and I experienced true free, sensual joy with Fez. We played out our aberrant imaginings, our dirty, fun games and, over two days and two nights, it never stopped. Over hill and dale he took me. Emotionally, intellectually and sexually, he was the best companion.

I, of course could never disclose anything about my real personal fantasies to Fez in regards to MacLean. Certainly not, since things were about to come to a head between my professor and me. We were about to cook up a storm, I keenly sensed. And I determined it would happen because I planned to continue to act saucy and provoke him. I had to go to the ends of this experience; it was just too much of a turn-on.

But Fez should never know; it wouldn't be fair to him. I wanted to live the rest of my life with Fez and I simply had to get MacLean out of my system. Clean out of my system. And there was only one way to do that.

Meantime I continued to have the unfortunate problem of absolutely savouring the thrill and madness that the fantasy fed my brain. I could touch this fear of authority, and the disdain, the uncertainty and the horny feeling at the thought of my teacher naughtily touching me – touching the disobedient law student.

Wasn't it ironic? MacLean was so very unpredictable yet infuriatingly attractive. Danger. That was what he provided to a girl like me. I wondered if his wife thought of him like that. I had to admit I could go there with Fez too, albeit in a more loving way. Whoever went with me to that deviant place, it was always much stronger if it was forbidden. In a sense, I felt I wasn't yet ready for Fez because he was everything, waiting for me. My true love ... who maybe one day I could trust with my inner self and contradictions. For now, I loved him and deeply appreciated the courage and vulnerability he'd shown me.

With the weekend spent with Fez, I'd had little time to anticipate MacLean's next move and this was not good. When I thought of the paper I'd recently submitted, the prevailing feeling it brought was highly charged anxiety. I could barely think about it.

11

Monday came and the day was marked for disaster. After I returned home from my weekend with Fez, I had a restless night of sleep and I woke up late that morning. So I needed to dress quickly to get ready for class.

How premeditated was it that I chose to wear my new short, gauzy skirt for my Monday class? I wondered what Bee would think if she saw me wearing that skirt in the halls of the university. She hated that skirt; she'd objected to my buying it in the first place. She said I wouldn't wear a slip. But maybe I should also wear it without any panties underneath, either. It was a momentary thought. I would look indecent, showing my silly naked cunt. But momentary thoughts are fun, aren't they? With such a skirt I could display my nude pussy in class even more easily than the last time. Fine. I would wear underwear. But I would not be so decent as to wear a slip. Bee's prediction would be correct.

MacLean was even more crusty than usual in his lecture. He seemed to be even further dissociated from the subject he was teaching. During the class he didn't look at me at all, or my legs, as was his usual habit. Like the fool I was, who liked danger, I'd come dressed and ready for any occasion which would lend itself to his advantage. But I was going to remain low-key. In fact, I tried to be indifferent too, even though half the time my mind travelled ahead to the end of class, where he would doubtless speak to me about my work. Would I then perhaps have to swoon before him again, like Yvonne Dupres? Dared I give him an opening, serve myself up on a platter? God, what was I thinking? I was planning too far in advance in my deviancies. God forgive me. God preserve me. God prevent me.

That wasn't the way it happened at all. It truly shocked me when I saw MacLean leaving the lecture hall directly after class. Maybe he'd made up his mind that I was a hopeless student; that he'd given me the chance to make up the work and I'd blown it. Maybe he didn't find me attractive at all! I was the last student to leave the room. I held onto the hope that that he would return to find me there alone, as he may not want anyone to notice him talking to me outside class hours. That would be the wisest thing for him to do, I thought reassuringly to myself. But after a few still moments in the empty lecture hall, I decided to no longer linger.

Down the hall I sped. I suddenly felt self-conscious and couldn't wear the skirt anymore without a slip and had to go home to change after my disappointment at seduction. Who did I see coming towards me but Bee, who knew this stupid skirt all too well. She seemed in a rush, too, and I was glad that she may not want to stop to talk. She waved at me in a 'see you after class' way, but then she changed direction and came towards me. My skirt was what her eyes were focused on.

'You're wearing that skirt,' she said as she neared me.

'I'm really uncomfortable in it. I'm going to change,' I explained quickly. 'You must be late for class. Let's meet after then?'

'Santa, you've got some kind of flair. But you need a slip m'dear. See you then,' was all she said, and with this Bee was back on her way to class.

I carried on down the hall, and when I reached the exit I turned to look back. Just then, Bee had also turned to look back at me. She had a worried expression on her face. Feeling the whole situation was too funny, I rolled my eyes at her. I rolled my eyes at the thought of myself in particular. I was too funny.

Later, while I was waiting to meet with Bee, I started to convince myself that MacLean simply hadn't had the time over the weekend to read my work on the defence of Yvonne Dupres. Surely I'd done a satisfactory job on the case. I hadn't omitted information necessarily. I'd simply argued the points for her side and that was the task, was it not?

'Does it shock you?' I asked Bee as soon as she sat down at the outdoor cafe on campus. 'Does it shock you I wore that terrible skirt? Geez, where's your sense of humour?' It just came out. I guess I was perturbed that she should pass any judgment on how I dressed, or that anyone would, for that matter. I hated to think that I could have made a fool of myself, but even if I had, wasn't that my choice? And did MacLean see right through me too? This thought, of course, made me painfully paranoid. I had to ask Bee, indirectly trying to get a reality check.

'What?' She smiled, looking away. She knew that she was being a super bitch to me at that moment.

'OK, Bee, the skirt, OK? Just tell me.'

'You can see right through it, Santa, and it's super short, so what do you want me to say here?'

'So fucking what? What are you, uptight all of a sudden?' I was off-the-hook saying all this, but I felt downright defensive.

'Fine, if that's how you want to feel. Don't ask me about my own personal madness,' she replied indignantly.

'I told you I was uncomfortable in the damn thing, what, you want me to admit I was fucked for putting it on? I don't think so, anyone can make a mistake. It's just a skirt, for God's sake! And you're the sanest person

I know. What are you talking about, your personal madness?'

'Nothing.'

There was a pause in the conversation. I put my head in my hands and said: 'Can you imagine Fez's reaction if he'd seen me in it?'

'No.'

'Actually, I can't tell how he would react. Quite likely he would think it strange at the very least. It would perhaps anger him,' I admitted.

'Do you think it was a strange thing to do? I mean, why did you decide to wear it?' Bee asked.

'God, I'm losing my mind. I think I'm trying to distract Professor MacLean from thinking I'm a shitty student.'

'Begs the question, how far would you go to score a good mark?' she said lightly.

'You've got to be kidding, my friend.' My face grew red hot. How transparent I was! I was burning to talk about my insane lust. But instead I asked her, 'Tell me what you meant about personal madness.'

'Well, just take my word for it, I don't judge. I don't dare,' she said intriguingly.

'What are you saying?'

'I was having some difficulty with my stats course last year ... it required some special tutelage with ...'

'Professor Unruh?' I interrupted. 'My God, Bee, I had no idea! What happened?'

'Professor Unruh. He wasn't bad, actually. Just once, you know. Actually, I could have fallen for him, but he was married. He passed me and that was the ultimate goal.'

'Tell me every detail!' I shrieked.

'First, first, what's up with you and MacLean?' Her eyes burned into mine inquisitively. Hesitating, I tried to gather my thoughts, for surely I couldn't tell her all my weird imaginings – the strange way he behaved, about how I lost all composure around him. Or how I wanted to play out the story of Yvonne Dupres and Father Lemartre with him.

'I've seen the way he looks at you,' she continued.

'Really, and how's that?' I asked, desperate for any detail to justify my desires.

'He just seems to study you like a wolf does his prey.' She shook her head. 'It's always been obvious to me. Fez even mentioned it once.'

'What?' My heart was racing. 'I mean, I guess he's said something to me as well.'

Where was this conversation supposed to be going? I mean, it was one thing for Bee to make confessions about something past, but for me to confess to something that may happen, or in fact *was* happening, seemed unwise in the extreme. 'But there is nothing going on, Bee, and nothing will go on,' I countered. 'I don't care what you may have done with Unruh. And I, just to inform you, handed in a mean paper, a defence case, just before the weekend. Fine, I wore the skimpy skirt today in hopes that if he didn't like my work he may go easier on me, that was all. But I'm terribly confident that he'll be duly impressed.'

'I see. Well good. I hope you're right, because he gives me the creeps.'

'I agree.' How terribly sinister he was indeed. But Bee would never know the extent to which this excited me.

'Unruh, on the other hand, wasn't creepy, he was kind of sexy. Who knows what would have happened if he hadn't been married,' she wondered out loud.

'Sounds like you got a little attached there. Tell me what happened.' Bee was about to answer me when Joey and Fez appeared on the scene.

'Another time,' she whispered. Then she called over

to the boys, 'Just in time to pick up the bill, guys!' Bee leaned in to whisper nervously to me, 'God, do you think they overheard?' I shook my head.

Joey and Fez sat down with us. 'What are you guys talking about, then?' Joey asked.

'Yes, looks like they've been telling secrets, eh Joey?' Fez said, looking at me intensely.

'Just silly girl stuff, I suppose,' Bee answered with a smile and a shrug.

'Hi, my honey,' I said reaching up to kiss him. 'I was just telling Bee what a fabulous weekend we had at your dad's cabin.'

'Oh yes, yes, we had a wonderful time.' He smiled at Joey and Bee. 'This summer we should all go for a weekend. Joey, you can escort us as we swim across the lake to this haunted island.'

'Excellent idea!' I cheered.

'Santa, would you dare? I mean, I'd just freak being so far from shore!' Bee exclaimed.

'I really want to try!'

Joey and Fez laughed. 'You've got yourself a real adventurer, eh, Fez?' Joey said, looking at me appreciatively. And the way Fez nodded in agreement made me a little uneasy.

'I've got to get to my next class,' I said, consulting my watch as I rose to leave.

On my way to the class I did wonder if the two guys had overheard our conversation. I dearly hoped not, or we would both be in severe trouble. Back at home later, I called Bee to see if the boys had said anything about overhearing our private conversation, but when I rang there was no answer.

So Bee wasn't beyond her own misdemeanours ... If anything were to happen to me, therefore, or if I should bring something upon to myself, I knew I could ultimately confide in her, even if she did think MacLean was creepy. More than creepy; he was truly insidious. More pressing was the mystery of why he hadn't addressed the subject of my paper – especially when he made such a big deal of the urgency of it being completed. I didn't have another class for two days. Perhaps by then...

Could it be that it was my choice of attire put him off? I did so not want to put him off. I wanted him hard in his pants and desperate for me: to force me into the bathroom and throw me up against the wall and have me. And so I was to continue in my descent into my hellish, fascinating fantasy. How did Yvonne Dupres present herself? Amongst the research I'd been given about the historic legal battle, there included artist's renditions of the two protagonists, some of which depicted the strangeness of their relationship. Naturally, given the times, Yvonne was attired in long dresses and high collars, suitable for one who resided in a convent, and particularly one supposedly possessed with such great religious conviction. Over her long and many layered dresses, she also wore a veil and a coif. And so, there was nothing outwardly sensual about her presentation; although I understood from my readings that she was extraordinarily beautiful. More than anything, she seemed to have embodied innocence itself. Although during the trial Father Lemartre had put forth evidence quite to the contrary.

How could Yvonne have uttered such things as she did in court? Testimony came from her own lips as to how she would allow Lemartre to subjugate her. She told the court he would use a whip or a cane. Then he would kiss her where he'd struck her naked body, which would be anywhere from her breasts, her underarms, every nook and cranny in-between her thighs. Sometimes this would happen when she fainted, which I just knew she'd faked. She was far more possessed with an unhealthy love for the Jesuit than I was for my law professor, though I wasn't too far off.

Like Yvonne, I would let MacLean subjugate me. His words flowed back to my mind telling me that this is what Father Lemartre had done to Yvonne Dupres, and that I must experience it to truly understand her. He'd raised my shirt and fondled my bare breasts. I remember how hungry my desire for this sensation had been, but how could I allow myself to arch my back with pleasure, reaching for his smooth, almost slippery touch. I wanted to groan with pleasure too, but I had to play the part of an innocently slumbering girl. I remembered how my panties were so wet while I lay there helplessly as his hands caressed and ignited me, and MacLean whispering the words, 'I want to make your bottom sting.' How far would he take that? Remove my underwear next? Strike me with a ruler, a belt? How could I ever allow such a thing? Yet I could barely contain my sense of arousal over the prospect of this happening. I could imagine the things he would say to me to ensure my cooperation. And so I fantasised.

Like if tomorrow after my last class of the day I would make my way to the library. It is on the second floor at the north end of the building. One must first pass along the corridor where the faculty members' offices are located. I encounter no one in the hallway as I continue on my way. My curiosity is stirred as I move past MacLean's door, so I slow down. All by itself, my head turns to look in. It so happens that the good professor's chair is facing the doorway, and that he is looking straight up at me. His regard is one of dark condemnation. With a great sense of personal certainty that I am going to be appropriately admonished, I stop in his doorway.

'Hello, professor. How are you today?' I ask, my nerves coming through in the timbre of my voice.

He opens his hands and says: 'I'm quite concerned about how you are. Indeed, how are you?'

'I'm fine,' I answer.

'No, I know you're not. I can see that you are not. You look a little pale,' he says studying me. 'I have evaluated your work. Would you come in for a moment, pray?'

He rises from his chair in such a way that reminds me of a great skulking cat. Being within a few steps from his door, he requires but two smooth strides to reach my side. I feel his breath on my neck and this serves to inebriate me fully. 'I have examined your defence case. You hurried through it, I suspect, like with so much of your work,' he says reproachfully.

'Not so.' I can't believe the composure with which I speak. 'I studied every aspect of the case, and so put forward my defence.'

'Well I didn't see any evidence of that. Come into my office and let's take a look,' he says decisively. Compelled, I go ahead of him and into the small space and he clicks the door shut. The noise stops my heart and causes me a sudden outbreak of sweat down my back, my notorious crotch area, my belly, my underarms, breasts and nipples. Here we go; here it is going to happen.

Small, the office contains his desk, his chair and another hard seat. Then there is the piece of furniture with which I am already acquainted – the red chaise-longue. I stand there, weak-kneed, not knowing what to do, or where to sit. He gestures to one of the stiff chairs and I sit while he remains standing by his own chair.

'Had you read the literature inside and out? You don't understand the parameters of the case. Your work is deficient. You didn't take into account her highly devious behaviour.'

'She was naughty, but that was all. He was plainly in authority and used it over her.' I wonder if I am getting into deep shit here. I feel like I myself am pleading innocence, and he is the lewd one with all the power; the one with the slithering snake's tongue crouching, ready to strike from within his mouth into mine.

'She put at risk her immortal soul by the things she said and did. It wasn't naughtiness, it was depravity. Do you realise the evil acts she committed in the name of the Lord?' At this he sits down, drawing his chair up to mine.

'She loved the Lord,' I say as I sit back into my chair. In doing so, I raise my pelvis slightly. Under ordinary circumstances this is a natural enough action, but not in front of him. My underwear is, I pray, not too visibly wet because my skirt is short enough to see under and I naughtily part my legs a wee bit, but only momentarily. But with this slight move, I am inwardly aroused. I want to show him my clitoris and all my wet folds. It excites me that I am only subtly trying to hide this suggestion of pleasure. Soon I am awake to the fact that I have crossed over into another more dangerous zone with my professor.

I become frightened when he continues: 'Loved the Lord? I saw what you just did, you bad girl.' He leans forward, resting his hand on the arm of my chair. 'I also saw what you were doing the day you pretended to faint in my class. Do you remember how you were exposing and touching yourself for more than a half hour?'

'No! Look, I'm just trying to discuss a point,' I say, hoping my intellect will save me. I cross my legs protectively. I am mortified.

'She had no hope of being a saint, but good for her for trying!' I argue with sudden vehemence.

'Oh no, she had no good intentions. Her motives were far removed from the things she professed to believe in, like Christ. Like God. The furthest thing from it,' he says, summing me up altogether.

'She truly believed and she was much misled by Father Lemartre, Professor MacLean,' I further protest.

'Yvonne Dupres didn't know any better and neither do you, he avers. 'That makes you weak and full of doubt and so full of temptation.' At this, he proceeds to lean forward and slowly raise my top. This I allow, helplessly. 'You are tempted. *You* tempt.'

My breasts are exposed now. He does not touch me yet. Instead, he gazes upon my naked femininity and seems angered. 'You do not know anything. You do not know the purity which you've been given. Look at you.' He gives each breast a light slap. Now he is going to play Father Lemartre and I Yvonne. 'Pray to God, then,' he says. And he guides me over to his hot-red chaise-longue where I plonk down my helpless bum. It is long and like a bed. I stretch back on it. He has me in such a highly suggestive state at this point that I wait for his next whim. My head starts to swirl like I am in a too-hot bath. Silly girl, pull out of it, I tell myself; and so I sit as upright as I can in the long soft chair and cross my legs.

'Don't do that,' he says.

I don't move, and he parts my legs. I am fully dressed, but I feel nude: that there is nothing between his eyes and my pussy. He knows of the wetness in-between my legs; he sees the damp spot on my underwear.

'You're all wet,' he says with condemnation. He flips my skirt up without ceremony. 'I can see your underwear is disgusting with your moistness. God can see. Let Him look upon you in all your sin and ask forgiveness. I will lead you to repentance. Lie back.'

As I do so, he rather roughly pushes up my shirt to expose my breasts and I gasp. He pinches my nipples quite hard and my back involuntarily arches towards his vigorous touch.

'You need to be punished very badly,' he says solemnly. His eyes travel down to my wet panties and he moves into an advantageous position to better see it. Pulling aside the crotch, he looks now upon my naked sex. As his fingers hold back the narrow strip of underwear, he uses his free hand to probe my slippery folds. Next he pulls down the crotch of my panties until I find myself fully open to his gaze and my underwear is being slipped down to my ankles. There he leaves them. His hands grasp my feet and he places my heels together, pushing them upwards and thus fully parting my knees. With his eyes never leaving my exposed cunt, he presses my knees down and my heels are almost in contact with my bare pussy. Then he dirtily takes this move a step further and makes my heels rub into my moisture so that they are wet too. As I watch him, his eyes ignite with fire and he looks up at me and slides my heels a little away from my pussy.

'Close your eyes,' he says sternly.

My breath is shallow and I have the overwhelming desire to touch my clitoris right before his hungry eyes. The need is soon assuaged, as I feel his fingers now parting my lips, and he tills a long slow line right up to my clitoris, where he then places a finger on each side of my swollen protrusion and pushes my lips away so as to cause my bud to jut out in a most unseemly way.

'This is the problem, right here,' he says as he pinches my slippery clit. And with that he releases his grip and moves over to his desk. Of course, I am not able to bear to keep my eyes closed any longer, so curious am I to see what he is about to do. I observe him as he takes out a ruler from his drawer, and something else that I can't quite make out. During this time, I have reached down to massage my aching need and, turning quickly, he catches me performing such a thing on myself. With one long stride, he is once again by my nude side and swiftly strikes my hand with his ruler. It stings and I close my legs in reaction.

'Expose yourself!' he orders.

I part my legs again, and gush forth more sexual juices in my excitement. 'Be a good girl now,' he utters and, with the ruler, he serves me sharp taps on my pussy, paying special attention to my clitoral area. I feel like I might come and so raise my cunt upwards to receive the rhythmic blows that he ceaselessly repeats. My suspicions that the ruler must be very wet are confirmed when he next wipes it across my nipples, leaving them wet and cold, but not before he has brought the instrument to his nose to inhale the scent.

'Now I will soothe your wretched, punished body,' he says. Just like Father Lemartre and Yvonne Dupres, my professor kisses me where he struck me. All over my pussy, he kisses and licks and probes with his tongue until I am pulsing with exquisite orgasm all the way from my clitoris to my anus and back again, and deep within my core and through the tips of my many folds, and up again through to the tip of my protruding, burning clit.

And so my fantasy ended in typical style, with my ultimate release and, beyond that, it left me with many more variations on the theme to play with in the future. So charged was I with these images, this ongoing story, that I thought I may not be able to control myself next time I encountered MacLean. I would like to faint in order that he defile my body as completely as he had done in my imaginings.

With these thoughts running through my deviant mind, I tried to sleep but couldn't, and so set to some school work that needed accomplishing. I would be tired the following morning, I knew, but I was caught up in

173

my work, so it was worth it. Anyway, I had a late morning class. Finally, before I slept, I chose my outfit for the next day. It would be my long dress and shawl. I would wear no underwear and no one would be the wiser. Tomorrow, I would so subtly attire myself like the notorious Yvonne Dupres who made her bizarre mark on history so many years ago. It was my fond hope that when Professor MacLean would see me, and he would be angry, and his cock would grow hard as he would register what I was trying to suggest with my costume. I was quite certain this little game was being entertained in his mind too. Goodness knows what he truly had planned for me.

12

Next day, it was Fez who spotted me in my unfashionably long robes. He approved and said so. In fact, he went so far as to say that I looked heavenly, even saintly, in my dress. It made me laugh inside, as I was wearing no underwear underneath. Momentarily too, neurosis waved over me as I felt that he was well aware my true designs. But that couldn't possibly be.

'It sure beats the outfit you'd come up with yesterday, from what I understand,' he went on to remark.

'What do you mean?' I asked nervously.

'Well, Bee told me about the outrageous skirt you wore to MacLean's class yesterday. It made me really quite angry to think about it.' He looked at my face while it turned beet red. 'And why weren't you answering your phone last night? I would have come over. I was going to stop by after work.'

'My phone? Well first of all, it never rang once!' I said defensively. 'And why would Bee report such a thing to you? Is she your spy?'

'No, not at all, she's just a little concerned about you, as am I,' he trailed off. 'Don't worry, I love you. I want a lifetime of weekends with you, like the one we just spent. I want it day after day. I'm waiting to hear about all your fantasies, plus those that include MacLean, and you will tell me one day. But for now, has anything happened with him? I mean, are you having strange interludes with him? I must know because I will have him punished. Murdered. And I will punish you, too,' he said in the meanest whisper.

'God, I don't know what you're talking about! Leave me alone!' I raged. 'And I would dearly hope you aren't capable of murder. That's outrageous!'

'Quiet and calm, darling. I am going to keep a close eye on you and will prevent you from doing anything foolish. Now I have a class. Will you allow me to buy you dinner later today?'

'Possibly,' I relented.

'I will pick you up, then, at six.' And with that he entered the building and disappeared. I felt so exposed, yet he really knew nothing at all; not more than an inkling. He still loved me and that was strange and wonderful; but it was scary how his macho Italian side, obsessed with honour, would flare up occasionally, as if he was remembering he was supposed to be the tough guy. I would have to be very careful about my intentions with MacLean, or rather MacLean's intentions with me. Real important stuff could hang in the balance.

But Fez couldn't prevent me from the mental side of my devilish pursuits.

When I saw Bee for a cigarette break outside the university, I laid in heavy on her about her indiscretions to Fez about me and my skirt. 'I could so easily tell Joey about you and Professor Unruh, how would that be? You expect me to take you into my confidence and this is what you do with my private information?' I complained to her.

'Hey, that is so much another matter. You wouldn't dare do that, would you?' she asked angrily.

'No, never. It's just that Fez gave me total shit for it.'

'You know, Santa, first of all, Fez loves you to death; secondly, he presses me for information; thirdly, your behaviour is a little strange and as two people who love you, we just sometimes discuss, well, you. But I am sorry. I want your trust. I won't do it again.'

'You were both mocking my stupid skirt. Did you have a good laugh?' I pouted.

'No, he'd asked me where you were and I said you went home to change. Then he asked why,' Bee explained.

'And you had to describe my foolish skirt?'

'Well, he naturally asked if it was too short and stuff.'

'You didn't tell him it was see-through,' I said hopefully. Now this line of questioning had nothing to do with my wanting to conform to Fez's version of propriety or anything. It was just that it was embarrassing, that skirt, and everybody had seen it and I didn't like thinking I looked an asshole. Even though, underneath, I defiantly thought everybody could just go straight to hell.

'And why the devil are you so bloody worried about me?' I inquired.

'Well, it's slightly selfish on my part, I guess. It's just that you're a little preoccupied, and you're keeping me out of, well, what I mean is, your sense of privacy lately just makes me wonder,' she said softly.

'God, I'm just trying to work, Bee,' I said in an equally gentle tone.

'I know. I'm just as insecure as you and it's a little alienating to me at times. I guess I miss you in a sense,' she explained.

'It's OK,' I told her.

It was the whole moving-in thing that was eating her. I knew it. It was that she felt Joey didn't love her enough. I wondered momentarily if she was trying to sabotage my relationship with Fez by talking about me when I wasn't there, but my good friend would never do that. She was always saying how she believed he was so in love with me. No, Bee really wanted the best for me, I had always sensed this and I wanted the same for her. Sometimes I wanted to kick Joey's ass for making her feel so unimportant.

'Yeah, I am preoccupied with my marks, that's for sure. God help me if I fuck up, you know? But you're the closest thing to me, to my heart, don't ever doubt that. I'm sorry if I've been distant.'

Neither of us spoke for a moment. Then she said: 'I do like your outfit today. You could start a whole new trend here.'

'You think?'

'Where did you get those funky shoes? They look like they're nineteenth century or something.'

'Found them in that little antique, second-hand shop on Princess Street,' I said happily.

'How do you get those buttons done up?' she asked, looking closer at them.

I opened my purse and showed her the trick – my special tool. 'It's a button-hook. Neat, eh? It still takes about ten minutes to do these up, though.'

'I love it!' she said, taking the button-hook to examine it briefly.

'Hey, did you think the guys were acting weird yesterday?' Bee asked.

'I don't know. Do you think they heard us talking?'

'Mmmm.' Bee looked down. 'You know, I think Joey knew last year that I had a fling with Unruh.

'Really ... how?'

'I don't really know. It's just an inkling I have.'

'You were already going out with him by then, right?'

'Just starting, it had only been a few weeks.'

'Then theoretically it wasn't cheating because you weren't even really monogamous yet,' I said to her, just as much as to justify myself. Fez and I had only been going out a few weeks ourselves.

'How are thing going with you and MacLean? Did

you get your paper back yet?' she asked, looking straight at me, studying my reaction.

'There's no need to wonder about the professor. There's nothing going on. I handed in my paper the other day. I'm still waiting to hear, but if I'm in the clear, then I'll be back to my calm old self,' I laughed.

We both laughed because we knew I was never calm. And though all I wanted was to reassure her, the subtext inside my head was reading that I didn't want to be clear of my professor. I wanted to be near him. I wanted him to get inside me. I wanted him to plunder me with his self-seeking pleasure, and forcibly too. I wanted him to forget about me, think about himself and use my body so that I could succumb to him and have my own crazy pleasure. I was the dirty girl. I so fully had the saint/whore complex.

But I was playing with fire with MacLean. He wasn't about to be nice dada. Of course that was the tantalising thing. I couldn't predict him. And the next day I would be surprised again. The next day, when I would see him in class and, hopefully, after class.

'And if he fails you, what would you do? And what if Fez finds out?' Bee asked.

'I object,' I said defensively, my thoughts confused about Bee's intentions here. 'Why would you assume I'm going to fail? What, do you think I'd suck my professor's cock like you did last year? And stop talking about me and Fez that way.'

'What way?'

'Well, are you after his butt or what? You sure like to have your heart to hearts with him about me,' I added accusingly. I was going too far, I knew it. I was trying to derail her, to put her off course because she'd now correctly identified the truth and it was none of her business. Moreover, it really did bug me the way she and Fez were talking.

'He loves your ass so much. He's not interested in me and I'm in love with Joey, which is my own cross to bear. Anyway, it's nothing like that, and how dare you!' she exclaimed.

'Well I never!' I said as I deliberately dropped the remainder of my coffee on the spring grass. I looked at her, shocked and appalled for a moment, and then we both started laughing like goofs.

'I know, I know, Bee. You would never want to hurt me,' I admitted to her sincerely. And really, really, she would never. It was just a diversion to make her think I was jealous of her and Fez, but didn't it work well? If she were more self-conscious, then the less I would need to be. And who had something to hide here? Bee had her liaison with her professor over a year ago and was just now telling me, her best friend. I hadn't even gone anywhere near as far as she had yet. She'd actually had real full-on sexual contact with Unruh. But it seemed in the end that I had much more to hide, for my deviant imagination went to far flung fields that were surely difficult to match.

Bee was such a great friend and there I was playing mind-games with her. It wasn't so serious, though. I had the right to my privacy and she and Fez were prying. If only I could have stopped acting so weird, but that was just the way it was; this was a time in my life where I had to wholly go to the extremities of experience or else life was just too deadly dull!

Bee was off to meet Joey. In parting, she told me sadly that she suspected Joey was seeing someone else. I told her there was no way. I sure hoped that Joey wouldn't do that to Bee after they'd been seeing each other for over a year. Something marked a difference between Bee and me – she was ready to settle down with one man, while I was unbearably tempted by so many. Soon I might have to be ready to commit fully to

Fez. Poor Bee, it seemed she couldn't have the very, very one she loved.

As I wandered through the university hallways, I wondered how I could ascertain that Joey wasn't fooling around on Bee. Spy work. More intrigue in my life. I'd have to think of a plan or just keep my eyes peeled. I could always press Fez to find out.

With no particular direction or goal, I continued to stroll around the university. Quite unexpectedly, I found myself in the corridor down by the law faculty offices. Yeah, right, I wanted him to see my dress. I slowed and literally held my breath as I passed in front of MacLean's office. The thought of my recent fantasies reverberated in my mind and I had a great urge to touch myself as I passed in front of his door. How disappointed I was when I discovered his door was shut. I paused and did touch myself through my skirt. I wasn't wearing any panties underneath. It occurred to me to even pull my skirt right up then and there. But that was out of the question. The only way my skirt should be raised and my pussy exposed there in the hallway would be if MacLean himself were to do it. If he came along, I would submit.

I heard a door open and shut behind me and I hurried away from MacLean's office. As I turned the corner, I quickly looked back and saw MacLean standing in front of his office door. Our eyes met just before I disappeared down the hall with a swish of my long skirts. He must think I'm mad, I thought, and he was counting on it, if my instincts served me.

Next day I returned to school wearing the same outfit. I hadn't had to wash any panties for two days now, and I reckoned it was probably healthier to go without. Plus, it brought me such an incredible sense of freedom and stimulation. I felt like I was more awake and definitely sexually aroused at all times. What a dirty girl I was!

In class, I tried not to wriggle in my seat, but I couldn't help it. It was the way he was looking at me. He'd registered something about the way I was dressed, that was for certain. In my mind, I was only a lifting of the skirt away. Was it the same in his mind? The thought of this made me shudder and my clit twitch. I took down my notes, drawing pictures on the side of rulers, fingers and hands. It was cigarette break time.

Now that it was a warmer season, Bee and I were regularly meeting outdoors for our self-assigned breaks. I hoped I was pissing MacLean off again. He was certainly pissing me off with the way he was making me wait for him to return my paper. It was ten minutes before the break and I left class early for a smoke. How cocky. My, oh my, my disregard was evident and right below the window of MacLean's lecture hall was where Bee and I stood smoking. I could hear MacLean's voice droning on and on. Despite my bravado, I was anxious. I urged Bee to move away from below the window and to go around the corner of the building; it was too much for me. I wondered if he could smell the smoke or hear us talking.

At the end of class, like the very time before, MacLean simply left the lecture hall without as much as a mere glance in my direction. Was this part of the game? Did he mean to have me come to him? Or had I lost his attention? Did I ever have it? The paper I submitted probably left him so cold that it sealed his decision to fail me as a student. Oh, I couldn't let it go at that! Maybe I should find him and confront him. I looked at my watch; it was nearing lunchtime.

So much hung in the balance for me, for if I failed his class there would go any chance of my getting a law degree. The lecture hall was empty and I still sat there, immobilised. Slowly, I gathered up my books. Perhaps it was time to go by his office, once and for all.

Three times I knocked, but not as hard as my heart was knocking against my ribs. He wasn't there. Once again, my urges took hold of me and I lightly scratched the front of my skirt, where underneath I was sans underwear. How good it felt! I did it right in front of the keyhole to his office, and it titillated me that he might be looking. Being terribly excited about that, I continued my fondling for a short time but soon my better sense made me stop. But I did lean down to look through the keyhole. My heart stopped when my eye caught a small flash of movement from within. Startled, suddenly losing my nerve, I fled.

I headed to a small restaurant tucked away on a street behind the university. It was late-morning and the place was quiet. It wasn't ever that busy anyway as the place was quite a hole. When I entered there were only a couple of lone customers parked at a few of the tables and the whole place had a heavy mood. I was glad the lights were dim and I took a seat at a small table in the corner. Soon a server came to take my order. I ordered a grilled cheese sandwich plus a glass of wine. It was hardly a midday drink, but I had to settle my nerves a little.

The waiter brought it and told me my sandwich would be ready in a few minutes. My stomach was empty and so I felt the effects of the wine within the first few sips. The persistent possibility that MacLean was looking at what I was doing to myself through the keyhole to his office door made me cringe with delicious fear. It was too much. I must relax, I told myself, and I sipped my drink as my sandwich order arrived.

As I proceeded to eat and drink, my feelings about the whole thing shifted from shame to anger. I ate my sandwich quickly, but it wasn't very good and I wondered why I'd not gone somewhere that served tastier food. I became determined that everything was all to be resolved today with MacLean, one way or another. That my grades were not in jeopardy and that my good professor was not ready to treat me unfairly. I drank quickly, my cup of courage, as they say. I loved to live with abandon and today was no different. I liked being alive and I liked my fantasies, though it seemed these days that those two worlds were growing closer together.

I was working myself up to confronting him. The hallway of the faculty of law was to be my destination shortly and I slammed my money down with great spunk and determination. It was time to go.

Though I should have headed straight home at this point, instead I'd determined to head back to the university to ask whether I was failing his lousy course or not. I giggled at myself the whole way. What the hell was I going to say to him? And once I'd reached the university building doors, I lost my nerve, got real, and decided the only thing I would do was to spy on him. I didn't have the nerve to talk to him. First, I'd get away from the crowds and see if I couldn't spot him in the library, where it would be easiest for me to hide. So I went along through the usual corridors but where did I actually find myself? In the faculty of law on the north side of the building, where MacLean was much more likely to be.

It was quiet as always. I liked the place, really; it smelt of books and wool suits. Perhaps the sweet odour of pipe tobacco too. I remembered for a moment that I'd once seen MacLean with a pipe. Maybe he was around, down in his office right now.

At the top of the hallway, I calmly stopped for a drink of water at the water fountain. I hoped my breath didn't smell of wine. Water may help, and it was refreshing. In truth I felt the time was ripe for this meeting with my professor, though it was unscheduled. I was readier than ever, and it was simply time to have a student-teacher conference.

I burped and then proceeded to walk down the hall. His office was midway down, and it took me much less time than anticipated to reach his door. In seconds, I was there. His door was closed and I stood before it and tried to listen in. Silence from inside. I then knocked twice, perhaps too softly. There was nothing to be heard from inside the office. Was my knocking not loud enough, I wondered? Of course it was. But no one came to the door. Well, he wasn't there after all, damn it.

Should I go try the door, I asked myself? Maybe my paper was on his desk? In a matter of a quick move, I tried the knob and discovered that his door was locked. I should have left then and there.

13

I suddenly remembered I had my button hook. I took it from my purse and studied it a minute. It could serve as a key, I realised. So the next thing I did was slowly ease it into the keyhole and wiggle it a little. I didn't want to break the lock on his door, by any means. What did I think I was doing? Indeed, what did I think I would do if I'd succeeded in penetrating his office? Lie there nude and wait for him? I think not! Perhaps I could look for my marks in his files. Yes, that'll do, I thought. As I continued my antiquated game of spymaster, guess who appeared at the end of the corridor?

If I could have run away, I would have, but my button-hook was jammed in the lock. MacLean was coming up on me while I stood trapped in the most absurd situation. Laughter at the situation was pouring forth from within me, but I was overflowing with embarrassment. He simply continued towards me, his face expressionless, which only made me laugh harder. By the time he arrived at my side, I was practically doubling over because my button-hook was not going to come out again. It was absolutely stuck in the key-hole. The whole thing was hysterical and horrible. I was in so much trouble.

'What do you think you are doing?' MacLean asked in his usual understated tone. I still couldn't stop myself from my fits of laughter. 'Do you like to get in trouble?' he inquired neutrally.

Still vainly trying to remove my button-hook, I shook my head vigorously. 'No I don't.' I was going about a billion miles an hour and he was moving in on me with the slow, steady pace of a great indescribable beast sure of their unmistakeable power and inevitable domination over the prey.

'Stop that nonsense!' he ordered in a low voice. I removed my hand from my button-hook that was for ever stuck in his lock. I tried desperately to collect myself, so I drew a deep breath and feebly tried to explain.

'God, I don't know what I was doing,' I protested frantically. I thought I could still smell the wine on my breath, as no doubt could he.

With infuriating ease, he reached out to remove the button-hook from the lock in one easy movement. He held it and examined it and a wry smile crossed his face when he looked down at my old-fashioned boots. With his free hand, he rummaged in his pocket and made a jingling sound. His smile disappeared and he looked at me with an even expression, then lowered his chin so his eyes peered at me from under his dark brow. It was a look of knowing something the other person did not, and was intended to cause consternation, to put the other person off balance. Well, it certainly had that effect on me, causing me to cease my nervous giggling.

Casually, almost sensuously, he pulled his key from his pocket and slid it into the lock.

'I so much want to be a good student,' I blurted out stupidly like I was trying to beg for forgiveness. And well I should, I knew. I was just now trying to break into his office! Help. I was in such deep trouble.

He looked at me briefly, opened the door and said, 'Inside we go.' With that he urged me with a light, but oh so burning hand touching the back of my vulnerable neck; my professor's authoritative hand. He guided me in front of him and into his office and followed close behind. I heard him close the door and say in a reprimanding but amused way, 'Taking up crime, are we? Well, that's one way to learn about the field of law. Isn't it?' I let out a nervous chuckle in response.

He laughed with derision, making me feel like never a bigger fool existed at that moment than I. The way he was laughing at me literally made me unsteady on my feet, although I was ever so slightly relieved. Here I was at the much-anticipated and dreaded meeting and I was now feeling entirely like the little idiot student. In effect, I knew that was the way it was supposed to be. Somehow, though, I wondered if I may have misled myself into thinking he'd ever noticed me. Maybe now he was going to call campus police and have me escorted off the property for good! And that all the other silly stuff that had happened between us only caused him some passing amusement and now he was now going to mock me for being such a foolish girl. All my fantasies about my professor were a crazy girl's wishes and the whole while he had no urgings towards me at all and I was simply about to fail. I'd totally blown my whole law degree.

Well, he loved the look that must have crossed my face. The bastard. He said, 'Close the door, close the door.'

'Pardon me?' I asked.

'Close the door.'

But the door was already closed. And I repeated what he said to me while looking at the closed door. I went over and pressed my hand against the already closed door and from there turned to him with my eyes narrowed; was it some kind of weird foreplay, perhaps?

'The door is closed,' I heard my own voice say.

I had to pass by him now in the close quarters of his office space and I felt that my body heat was about a million degrees Celsius and was filling the room. I tried not to brush up against him as I moved by him to walk to the chair he gestured me to take, but he made it difficult not to rub up against him. I couldn't avoid feeling the light, physical nuance of his hardened prick inside his pants as I slipped by him to my seat. I felt it against my backside because I passed with my ass to him.

The feeling of his actual cock sent a sudden spasm right up my pussy, so as to make me almost stumble. Then I said in a shaky voice, 'Look, I don't want to fail the class; I don't want to get expelled. I worked hard on that paper. I just needed to talk to you about it.'

I felt a little braver having said that. Here now! I wasn't going to give him any power! I had come to talk about my paper, even if I had been trying to break into his office. That might well be true, but we were going to forget about that, I decided. Saying it like this inside my own head gave me even more confidence, and, plus, goddamn, I knew how hard I worked on that case study of Yvonne Dupres for his bleeding course. So I said to him: 'So, what did you think of my written defence case for Yvonne Dupres?'

We looked at each other and he sat down. He was grinning now and he sat back in his chair and lazily let his eyes graze slowly up and down my body. He was looking at my long skirts as if he might lift them up at any moment and touch my naked pussy. No doubt he was thinking about how he knew I was wearing no panties and also of how I was dressed exactly like Yvonne Dupres. Despite the long skirts, I was not at all innocently dressed. He had a terrible twinkle in his eye as he registered this fact. Who was trying to seduce whom here was the question in the air. He was thinking he'd win the argument – that I was the one, the seductress, which exonerated him from whatever he was planning to do to me. And now that I'd gone this far and I was going to get a pulled-down-panties spanking.

Bare-bottom hard slaps is what he was fully within his rights to do to me at this point.

And I would let this man touch me all over – especially my cunt. Indeed, I'd show it to him first.

The bugger was taking the time to ponder how much he had on me at this point. My button-hook caper, for instance, where I was trying to illegally enter his private office. Then there was my cigarette smoking in the girls' and being caught. And, horribly, let's not forget my exposing myself to him in his class, when I showed him my naked cunt for a last half hour of a class ... shaven pussy, no less, and then my pretending to faint. And my pretending to be asleep in his office while he fondled me. And, finally, now there was my failed paper, possibly.

'Your paper may no longer be relevant,' he said. 'At this point I may have to take other things into consideration.' He gestured to the chaise-longue.

As I sat down I almost touched myself between the legs, but I stopped myself and rested my itching hand on my lap. I didn't care about a law degree any more; I just wanted him to touch me intimately while I lay back like a good girl. But I was going to be a saucy girl instead and said coolly, 'I demand to know about my paper, and my defence case about Yvonne Dupres. Surely you have some comments? You received my paper; I hand-delivered it to you.' The cheek.

He took up my paper from the top of his desk and rolled it tightly into a tube. 'You're just like her, aren't you? You know what a bad girl Yvonne Dupres was?' He pointed my document casually at me. 'You've been an unruly student, smoking on campus, exposing yourself in my class and attempting to break into my office.'

I began to object but then he approached me on the chaise-longue and, before I knew it, he had a grip on my thigh and pushed me over onto my side and had served me a sound wallop right on my bum with my report. It stung and he released me. I rubbed my ass as I looked back up at him, half challengingly, half terrified, as I slowly turned back over. He pulled his chair over by me, sat squarely on it and told me matter-of-factly, 'But you're going to be a good girl now, aren't you?'

I was looking at him like a caged animal.

'As for your report, you have presented a case as flimsy as the skirt that you were wearing the other day,' he said, and leant forward to touch my skirt. 'And so, now, how do you dress today?' he asked. 'What do you wear? Do you look like her?' He studied me appraisingly.

'Who?' I asked feebly and squirmed in my seat. The caged animal was now having a stick poked at her through the bars of her cage.

The sadist.

He laughed. 'Do you wish to look like her? She was very beautiful and she was very naughty too.'

I was going to ignore his last question. I was sure he didn't intend for me to answer it anyway. 'I would like to read your comments about my work,' I said as I crossed my legs and held my hand out.

He snapped my paper in his hands, not releasing it to me. My cunt fluttered involuntarily and I meekly put my hand down.

'Do you believe Yvonne Dupres was a saint?' he asked.

'Certainly not after Father Lemartre corrupted her,' I replied.

'She was prepared to do anything to achieve her ends.'

'That's what the other side would argue.'

'What would you have done if you were her? She was very ambitious,' he stated amusedly.

'He bewitched her, so she claimed,' I said as I sat there dumbly looking up at him, painfully aware that I too was being bewitched.

MacLean stared at length into my eyes with his usual lack of expression that was so unsettling. 'She had a weak will and a wild imagination. That's why I thought this case suited you.'

'Does that mean you are unsatisfied with my work?'

'Are you?' he asked with a challenging tone in his voice.

'I think I have a talent for law,' I boasted and sat back slightly on his chaise-longue. Not so subtle, though, was the gushing of wetness between my legs. I thought my skirt may be noticeably wet as I wore no underwear. I looked down to see and back up at him. His countenance was even, though I could still see a smile behind his expression.

He rolled up my paper until it formed a tighter tube. 'You smell of alcohol. Have you been drinking?' These words made my head swirl and, to steady myself, I placed my hand on my forehead and laughed a little. 'You're very naughty, just like Yvonne Dupres, aren't you?' He leant in closer.

'You've got me all wrong, good sir.'

'How dare you come to my office in your shameful condition? You're no more a student than Yvonne was a saint.'

I tried to get up to leave, but he blocked me. 'Lie down and be a good girl,' he said, pushing firmly me back with the palm of his hand against my upper chest. 'I think you understand Yvonne Dupres far better than you were willing to demonstrate in your defence. I know you're not wearing any underwear. Imagine yourself as Yvonne, then, and pray for forgiveness. Turn over like a good girl.' He laughed at me mockingly.

Shocked, I remained motionless, but he was not going

to wait and in one swift move he firmly turned me onto my stomach himself. I said in a pleading voice, 'I'm sorry, professor.' Being on my belly aroused me to the point where I couldn't help but squeeze my thighs together. Again, I released more moistness from between my legs.

'You need to be punished. Sh! Be an obedient girl, now. I know what to do with a student like you,' he said gustily and whacked my ass a couple times with my term paper. 'You pulled your panties down in front of me in class; you showed me your naked pussy, didn't you, you bad girl? Pull up your skirts now for a spanking.'

From on my belly, I slowly pulled my skirts up a little for him but had to stop halfway up because I had no panties on.

He swatted my bum again, and the pain was delicious. I whined and squirmed and his blows grew harder and harder until I tried to escape from underneath. 'Are you going to be a good girl and show me your bare bum?' Whereupon I quickly pulled up my skirts to expose my bare behind, already red for certain from his punishment upon me. When he saw this nakedness, I heard him say, 'You need a sound lesson.' After which he spanked me hard again, continuing to deliver blow after blow on my poor bare bottom until it was red with heat. 'No panties, you wear no panties. You're such a dirty girl.' He stroked my ass, feeling the heat of it, and he said in a stern voice, 'Turn over now.'

I didn't dare not obey and slowly shifted my hips so I could roll over.

'That's a good girl,' he said softly, as if to carefully teach me how a good girl should behave. 'Raise your dress up better so I can see what you already showed me in class.' And he fixed his eyes on my hands as I hesitatingly pulled my dress up above my cunt to my belly, and then, as I helplessly lay there, his eyes studied my naked, shaved mound.

'Bare, bad pussy,' he said and he lightly patted my sticky cunt lips with his hand. 'You're already wet, you dirty girl. Do you masturbate in my class? Do you want me to look at your naked cunt?' And then he stroked me for a moment all along from my hole to my clit, parting my lips a bit as he did so.

He momentarily stopped touching me so he could place my rolled-up manuscript that he was holding in his other hand neatly upon his desk. Then he stood up over me. I squirmed a little, my pussy lips swelling even more so and becoming even more moist with bad girl juices. I covered my clit and pussy self-protectively, taking a moment to massage myself there.

'Sssh,' he rebuked me. 'Take your hands away.'

I did and squirmed a little more.

'Keep your naughty cunt still,' he ordered me. Then he parted my legs ever so slightly and spanked me again a couple of times with his hand. But that was just the beginning of what was to come. He made me spread my legs even more as he pressed my knees apart. It seemed he didn't need to talk to me any more; he was in full command of the operation as he raised my knees up to my chest, spreading my cunt out to the fullest extent. It was then that he started spanking me sharply in-between my legs and fingering my hole.

'Does it hurt?' the professor asked, never taking his eyes off me.

'Yes, please stop,' I begged, squirming, and he resumed his spanking of my cunt as I lay open on his chaise-longue. Was he never going to stop with his law professor's disciplinary hand? I hoped not; it felt so good and I moaned.

'Sshh ...' he whispered gently, and he stopped being so strict towards me as his hand now patted my mound and stroked it and I gratefully raised my pelvis. 'It feels good, doesn't it, you bad thing?' He stroked and stroked and tickled my slippery folds, his finger tilling the length of my cunt until he felt my dripping wet opening, which he stroked over and over, bringing the juices upwards to my clit as his finger slid along. He groaned at the discovery of how wet I was getting and shortly he instructed me to spread my legs a little more.

'You're a bad girl for being so wet. You like being dirty.' He smiled down at me knowingly. 'Did you masturbate when you were writing the report for me?' he whispered, looking at me in the eye.

I squirmed. 'Sometimes,' I admitted. I so wanted to be a good girl, tell him everything while I would let him just keep touching me. I opened my legs even more and he said to me, 'I'll bet you masturbated a lot.' And he further pressed my thighs apart – this time, to their fullest extent. He stood up and, with his bare hand, he spanked me lightly at first, then with increasing force he slapped my wet open pussy again and I started to close my legs.

'Sshh,' he said to me. 'Open up a little more like a good little student would,' he urged. 'Now touch your clit.'

He inserted his finger in me, sliding it in and out. I started to have light spasms at this point, but I wasn't allowed to orgasm for soon I was moving. He told me to make like a doggie and, when I went on all fours, he pushed my knees far apart under me, to the furthest point, and raised my bum high into the air with his one hand between my legs. He swatted me underneath, on my bum, on my exposed asshole, on my pussy and on my clit in a deliberate sequence. He spanked me all over. I made soft moaning sounds, mixed in with cries of protest, to which he responded with a rough, sharp, 'Sssshh!'

And he struck me harder the more I protested. Then he finally said, 'Bad girl, now turn over and show me what you were doing in my classroom?'

'In class?'

'I saw, you disgusting girl,' he replied.

'Please, I don't know what you mean.'

'Show me,' he said, leaning back in his chair.

'I am ashamed to,' I confessed to him.

'Let me see you in all your dirtiness,' he murmured.

'No, please ...'

'Show me,' he said again.

'What?' I asked most innocently.

'You know, and you're going to show me.' Next he unbuttoned the top of my dress so as to expose my breasts. And he felt them awhile, and he lightly stroked them.

'Hmmm, you like that?' he asked. Shortly he turned away and went over to his desk.

Into his desk drawer he went and equipped himself with something I could not see. He came back over to me. In my half-dressed state I sat with the top of my dress open on his chaise-longue. Holding up two paper-clips he showed me that he was parting them slightly at their metal folds and I then realised what he was going to do with them as he first stroked my nipples and squeezed them so as to make my buds as hard as possible. Separating the paper clips a little more, he promptly placed one on each of my nipples. They pinched as he slid them crudely across my buds and attached them there. Once fixed, and he seemed so expert at doing so, they felt tight and punishing. It made me feel like I might faint possibly, so good was the pleasure of it and the pain.

'Now you are going to show me,' he said once more as he pushed up my skirts to better see my aching naked cunt. I squirmed helplessly and I pushed myself slightly outward to my bad professor. He roughly parted my thighs and reproached me. 'You refuse to accept my lessons in the classroom, so now's your chance to show me that you are a good student. Show me that you understand the case of Yvonne Dupres. Expose to me the origin of her impurity and of yours.'

I knew what he'd meant for me to do. Ambitious to be a good student, and deeply aroused, my fingers shyly, tentatively, made their way down to my clit. He held my legs apart and watched with cruel hunger in his eyes. It was slippery down there, and as I tried to part my lips before his eyes, my fingers slipped, but finally I did expose to him my firm, fully erected button. This caused my entire cunt to spasm with pleasure. It was terrifying, what I was doing ... what he was compelling me to do.

'That's right, you dirty girl, that is the centre of your depravity,' he condemned me, and he poked my clitoris hard with his fingers, causing me to release more juices from between my legs. He then produced yet another paper clip and said, 'Push it out.' I squeezed my clit so that it was further exposed to him and held it there while he gently applied the paperclip. The total pervert. It slid onto me and the pressure of it caused burning spasms. I lay there, immobilised with the intense weird pleasure of it all. But I could not resist plunging my fingers down into my pussy to gently massage myself. He immediately reached for a ruler on his desk whereupon he flipped me quickly over onto my belly.

Then the spanking began with a ruler while I rubbed my pinched clit underneath me. Then the reality of everything overtook me. I was coming, finally, under MacLean's ministrations. His punishment continued until my orgasm rocked me deeply, inside and out. It was the longest, most excruciatingly hot climax I'd ever experienced.

I was winded by it, it was so intense.

He watched me the whole time, writhing in my ultimate pleasure.

'Turn over,' he said finally. Whereupon I looked back at him and saw that he'd begun to unzip his trousers. My eyes widened, or must have, since he said, 'It's all right, don't be frightened.' I turned onto my back and he knelt beside me to examine my clitoris. The paperclip had slipped off and he began to kiss my clit, ever so lightly at first, then he dug gently and slowly with his tongue, circling the sensitive bud that jutted out from between my lips. I felt wet and warm and relaxed and soothed. But he was greedy, too, because almost sadistically he began to thrust his finger in and out of my cunt at the same time. He must have been about to burst, having this young girl coming in front him, in his office, in the middle of the afternoon.

This made me more slippery than ever as he scrubbed my folds and my aching channel so deep and raw. He probed at me, all the way to the uppermost, tenderest part of my being. Every time he dug in with his long finger he grunted as he found me wetter and wetter. God, he was so bad as he plunged his finger in and out and I realised that he was stroking his cock at the same time.

Now his mouth moved away from my clit and his tongue licked my softer, wetter spot. I could not help but raise my hips to his urgings, as his tongue moved in and out until I couldn't stand it any more. He didn't care; he turned me over to pluck at my folds from behind with his fingers, then I felt him insert his finger into my asshole, so smoothly. I raised my bum to the occasion and the waves of orgasm started to come from within me again, and I came and I came. I died. First my clit burnt so that I had to thrust against it, then the pleasure massively waved along my folds and up through my pussy, pulsing through and through, right to my innards; my very womb vibrated to the point where I had to gasp for air.

'Fuck me, professor,' I heard myself say.

His anger rose again in the face of my pleasure. My orgasm condemned me for a second time. What a dirty girl. He ordered me to lean over the chaise-longue.

'All the world and creation should see what I am about to do to you now, but you shall speak of this to nobody.'

These were the words of Father Lemartre, those same words that he had spoken to Yvonne Dupres.

MacLean penetrated me, his cock exploding into my pussy. I could feel his whole body behind me, banging up against me with his hard thrusting cock inside me. He had his full way with me he filled me up. At that moment, my sex was my amoral centre – and it was being filled. Now his true authority pulsed within me, deeper and deeper with every thrust. I lay myself fully open now, to avoid any future pain. I wanted to obey him. While he was having his raging pleasure with me, I had my bum high in the air and fell into another orgasm, this one shorter than the first. How much more could I take? Then he exploded his come inside me. He croaked: 'Santa, Santa, that's a good girl now.'

After he withdrew from me, he took out his handker-chief and gently wiped me up, saying, it seemed more to my pussy than to me, 'I've been waiting to meet you for a long time and I must say, it's been a great pleasure.'

'You did have a little encounter with my cunt on the dance floor, didn't you? It was you, wasn't it?'

'Oh my, yes, and a delicious one at that!' He laughed and looked up at me.

'You shouldn't have stolen my mobile phone, sir,' I told him.

'Your neglect isn't to be misinterpreted as my dishonesty. Anyway, I was going to return it to you first thing Monday morning.'

He finished wiping me up and placed the handkerchief back in his pocket. With that, he straightened his clothes and left me in his office alone with a warning: 'Now rewrite that paper,' he said on his way out, and tossed the rolled-up report onto my naked lap.

Rewrite the paper! What an outrage! I wanted to hate him, but couldn't. He was a second-rate professor but he was still my professor. I loved him, just like Yvonne had loved the rotten and corrupt priest.

I took my paper and went on home. I didn't call anybody. My message machine was full and I listened to everyone's calls, from Fez to Bee, and there was even a message from Joey. It was as though somehow all those close to me knew of my terrible deed. My surreal day. There was no way they could, really, but sometimes forces conspire to whisper our secrets in the wind. Moreover, I feared that if I spoke to anyone, my voice alone would betray all.

So I ignored these messages. I couldn't possibly talk to anybody today. Instead, I'd locked myself up to reflect on what had happened, and to prepare to rewrite the damn paper.

I could feel Father Lemartre's shadow on me; I could feel MacLean's breath on my neck as I read his comments about my defence. They went as follows:

Upon reading the defence prepared for Yvonne Dupres in the eighteenth-century case against the church, or, more specifically, against the Jesuit priest, Father Lemartre, I come to two conclusions. Firstly, the defence is much misled in omitting certain evidence that would serve its greatest point. Evidence that Yvonne herself seduced the priest was a fact that was widely known. It would be far more effective to argue that she prostituted herself to advance her cause and he breached his contract to her, which was, in fact, his verbal promise to her. Secondly, in her desire to be honoured with sainthood as payment for this prostitution, the plaintiff should instead seek costs and damages.

While you did have some good arguments in making her out as the victim, next time, make a more practical argument.

Oh brother, I thought, and laughed. Was he was going to give me a good mark on this after all? And when I looked at the bottom of the page, I saw the mark he had assigned. It was a decent 'A'. Whew, boy, I thought, there was nothing left to worry about. I needn't rewrite the paper! He was teasing me the whole time. What an infuriating man! I could finally rest, and to bed I went.

14

The next morning, I answered a persistent knocking at my door. Bee piled into the apartment and blurted out to me, 'Me and Joey split up yesterday. Where have you been? I'm completely destroyed! Oh, Santa!'

'Bee, it's not true! What happened?'

And she wept so hard I had to embrace her; my dearest friend was never more broken up. She sputtered that Joey was seeing someone else, that she didn't know who it was, and that didn't matter anyway, except for the fact that she'd hoped this bitch-whore would die. I told her I just didn't believe it. After she calmed a little, I called Fez.

Of course, before I could say anything, he had to get super mad at me.

'Where in the bloody hell have you been? How dare you not call me back!'

'A total of six messages, I know. I was surprised you didn't drop in.'

That was sneaky of me, wasn't it? Throw a little guilt in wherever I could. Don't pester me, I was implying. The good bitch didn't miss a beat and I went on fabricating my story. 'Believe me, I'm so sorry, Fez! But I had to deal with my paper, and I thought MacLean was going to fail me. I was just in no state.' I was putting it all on so thick that I started to cry.

So I continued my sobbing and appealed to him. 'But that's not the crucial point, Fez. Listen, and tell me the truth ... is that jerk Joey fucking around on Bee?'

There was silence on the other end of the phone. I

suddenly realised that I'd also just finished betraying Fez with my latest encounter with my instructor. That was a brutal reality, because I would absolutely hate for Fez to have an affair. What a hypocrite I was. Although I didn't really regard my liaison with MacLean as being at all about cheating on Fez. On myself, yes, and how dirty and lovely it was! But that whole episode was in a totally different orbit; not even of this world. My extreme collusions with MacLean were not even remotely threatening to my dearest Fez, and now the whole thing was actually a closed chapter when I came to think of it. I had gotten MacLean out of my system and I was more than ready to commit fully to Fez.

Fez finally broke the silence on the phone, 'Sshh. You're not going to fail. And let me come over and talk to Bee. And see you, finally.'

'I wish we were at the lake,' I said.

'Like the last time. That was so nice. Do you still love me?' he asked sweetly.

'Yes, I do.'

'Can I come see you, right now?' he asked.

'Can I say something reassuring to her, meantime?'

'I've kept my word to Joey,' he let on.

'What do you mean, is there a secret?' I asked.

'A good secret.'

'How could that be? They've broken up. She thinks he is seeing someone else.' I argued with him.

'I think there may have been a misunderstanding, really,' he said.

'She's really upset, my love,' I urged him.

'I'll be right over.' He hung up.

Bee was waiting in the kitchen and I went in and put on some coffee. I turned to look at her, all heaped over and sorrowful on one of my kitchen chairs. I hugged her again.

'I was so mad because I thought he was seeing

someone else and then I tried to hurt him by telling him about my affair with Unruh last year. Then I said I was through with him. Santa, it's all over and I love him so,' she sobbed.

'How can you be so sure he's seeing someone else?'

'I don't know, he just never seems to be around, never wants to spend much time with me any more, never has me over to his place, like he has something to hide. What else am I supposed to think?' She wept so bitterly.

'Fez's on his way. He seems to think that there's been a misunderstanding,' I said reassuringly.

'Good, so someone else who can come see what a loser I am,' she wailed so mournfully. Joey couldn't not love her any more ... there was no way! But what if he had wandered from her and found someone else? It was too bad that Bee had told Joey about Unruh, though; that was not a good move. I would hate it if Fez learned of my liaison with MacLean, though I didn't truly feel I was cheating on Fez. I mean, we had only just started seeing each other, and our commitment was, as yet, unspoken, or so I felt (even though he'd asked me to move in with him). But what I did with my professor was just too bizarre and it started long before Fez came into my life. Now it was out of my system and I knew no one could ever come close to my heart like Fez. The door sounded. It was Fez already.

'My dearest friend, it will turn out OK,' I said with certainty. 'I'm getting the door now.'

'Hang on, let me dry my tears first. Jeez, I hate this!' Bee was overcome again and I achingly watched her as she tried to dry her flowing tears with the tissue I held out to her, but then I finally had to go to answer the door.

When I saw Fez on the other side of the threshold, I was myself overcome with tears. I feigned that I was crying for my dear friend's sorrow, but really it was for him. Had I betrayed him with MacLean? No!

'Bee's destroyed by this, Fez, what are we going to do?' I sobbed.

'Sssh.' He kissed me long and slow and sweet.

Abruptly, I pulled away. 'Thanks for coming so quickly. So what's up with Joey, then?'

'Let me see Bee first.' He moved past me and into the kitchen.

'Oh, Fez, why is this happening, please tell me?' Bee asked so softly as he entered the kitchen, as if inside her breast, her heart, were made of glass and would break if she spoke too loudly.

He knelt by her chair and looked back at me with an eager smile as I came to stand in the doorway to the kitchen. Why was he smiling like that, I wondered?

'Are you ready for this, Bee,' he said teasing. 'Are you ready?'

'No, for nothing,' she wept, and he put his hand tenderly on her shoulder.

'You're not ready for this. Yes, Joey's furious with you about Unruh. But he said he's punished you enough and he's waiting downstairs to see you. Joey's been keeping some of his own secrets, it's true,' Fez said as he smiled up at her.

She looked at him. 'What, who is he seeing, has he come to tell me who the dirty slut is?

'You don't know if he is seeing someone else, now do you, Bee? But he knows all about you,' Fez said a little darkly, which caused Bee some renewed consternation.

'That was when we'd first just started going out. I'm not having a affair a year later like him. I wouldn't pick up with someone else after being in a relationship this long, Fez,' she argued, and she made her point well, which made me feel better about MacLean.

'And I know he's seeing someone else,' Bee continued. 'Where's he been lately? Why has he been so secretive? I don't want to see him ever again!' she said angrily. 'He's left me for someone else.'

'He's outside waiting for you right now, Bee. He wants to tell you what's really going on. Look out the window, you'll see him down in front of Santa's building,' repeated Fez. With that, Fez took Bee's arm and brought her to stand at the window. I looked at her and smiled, bewildered and hopeful.

Now over at the window, in my living room, Bee peered out to discreetly look down onto the street below. She said quietly to herself, 'He is out there,' as if she didn't believe that he would be, and she continued gazing down at him for a short spell.

Bee turned to me and asked, 'Do I look OK, Santa? My eyes must be all puffy. I have to go put some make-up on.' She didn't wait for me to reply and went into the bathroom holding her purse. I smiled at Fez, feeling sure something good was about to happen.

'What is it, Fez, what?' I asked enthusiastically once she'd left the room.

'Sssh.' Fez gestured towards our Bee as she came out of the bathroom. She looked over at us as she went for the door.

'I'll be right back,' she mumbled, and the door clicked shut behind her.

Fez rose to go over to the living room window. I joined him and we both perched on the ledge and looked down at Joey waiting below.

'He's going to ask Bee to move in with him. All this time he's been fixing his apartment up so it's super nice for her. He wanted to keep it a secret because he knew she wanted to move in so much,' he laughed.

'She'll just die! So there is no one else, he's just been holing up and preparing all this for her?' I asked.

'Pretty much,' Fez said, and we were silent a moment as we watched the two lovers meeting downstairs.

'The great pleasure and pain of love,' I said, somewhat forlornly as I watched Bee and Joey embrace each other down on the street.

Fez took my hand and held it fast to his chest. I noticed he had an odd twinkle in his eye. 'Yes, so Joey found out about Bee's little escapades with Unruh quite a few months ago, did you know? Never said anything to her about it and he didn't tell her about his plans to ask her to move in so he could leave her to suffer for a period of time because he wanted to punish her a little.'

Fez pulled me up and made me stand close to him and he laughed deviously as he grinded me with his groin. He was acting a tad weird, I thought.

'I have a little surprise for you too, Santa. I know all about how you've been flirting with MacLean, you and your see-through skirts. I have a little surprise for you.' He chuckled to himself again.

'What do you mean?' I asked.

'Sssh now. Take this.' He reached into his shirt pocket and presented me with a small jewellery box. It was tiny, smaller than a ring would ordinarily be contained in.

'What are you doing, Fez?' I asked him, and took the gift from him, perplexed. I slowly pried it open and inside I discovered a very tiny ring that I guessed was a single earring. It had a small diamond set on the band, like a miniature engagement ring for my ear. I shone my eyes at Fez and held the ring up to my ear. 'It's beautiful,' I said.

'No, it doesn't go there,' he said playfully and smiled as he looked down at my thighs.

'Oh my God, Fez, you've got to be kidding,' I said, wide-eyed.

His face grew serious and he shook his head. 'I'm

taking you to see a friend of mine who owns a tattoo and body piercing shop.

'Fez! Stop.'

'Oh yes, my dear. I'm making you mine and this is step one.'

15

Later that day, we set about seeing Fez's friend, who was to professionally fix me up to wear his gift to me – this strange and beautiful ring. The location on my body I was to sport said ring was on an unspeakable region. Oh my, oh my. Would it hurt? I wondered. And his friend was to see, examine, touch and finally pierce my most intimate place. A complete stranger, no less! I couldn't believe Fez would allow such a thing.

But I had to be tamed, Fez told me, referring to my misdemeanours with MacLean. Well, I confessed to him that the relationship I had with my professor had come to an end, like with the university session itself.

'Besides, he seduced me!' I said defensively, but Fez only shook his head; he knew all about me.

But my deranged affair with MacLean was over. And truly, I was more than over-satisfied with my experiences with my instructor at this point. (I hoped.)

This terrible new prospect was now on the horizon for the bad and untameable girl. But I had to be tamed, Fez told me, referring to my naughty flirtations with MacLean. Well, thank goodness he didn't know the whole terrible truth of it! And I was grateful for that.

Fez was initiating a whole new dimension into our sex life and it was intriguing as hell to me.

Beyond the promisingly erotic procedure, which was going to have the hood of my clit pierced by a total stranger, I kept wondering how sex would feel afterwards with the tiny ring attached to my most sensitive, highly-private sexual spot. Fez meant to affix this glori-

ous little piece of jewellery into me to effectively dominate me and possess me. Plant his flag on me. He said
he would be there to attend to the whole proceeding.

I said to him on the car ride to this unknown shop,
'You mean, I'm going to have lie down nude, in front of
your friend, spread-eagled while he pierces my pussy.
What, Fez, are you crazy?' I couldn't believe he would
allow such a thing to be done to a woman he apparently
felt so possessive about.

'I can't do it myself, my dear. So this is the solution.
Don't worry, I'll be there the whole time,' he said with a
sexy command in the tone of his voice. 'He's an expert,
my friend, Jean-Jacques.'

I was nervous and aroused by the thought of two
young men performing this kinky operation on my bare,
easily aroused pussy. That would mean I would have to
undress, lie down and spread my legs so that it was
fully open to their eyes. I was already getting unbearably wet on the car ride there thinking about what was
ahead. It wouldn't do to be all slimy and aroused in my
panties. I was about to have a piercing of the unbearably
horny cunt. It was too much to endure!

Would it hurt? I had a sneaking suspicion that it
would feel good. Of course, I gushed again with wetness
as we pulled up to the place of possibly my sexual
ecstasy or doom.

The colourful storefront window displayed the usual
sort of paraphernalia for a tattoo shop: funky mannequins with crazy wigs wearing rock band T-shirts and
heavy silver jewellery. These same dummies had
sketches of intricate tattoos drawn across their plastic
arms and legs; images of heaven and hell as depicted in
predictable iconography – tattoos of clouds and wolves
and fire and so forth. There were gold or silver rings or
studs planted on ears, lips, or on the noses on these
same zany, lifeless models. Curious, little forms bulged

visibly under the thinly sewn underwear that the mannequins wore.

All sorts of things were going on inside this building, I supposed. Was Fez associated with this sort of thing? I'd always thought of him as a little more traditional than to go in for such stuff. Like, I never had him tagged as a Goth, or the prince of darkwave.

'Come,' he said as he pulled me out of the car. 'Ha! And afterwards we will go to church, catholic girl!' He laughed at this and I laughed too, in spite of myself. Well, I guess I did trust him in the end as I let him lead me into the shop. Go to church! Blasphemous man! He was a catholic like me!

Inside he introduced me to his friend, Jean-Jacques. The moment this guy laid eyes on me, he offered to provide his services for free. Horny boy, I thought. Well, of course Fez said no to this offer and pushed his friend playfully away, insisting he was going to pay the bill and that there wasn't going to be any funny stuff about it.

'You keep your dick in your pants, my man, this is pure business, get it?' Fez informed him with his arm around my shoulders and they both laughed. My face went red and so I turned away and wandered over to a counter displaying merchandise.

While they carried on in their business discussions I looked at the lighters, key-rings, and T-shirts. There were earrings, keychains, and short and long necklaces. I idly wondered if it was here that Fez had bought the necklace he had given me. None of them looked exactly like mine, however.

A tulip-shaped lighter caught my eye. I loved it, even though looked like it might be awkward to use. It seemed to me that it was made of pewter and it would be heavy and too large to carry in your pocket. What a beautiful ornament it was, though. I thought I would buy it and turned around to speak to Jean-Jacques about it. The two were talking quietly but intensely about the deal they were making in the corner of the store. It seemed to me like they didn't want me to hear what was being said between them.

Fez seemed to be a little heated and was pointing threateningly at Jean-Jacques.

'All right, forget it,' Jacques-Jean said. He seemed to be conceding in some way and then they both looked over in my direction. Jean-Jacques had a glint in his eye, like he was looking forward very much to getting to work on me and piercing my pussy. Fez leant back against the wall and looked at me casually.

I cleared my throat and asked, 'Hey, how much is that little beauty of a lighter, Jean-Jacques, the tulip shaped one?'

He laughed, his eyes brightening. 'We'll have to see,' he replied.

'I'll buy it for you, Santa,' said Fez.

'It might not be for sale,' Jean-Jacques explained. I like having it on display, really. We'll have to see. Now, shall we?' he gestured towards the hall.

Jean-Jacques led us to a small, well-lit room in the back of the shop. 'There's not a lot of room in here. It could be a bit crowded, Fez. Too crowded for me to work with more than two people in one room.'

Jean-Jacques was avoiding my eyes; he was trying to be strict and professional about this, even though he clearly wanted to be alone with me for the piercing procedure. He was handsome. His arms were muscular and his chest was broad; two qualities in a man that I particularly liked. I thought it would be fun if he undressed me.

'Sorry, bud. But I will oversee the whole affair,' Fez replied tightly. And he produced the ring from his shirt pocket. That little ring designed for his purposes. After handing the jewel to Jean-Jacques, Fez came to stand beside me and began to unbuckle my belt. I giggled and pushed his hands away, but he came right back at me saying, 'Ssh, you're going to cooperate.'

With that, he unzipped my pants and had them half-way down and then he gave me a little kiss as I further submitted to him. He pushed his hand down my panties and gave me a little feel. I was definitely wet; his fingers slid so smoothly. Jean-Jacques enjoyed watching and when I self-consciously looked over at him, I noticed he was secretly rubbing the crotch of his pants.

Next, Fez had my panties down around my thighs. He was openly playing with my pussy and Jean-Jacques' keen eyes didn't miss a thing.

'Bring her over here,' he said, spreading a clean sheet across his operating table.

Fez continued to pull my pants and panties down all the way to my ankles. 'Step out of them, Santa,' he said. I looked at him as he knelt down at my ankles and he nodded up at me that everything was going to be OK. I held nervously onto his shoulders and he took advantage of the close-up contact with my moist sex as I stepped out of my jeans, licking my clit, quickly and lightly. I arched my pelvis, and Jean-Jacques watched the whole time. Fez then led me over to the operating table, where I stood, vulnerable and waiting.

'She should take off her shirt too,' Jean-Jacques added as he ogled my bare cunt and ass.

'I doubt that's necessary,' Fez returned.

'I like everything to be sterile, my dear man. This is my shop and my regulations.' And he nodded at Fez that he didn't want any argument about it. Fez patted my naked ass.

'You heard the man,' my terrible lover said to me. Fez was as naughty as I.

'I'll do it away from the table,' Jean-Jacques offered

and he led me a little away from the site of his oper-
ations. I followed without protest. I knew there was no
retrieving the situation at this late point. There, the body-
piercer slowly unbuttoned my shirt. As per usual, I was
not wearing a bra. I hated bras. My breasts were soon
released from the confines of my shirt and I was exposed
up top. My nipples were already hard and ready for him.

'Oh, my God,' he said, as his eyes took in my fully
naked form. Fez took up my shirt and placed it over my
shoulders.

'Like this, just leave it open. Give her some cover, I
mean, my God, JJ.'

'No, I have something better.' And JJ brought out a
short gown that covered me, but they wouldn't let me
button it up and brushed my hands away when I first
tried.

'Fez, I doubt I need to be totally nude for this,' I said
and spewed out a gusty laugh. There was no response
as I was led to the table by the two of them and
suddenly I felt like fighting them off. Why I didn't, I'll
never know, the little bastards. They were the ones who
needed a spanking. They were having a good eyeful of
everything. Taking liberties and coercing me into goodness knows what. Meanwhile, I was made to lie on the
table by both of them.

Fez wouldn't let anything bad happen to me even
though he was out to punish me for my illicit wander-
ings. Timidly, I kept my hands across my chest. 'It's all
right,' Fez assured me as he patted my pussy.

'OK, my little beauty, spread your legs apart for me,'
JJ requested.

They each took a knee and spread my legs far apart
for all to see. 'Ah!' I gasped, objecting.

'Oh, baby,' Jean-Jacques uttered breathily, looking at
my spread pussy.

My cunt was bare and out for both men to freely gaze

upon. Jean-Jacques leant in for a closer view and I felt his warm breath. I felt the warmth of his finger, before he even touched me; and finally, I felt him lightly flick my clit with his slippery finger. It wasn't his finger, but my cunt that was so slick. 'She's all wet,' he pronounced, and I died of shame.

'Yes she is,' Fez said. 'Are you all turned on, Santa?'

'No!' I said, denying it and pulling my legs back together, but how excited I really was. I couldn't stop myself from squirming a little bit as I did raise my crotch towards Jean-Jacques' face. I immediately regretted it as Jean-Jacques looked up at me and smiled and then grinned at Fez. It was all so erotically embarrassing.

'Well, we can't have you being all wet while I do the procedure,' he stated lustily and then reached for a cloth. It was a thin cloth, which he demonstratively placed around his middle finger. He then proceeded to part my legs gently again.

Exposed, my pussy felt so naked and cool and JJ and Fez looked down in awe at my wetness. Gently, the body-piercer inserted his finger into my dripping pussy. In order to tidy it up and dry it, he wiggled the thin cloth between my cunt lips and gradually dug it deeper and deeper, all along the way wiping the wet, inside walls of my sensitive cavern. His finger squirmed while the cloth became wetter and more slithery. I knew they could hear me breathing unevenly, and I had to close my eyes as he pushed the cloth deeper into me.

'Take it easy, Jean-Jacques,' Fez advised. I looked over at my boyfriend and saw him looking at me hungrily and somewhat uneasily as his friend continued his activities.

Jean-Jacques replied, 'I know I can't fuck her, she's yours, but we are, quite possibly, going to make another kind of deal.' He had now finished wiping my pussy and was drying the area around my clit.

'She's very nice,' Jean-Jacques commented, somewhat politely for his type, and he went on to say, 'So you got your heart set on that tulip lighter, Santa? Well, well, well, it may be for sale . . .' he said elusively.

'How much,' Fez inquired.

I said nothing.

'Mind you, it isn't really for sale. It's a very expensive display item,' he went on to say. The body-piercer swirled his finger around my slippery clit, but I was getting wet all over again.

'You snarky bastard, tell me the deal, already,' Fez urged him.

'All right, here it is,' Jean-Jacques began. 'I am always in need of models, and this one is beautiful in every way. I've seen a lot of pussy, man, as you may have gathered, but this is a precious specimen. My camera is first rate, so let's take some pictures. I need a before and after, well several. And chain too.'

Chain? What chain did he mean? I thought it was just going to be the ring. I gushed again from in-between my legs at the thought of him photographing my bare, shaved sex and I laughed uncomfortably and closed my legs and covered myself with my robe.

'Ha! You're going to have to pay her for that,' Fez said, laughing too as he reached over to cover my breasts a little better. This I did appreciate, if for no other reason than the fact I was a little cold.

Jean-Jacques paused. 'Perhaps,' he said looking at Fez. 'Would you like to make some money, Santa? You want the tulip-lighter? You want this session for free, Fez?' Jean-Jacques inquired, as he strode around his operating room setting up for the procedure.

'What's your offer?' Fez said amusedly.

JJ came back around to me and unveiled my robe from around me.

'Stop. I don't know!' I protested as he exposed me

again. I put my hands down around my crotch to stop Jean-Jacques from touching me again. Just then, Fez lightly slapped my hands.

'It's not your decision,' Fez informed me and smiled.

'Yes, yes it is!' I said.

16

'Will you need freezing or not?' Jean-Jacques asked.

I guess I knew the answer. And Fez did too. He knew what I would want, and it wasn't really pain for pain's sake.

Jean-Jacques said, 'I have some effective ointment that will numb you and make the experience very pleasant, or so I've been told. Some prefer it without. Oh yes, very much so,' he laughed.

'Fez, I can't do this, any of this!' I cried, sitting up quickly and gathering the robe around myself.

'Oh, Santa, you are going to. To atone for your silly behaviour with MacLean, remember?' He leant over and kissed me lightly on the mouth. 'As far as the pictures are concerned, that's your decision. I'll permit it only because you will look so beautiful. But just for the record, I would like to see you do it,' he added and he kissed me again.

I looked down silently and heard Jean-Jacques say, 'Tulip-lighter, my girl, tulip-lighter. I will give to you.' He was a terrible tease. I couldn't help but smile secretly to myself as I watched him prepare the needle properly for sterilisation. What a turn-on it would be to have Jean-Jacques take pictures of this act of domination Fez was enforcing upon me.

'What kind of pictures will they be?' I asked.

'You know . . .' Fez and Jean-Jacques said in unison.

'Close-ups of my . . .?' I couldn't bring myself to name it and I looked at them both as innocently as possible.

'Would you like JJ to keep your face out of it?' Fez asked me.

'No, she's very pretty, no,' Jean-Jacques protested.

'How much?' I asked.

'Well, let's see ... the lighter, the piercing ... let's say three hundred bucks,' Jean-Jacques offered.

I looked over at Fez for his reaction. He nodded his approval at Jean-Jacques' offer. 'Only sluts do this sort of thing,' I said sketchily, and Fez laughed a nasty laugh. And with that I had agreed. What the hell was I doing?

'Say, who's going to see these photos anyway?' I asked, thinking how nerve-wracking this was. I couldn't take my eyes off Fez who looked back at me approvingly.

'My clients. Dirty girls just like you,' Jean-Jacques said devilishly.

'You won't tell them my name,' I said.

'Of course not. Now, if you'll excuse me for a moment, I'll just get my gear.' Jean-Jacques left the room.

When we were alone, Fez said, 'Give me a blow-job, honey, and right now, you terrible, pretty thing.' And with that Fez pulled his cock out from inside his pants. It was all ready to go, I must say!

'Oh I see,' I said, as I crossed my legs. God help me, I wanted to give him a suck. Right around the tip of his beautiful cock, so slippery, he would be.

Fez approached. 'You are my love, and a very bad girl at that, and you always will be mine and you will suck on this for ever,' Fez said as he pushed his cock into my mouth. I sat up a little while he took hold of both my ears in his hands and moved his cock around inside my mouth, whispering filthy things to me. He must have been so turned on showing me off to JJ, that he climaxed within five or six strokes.

Jean-Jacques re-entered the room and I quickly turned my head to spit out my lover's come, but Fez said, 'No, you're going to swallow it, love of my life. Especially on this occasion.' And so swallow it I did. Oh my God.

JJ laid out his gear on his work table next to me. He screwed in his camera lens and checked that he had enough film. How much film did he need? I would agree to two pictures, one before, one after, with the jewel on. This was to be a picture with Fez's gift on my cunt – the tiny ring; his present to me and my present to him.

Jean-Jacques looked through the lens and pulled focus. On my cunt, no less! No! I suddenly freaked, and couldn't let him take a picture. There was no way!

'Oh, my God, wait a sec!' I said vehemently, not at all ready for this. I pulled my legs under me and immediately covered my face.

'Stand up and look at the camera as you remove your robe,' JJ instructed me. 'You are beautiful.'

So I stood up nervously, clinging to my garment. After a few deep breaths I let my arms drop. I tentatively looked at the camera and I felt beautiful. So I slipped off my robe and Jean-Jacques clicked the camera, his first picture for this session.

'Yes,' he said happily.

'Very nice, Santa,' Fez told me.

I looked over at him and smiled shyly. Click – another picture was snapped.

'OK, now listen to my direction. Santa, just touch your pussy a little for me,' JJ said. Well, to be truthful, I'd wanted to touch myself in front of them the whole time. I did it so sensuously. My, I was wet; and it did feel so good as I stroked my wet hole up to my clit. He took another picture, and another. 'Pull your lips aside so I can see your clit,' he said in a husky voice.

That's the second time I've been told that this week, I thought humorously to myself. Naughty girl.

I spread my lips and arched my lower back so my cunt would stick out more from between my thighs.

And from behind, my bum was all tensed muscle. I looked down at the detail I was showing the camera.

'Ooh, Santa,' I heard Jean-Jacques say, as he snapped the next photo. 'God, I want to fuck you so much.'

'Shut-up, Jean-Jacques,' said Fez.

The photographer came in for a close-up. I pushed out my pelvis even more, pulling my lips further apart. I felt I might orgasm at that moment, but, before I had a chance, I was led over to the table.

'Let's do the procedure,' ordered Fez, with a note of urgency in his voice while Jean-Jacques kept clicking close-up pictures.

As I was made to lie down, I became worried about the piercing; it shouldn't hurt too much. 'Put that ointment on first, Jean-Jacques,' I begged him. He snickered as he now took a picture of my anxious face.

'You can't use all these pictures,' I said to him in a semi-delirious state, for the situation I was in was so unnerving. He put the camera down and turned to get the numbing ointment. He squeezed a little out of the tube onto his finger and applied the cream all around my clit, rubbing it in for a while, making the whole area quiver to the point where I thought I would come to a climax. He stopped before that happened and went to ready the needle as everything was taking on a tingling, numbing sensation.

Fez was now at my side, kissing me on the mouth and rubbing my clit with his middle finger. The tingling sensation increased as his finger stroked me so lightly.

'Fez, you hold back her lips as I pierce it, OK?' Jean-Jacques suggested.

'Mmm,' Fez answered, and proceeded to spread my lips apart. New fingers probed my pussy as JJ pulled on the hood of my clit to extend it, so he would be able put the piercing gun around it. He massaged it in an outward direction. It was now so numb, I had to move more to feel it better, which was great, because I didn't particularly want to feel the jet of a sharp needle through it. But I would. Oh, I would.

JJ got the gun in place around the hood as I squirmed on the table. Fez spread my lips a little further. I was feeling my own breasts, and was beyond stimulated when the gun shot off and pierced the skin. It was a sharp, delicious pain and I went into orgasm at the moment of contact. Fez had meantime stopped kissing me to watch.

I let out a great groan and Fez was going 'Sssh,' but I couldn't stop. Jean-Jacques then was cleaning the area with some medicinal gel while I continued to orgasm. During this time the clit-ring was installed in the freshly-made hole. Jean-Jacques immediately went for his camera.

'It looks beautiful, Fez,' he congratulated him.

'Yes, doesn't it?' he agreed.' Then snap, snap, snap, as I simply lay with my legs wide apart.

'Nice and swollen, perfect, little clit,' said Jean-Jacques. 'Just right for a photo session. Oh Santa! You are incredible!'

My pussy experienced another little wave through it as I gently touched down to feel the lovely new ring. I ran my finger along his gift to me. I felt adorned by my Fez, like I was a princess.

'Now we'll have to be very careful with this next step.' Jean-Jacques snapped another photo and he went on to say, 'Don't want to make her sore.' This was to be the photo that would definitely be the feature for his business catalogue: a close-up picture of his more intimate work.

But as it turned out, there were a few more pictures that he and Fez planned to take.

'No, we don't want to make her sore,' my man said

as he picked up on his friend's point. I looked over in wonder at Fez. What indeed were they talking about? Be careful about what? I thought we were finished. I sure was. I'd finished orgasming and my ring was perfectly affixed and photos had been taken.

However, Fez next went about taking my chain off from around my neck – the one that he'd given me on that previous occasion when he first professed his love for me; the same necklace that reached down to my navel. It had his apartment key strung to the end of it. I loved that chain. Why was he taking it off me?

'Give it to me,' Jean-Jacques directed him. Fez gave the chain to him and JJ soaked it next in some kind of sterilizing solution. He then passed a pair of surgical gloves to Fez as well as the newly cleansed chain, or necklace, or whatever it was!

'Now you have to stand up,' Fez instructed me. He extended his hand to mine and helped me up and, with the small ring implanted in my flesh, I rose. During the course of which I became aware of how my newly decorated clit was coming out of the freezing, ever so gradually, and was starting to slightly sting and mildly burn.

Before me, Fez knelt down on one knee. 'Are you OK?' he whispered, looking up at me tenderly. He then brought the chain up to my pussy. I felt him attach my new ring to a link in the necklace. This he did most carefully, for my clit was so sensitive. I looked down at what he was doing. My pussy was engorged and slightly pinker than usual but it didn't mind a little soft touching. Fez let the chain go slowly and the full weight of it hung from my clitoral hood. Oh my, it felt a bit too heavy. But Fez picked up the end of the chain and held it up for me to see: it was like a leash and I giggled. Or maybe more like some kind of engagement and we were bonded at that instance. He tugged ever so slightly at the chain and Jean-Jacques snapped a picture of us both.

Fez said, 'Will you be mine?'

I laughed. We all laughed together and then my darling Fez said, 'When you're seventy years old, I will give you a new pussy ring with a very big diamond, because you are for ever mine.' And he stood up and kissed me. JJ placed my garment around my shoulders.

On the way home, Fez and I drove past his father's restaurant and he reminded me we were to have supper there with his parents that evening.

'Gosh, Fez, I'm not sure how comfortably I'll be able to sit down. Do you think I'll still feel sore by tonight?'

'Hmm, I don't know, but JJ gave me some ointment to numb you a little and I'd be happy to apply it for you!' He turned and looked at me, playful and pleased.

'Oh, you!' I gave him a light punch on the shoulder which made him laugh.

The other hand was curled around my lovely tulip lighter. It was worth the pain!

I was slightly apprehensive about going to the Augustos that evening. What about Fez's brother? Would there be another brawl? And would MacLean show up with his cronies like the last time, I wondered? My, how predictable was it that I hoped he would? Now that the university session was over, I may not see him again until the fall. Well, I had the summer ahead with my dear Fez, and I could hardly wait to swim across the lake with him, escorted by sweet Bee and Joey, who had finally sorted things out so nicely. We'd all have such fun, sitting around the campfire and going for long walks in the woods. I'd definitely get Fez to surprise me in the woods again. I'd really gotten off on that.

What a funny year, I thought. So many sexual secrets and intrigues. It was the best! I'd gotten away with it all! And at least my devious professor gave me a fair mark in the end. Perhaps more than fair. I wondered how he'd spend his summer vacation. Maybe he'd spend it with his wife, languishing in the sun. But that seemed unlikely; he was such a crusty old professor. He'd more likely spend it digging about some library, unearthing another bizarre case as a special assignment for his naughty student, with her pierced and glinting clitoris.

But I wasn't going to go down that track ... at least not now summer was here.

I was going to be a good, bad girl and have the best time of my life with my best buddies in the sunshine.

Visit the Black Lace website at
www.blacklace-books.co.uk

LOOK OUT FOR THE ALL-NEW BLACK LACE BOOKS – AVAILABLE NOW!

All books priced £7.99 in the UK. Please note publication dates apply to the UK only. For other territories, please contact your retailer.

FRENCH MANNERS
Olivia Christie
ISBN 0 352 33214 X

Gilles de la Trave persuades Colette, a young and beautiful peasant girl from one of his estates, to become his mistress and live the life of a Parisian courtesan. However, it is his son Victor that she loves and expects to marry. In a moment of passion and curiosity she confesses her sins to the local priest, unaware that the curé has his own agenda: one which involves himself *and* Victor. Shocked, Colette takes the only sensible option for a young girl from the provinces: she flees to Paris to immerse herself in a life of wild indulgence and luxury! **An erotic and beautifully written story charting a rural young girl's journey into adulthood and sophistication.**

UNNATURAL SELECTION
Alaine Hood
ISBN 0 352 33963 2

Hailey is an up-and-coming biologist, and sexual evolution is her passion. Natural selection works best, she believes, when a woman has lots of options. Between her studies and her job as a bike messenger, Hailey hasn't had time to do much more than be a voyeur watching her own species at play in the city's nightclubs. Everything changes when she meets Noah and Cade, two very sexy men who will overturn her views on human mating games. But Hailey knows a lot more about mating games than they realise and, before they know it, she's the one doing the hunting – with Cade, Noah, and a rugged big-cat handler named Rick as her prey. **A crash course in female sexuality!**

FIRE AND ICE
Laura Hamilton
ISBN 0 352 33486 X

Nina, auditor extraordinaire, is known at work as the Ice Queen, where her colleagues joke that her frosty demeanour travels to the bedroom. But what they don't know is that Nina spends her after-work hours locked into fiery games with her boyfriend Andrew, where she acts out her deepest fantasy of being a prostitute. Nina ups the stakes in her anonymous guise, being drawn deeper and deeper into London's seedy underworld – where everything can be bought and sold and no one is to be trusted. **A dark and shocking story of fantasy taken to extremes.**

Black Lace Booklist

Information is correct at time of printing. To avoid disappointment check availability before ordering. Go to www.blacklace-books.co.uk. All books are priced £6.99 unless another price is given.

BLACK LACE BOOKS WITH A CONTEMPORARY SETTING

☐ SHAMELESS Stella Black	ISBN 0 352 33485 1	£5.99
☐ INTENSE BLUE Lyn Wood	ISBN 0 352 33496 7	£5.99
☐ A SPORTING CHANCE Susie Raymond	ISBN 0 352 33501 7	£5.99
☐ TAKING LIBERTIES Susie Raymond	ISBN 0 352 33357 X	£5.99
☐ ON THE EDGE Laura Hamilton	ISBN 0 352 33534 3	£5.99
☐ LURED BY LUST Tania Picarda	ISBN 0 352 33533 5	£5.99
☐ THE NINETY DAYS OF GENEVIEVE	ISBN 0 352 33070 8	£5.99
Lucinda Carrington		
☐ DREAMING SPIRES Juliet Hastings	ISBN 0 352 33584 X	
☐ THE TRANSFORMATION Natasha Rostova	ISBN 0 352 33311 1	
☐ SIN.NET Helena Ravenscroft	ISBN 0 352 33598 X	
☐ TWO WEEKS IN TANGIER Annabel Lee	ISBN 0 352 33599 8	
☐ PLAYING HARD Tina Troy	ISBN 0 352 33617 X	
☐ SYMPHONY X Jasmine Stone	ISBN 0 352 33629 3	
☐ SUMMER FEVER Anna Ricci	ISBN 0 352 33625 0	
☐ CONTINUUM Portia Da Costa	ISBN 0 352 33120 8	
☐ FULL STEAM AHEAD Tabitha Flyte	ISBN 0 352 33637 4	
☐ A SECRET PLACE Ella Broussard	ISBN 0 352 33307 3	
☐ GAME FOR ANYTHING Lyn Wood	ISBN 0 352 33639 0	
☐ CHEAP TRICK Astrid Fox	ISBN 0 352 33640 4	
☐ THE GIFT OF SHAME Sara Hope-Walker	ISBN 0 352 29935 1	
☐ COMING UP ROSES Crystalle Valentino	ISBN 0 352 33658 7	
☐ GOING TOO FAR Laura Hamilton	ISBN 0 352 33657 9	
☐ THE STALLION Georgina Brown	ISBN 0 352 33005 8	
☐ DOWN UNDER Juliet Hastings	ISBN 0 352 33663 3	
☐ ODALISQUE Fleur Reynolds	ISBN 0 352 32887 8	
☐ SWEET THING Alison Tyler	ISBN 0 352 33682 X	
☐ TIGER LILY Kimberly Dean	ISBN 0 352 33685 4	

Please send me the books I have ticked above.

Name ....

Address ....

....

....

....

Post Code ....

Send to: Virgin Books Cash Sales, Thames Wharf Studios, Rainville Road, London W6 9HA.

US customers: for prices and details of how to order books for delivery by mail, call 1-800-343-4499.

Please enclose a cheque or postal order, made payable to Virgin Books Ltd, to the value of the books you have ordered plus postage and packing costs as follows:

UK and BFPO – £1.00 for the first book, 50p for each subsequent book.

Overseas (including Republic of Ireland) – £2.00 for the first book, £1.00 for each subsequent book.

If you would prefer to pay by VISA, ACCESS/MASTERCARD, DINERS CLUB, AMEX or SWITCH, please write your card number and expiry date here:

....

Signature ....

Please allow up to 28 days for delivery.